Maya's Story

Slipping between Time and Space

By
Diana Story

For Ralph Story

Author's Note

Three months after he died, my husband, journalist Ralph Story, came to me in a dream. At the time I was preparing to send his scripts and tapes to the UCLA Library Special Collections. In the dream he told me there was something in his material that I needed to write about. I indeed found something that interested me and then it took on a life of its own. This novel is the result.

Ralph has been with me every step of the way and I call him my ghostwriter.

Acknowledgements

After forty years of metaphysical study I have many people to thank. Far too many to list here, but I will mention a few.

Regina Jensen, Ph.D. Regina helped interpret my dreams and visions and opened up a new world. I will be eternally grateful for her friendship, council and encouragement. A truly beautiful old soul.

Deepak Chopra helped me explore that new world and showed me how to move into the adjoining dimensions. His help was invaluable.

Helene Shik, spiritual ambassador and fearless leader of her "Sacred Journeys," guiding pilgrims around the world.

Medium Robert Brown. I was on my way to one of his workshops when, over a six-hour period, the outline of my novel downloaded itself while I scribbled in a notebook.

Gabriel Blackburn, colleague of Krishna Murti, who opened my third eye and kept me tethered to this world during an extraordinary out-of-body experience.

Special mention has to go to my story editor, Eduardo Santiago. We found each other by accident, and, as I don't believe in coincidences, I knew that we were meant to work together. We connected and he understood the story I wanted to tell.

Rex John who helped me navigate the self-publishing business and created the beautiful cover art. His enthusiasm and faith in me as a writer still astonishes me.

Bradley Snyder for his patience, support, research, and technical help.

The line editing was a collaborative effort between Bradley Snyder and Rex John, and I am truly grateful.

My numerous workshop teachers, including Barbara Brennan and Master Stephen Co.

Brian Greene for his brilliant and easy to understand "Elegant Universe."

My women friends. For years they patiently listened to me talking about my novel. They are still my friends even though when the novel had me in its grip I retreated into my own world. I had no idea that writing was such a solitary endeavor.

And the amazing Carl Sagan.

Chapter 1

Magnus is worried. Worried that the incandescent sweep of glittering stars and constellations that surround him might be endangered. Worried that their light, which penetrates the infinite darkness and reaches into the farthest corners of the Cosmos, might be affected by what is happening on Earth.

Magnus, the Monoceros, or Unicorn Constellation and Patriarch of the Milky Way, has been watching planet Earth for several million years. He has seen the birth and death of many planets and stars, some collapsing in on themselves, creating black holes, and others becoming nebulae. He has also seen Earth survive several near misses with asteroids; but this planet holds a special fascination for him because of the life forms that have emerged from the oceans. Now the most sophisticated life form, Man, seems determined to destroy itself and the planet it lives on, thereby endangering the Milky Way.

Magnus has also been watching a young Earthling named Maya who, with the help of her grandmother, might be able to stop the destruction. Unfortunately, the negative force she is destined to fight is getting stronger and Magnus is thinking of taking the unprecedented step of interfering in Earth's development.

"Pisces, Cancer, Leo, can you hear me? It's Magnus."

"Yes, Magnus, we can hear you," reply the constellations.

The Unicorn Constellation's voice is soft because he is very old, and so very far away, but it is firm with the wisdom of millions of years. The constellations have great respect for him, and are flattered that the elderly unicorn has singled them out. In fact, Cancer, who is extremely insecure, is turning pink and making clicking noises as he turns around in circles, and Leo is positively glowing.

The other constellations are listening in on the conversation.

"I have been giving our predicament a lot of thought," says Magnus. "I was going to talk to Red Spider to see if she could weave Earth back together."

"But she's dying," chimes in Orion.

"Precisely," replies Magnus; "and now that she has become a Nebula, and is just a cloud of dust, I have a better idea. I'm going to ask her to fill up the hole in the ozone layer until the Earthlings are able to stop global warming."

"That will be the day," mutters Taurus under his breath.

"You know that, for some time, I have been watching a young woman on Earth who might be able to help us," says Magnus.

There's been a general feeling of gloom amongst the constellations because of what the Earthlings are doing to themselves. It seems as if they are destined to self-destruct.

"How can these stupid, arrogant Earthlings think that they are the only creatures who will be affected by their actions," says Scorpius.

"Save your breath," rumbles Taurus, "you know that they are still infants, with no idea of the impact their actions will have on others; they are not exactly heavenly bodies."

"Oh, very clever," sneers Scorpius. "But there is no excuse for their actions, I'm so angry I could sting someone."

"You'd better stay away from me," says Cancer, "or I'll clip your tail off."

"Please stop bickering, I know how you feel about Earthlings, but for our survival we have to help them, and you are starting to sound as infantile as they are."

There is shocked silence. Not just at his suggestion to help, but at his criticism of them. This must be serious.

"But, Magnus, we thought that it was impossible to interfere. You have always told us that planet Earth is an experiment. That they need to grow on their own, that they have free will, and that if they refuse to learn then they will literally have to sink or swim."

"At the moment it looks as if they are going to have to swim. If all the ice melts and the oceans envelope the land, they are lost," says Ursa Major, worried about the bears. He's been listening in on the conversation and is irritated that the Old Man didn't include him.

"Part of the reason that Earthlings are on the planet," says Magnus, "is to reach beyond themselves, to make a deeper connection to all that there is in the Universe."

"It is true that I told you that we couldn't interfere with the Earthlings' development, but if just one Earthling sincerely asks for help from Spirit then we have to help them."

"But we are not Spirit," say the shocked constellations in unison.

"No," replies Magnus, "but we are the instrument of Spirit, and if an Earthling asks for our help, then we have to give it to him or, in this case, her."

"Getting back to what I was saying, before I was interrupted. The 'her' I'm referring to is an Earthling who is trying to help the young girl I've been watching, and this Earthling wants to ask Draco for help."

"Draco!" say the constellations. "Why not us?"

"Brothers and sisters," replies Magnus, exasperated; "this is not the time for hurt feelings. The Earthling who is going to ask for Draco's help is called 'Grandmother'. Grandmother is in charge of training the girl, a very special girl, the girl who is going to lead them into a great battle."

"Do you believe that Grandmother has the necessary skills?" Orion worries.

"Grandmother is not a powerful enough name for a warrior coach," grumbles Taurus, bullheaded as always.

"I've had my eye on this special woman since the day she was born and I can assure you that she is more than qualified to teach the young girl. And, by the way, Grandmother's name is Vida, it means Victory; her name also means Life. Is that powerful enough for you?"

Chapter 2

It was 1962 when Vida came to San Francisco to visit her cousin Marta and Marta's husband. Knowing that Vida didn't have any money, Marta had sent her cousin a plane ticket, not realizing how this journey would change all their lives.

Born in a small Russian town near Belarus, this sheltered seventeen-year-old girl with a complicated past, fell in love with San Francisco and its people, becoming what her cousin called a "wild child." Nothing serious, smoking a little pot, dressing in colorful clothes, staying out all night and dancing in the streets, but she embarrassed her conservative cousin.

Vida's father, Uri, knew that his daughter had received a great gift, "the gift of sight," a gift that she had inherited from his mother, Dinara. Before Vida left for America he had given her Dinara's silver locket and explained about her lineage and the family secrets.

Aware that it would be dangerous for Vida to use her abilities in Russia, he was both happy and sad when she asked for his permission to stay in America; glad that his daughter could live without fear and escape the tyranny of an oppressive regime, but sad that he might never see her again. He later told her that when he saw her get on the plane for the U.S., anticipating that she would want to stay in that far-away country, he thought his heart might break.

Marta and her husband reluctantly agreed to sponsor Vida on the condition that she went to school, learned English, and that they would speak only English in the house.

Marta was impressed with how hard Vida studied and the long hours she spent on her homework, frequently working late into the night. She grudgingly praised her cousin's progress, and started looking for a man who might marry her and get her out of the house. The girls had never been close, and Vida always had the feeling that Marta was spying on her, that her cousin didn't trust her. But Vida had to admit that, when she arrived in San Francisco and got her first taste of freedom, she had behaved very badly.

While Vida was in school she made friends with a classmate named Katerina Korosidis. Her friend spoke English quite well but wanted to perfect it. She had dreams of becoming a translator and working at the United Nations.

Katerina was drawn to Vida; she felt that there was something special about this young Russian, and invited her to the family's home for dinner.

Because of her limited English, Vida was self-conscious, but Katerina's parents were kind and she was included in all their conversations. They were halfway through the meal when a young man strode into the room. Vida judged that he might be six or eight years older that she, and was very handsome. Before he sat down he apologized for his tardiness and introduced himself to Vida, telling her that his name was Athos. When they shook hands Vida felt a tingle of electricity run through her; it was almost like a shock of recognition and she knew that he felt it too.

Marta was delighted that her cousin was meeting what she considered "the right kind of people" and encouraged the weekly dinners at Katerina's home.

Over the next couple of months, when Vida could find some time away from her schoolwork, she would meet Athos. They would have coffee, stroll in the park, or walk the streets of San Francisco, fascinated by the exuberant and colorful people.

Athos worked hard in his family's import business, but always found time to be with Vida; he was almost hypnotized by her deep violet eyes.

When she had first met him Vida knew that she wanted to marry this special man and was thrilled when, six months later, he proposed.

Marta did little to disguise her joy and was grateful to Athos for taking Vida off her hands.

Vida hoped and prayed that her fiancé would continue to love her after she told him about her Russian family. She should have told him earlier, but just couldn't get up the nerve.

Trembling, Vida took a deep breath and told Athos what her father had told her.

Her grandfather, Fedor, had been a famous mystic and healer, and people would travel great distances for his help and council. He was also an advisor to the Romanovs.

After the royal family was assassinated, Fedor fled to England, where he continued to advise Russian émigrés, and there he met and married Dinara, a soft-spoken, demure woman with dark curly hair and startlingly blue eyes. He soon became aware that his beautiful and gentle Scottish wife was very powerful, with abilities that far exceeded his.

Dinara was descended from the Alexandrian Druids and was a Priestess in The Sisterhood. The Sisterhood was a group of Priestesses who spanned the globe and consisted of remarkable women with varying talents who represented many nations.

Although these were perilous times, after a few years Fedor and Dinara returned to Fedor's homeland. Moving to a small village, Fedor and Dinara had a son whom they named Uri. The revolution had changed everything and it would mean instant death for the entire family if anyone knew of Fedor's connection to the Romanovs or the fact that Dinara was a Priestess, so the family kept to themselves.

On a bitter cold fall night Dinara woke with a start from a vivid dream. It was a dream that predicted her death. Realizing that Uri needed to know about his lineage, Dinara knew whom she had to tell, her dream had made that very clear. Or had it?

Wrapping a heavy cloak around herself and pulling a wool muffler over her nose and mouth, she stepped into the freezing early morning air. Dinara looked around carefully to see if she was alone. Seeing no one she walked quickly to her neighbor's modest house. She paused before entering and wondered if she was making the right choice. Had she interpreted her dream correctly? This was going to be a life or death situation. Reassuring herself, she squared her shoulders and slipped silently through the unlocked door.

Alma was standing with her back to her.

"Hello," said Dinara.

Startled, Alma turned and, seeing the concerned expression on Dinara's face, asked, "What's wrong?"

Without answering her question, Dinara asked, "Where is your husband?"

"He's out trying to sell one of the chickens," Alma replied, "as if that's any of your business."

"I need to ask you for a favor," said Dinara, ignoring her neighbor's rudeness.

"What sort of favor?" asked Alma, suspiciously.

"I have to tell you a secret and I want to ask for your help," replied Dinara.

Alma crossed her arms defensively, covering herself.

"I don't want to hear any secrets. You've lived here for years and I know nothing about you or your family and I don't want to," said Alma, angrily.

"Uri plays with your children," said Dinara calmly, but wondering if she had made a big mistake. "I didn't tell you anything about our family because I wanted to protect you."

Fear passed across Alma's weathered and deeply lined face and, as she uncrossed her arms, her hands started to shake.

"Don't tell me any secrets," said Alma in a quivering voice. "I don't want to get into any trouble."

During the years that they had lived in the village, Dinara had watched her neighbor, and knew that the peasant woman had a kind heart; in fact her name means, "caring."

Although Dinara knew that The Sisterhood would protect Uri, he was only six years old and would need a family to care for him until he was a young man. She was having second thoughts. Did she really want to entrust the life of her precious son to a simple woman whom she hardly knew?

When Dinara told Alma about her dream, she could see that the woman was fearful and couldn't understand how Dinara knew that she was going to die. When Dinara told her that Fedor was a mystic, this was information that Alma could relate to.

Russia had a rich history of seers, mystics, and fortunetellers, and, although Alma had never consulted one, she didn't have the money, she knew that many people believed in, and relied on, prophecies.

Dinara removed the silver locket that she wore on a long chain around her neck and told Alma the rest of her story. She handed Alma the locket and showed her the secret catch that opened it. Inside was a picture of Dinara and Fedor taken on their wedding day along with a small piece of Dinara's hair.

Alma studied the photograph and gasped as she watched Fedor fade into the background and the image of Dinara begin to glow. The light shining from the woman in the photograph was so bright that it was almost incandescent. Frightened she snapped the locket shut.

Looking up, she could see that Dinara had a soft light glowing around her. Feeling faint, Alma dropped the locket as it started to radiate heat.

Dinara steadied Alma and picked up the locket. She tried to hand it back to Alma but Alma wouldn't take it.

Dinara asked Alma if she would care for Uri after her death, saying that, if she agreed, every few months the family would be blessed with a small gift. Perhaps their chickens would lay more eggs or a stranger visiting the village would have the money to buy one of their pigs, nothing to draw anyone's attention but enough to make their lives a little more comfortable.

Dinara could see that her neighbor was trying to think how she could use this information to her advantage. Dinara was getting nervous, but she had no other option; and she was sure that the woman had a good heart.

Alma was frightened by the information but, when she looked at Dinara, she saw that behind her determined expression Dinara's eyes were filled with desperation. This was a woman who loved her son and was tormented by the thought that he might come to harm. Alma could also see that Dinara was someone who possessed powerful magic. She wondered if she should tell the authorities, but they already knew that the boy was Fedor's son, so she had nothing to gain. There was no possibility of stealing the locket, she was afraid to touch it.

Dinara watched the woman as these thoughts showed themselves on her simple face.

Alma's attitude softened. She had lost one of her children to a fever and she understood a mother's grief. Taking Dinara's hand she agreed to care for Uri.

Dinara told her that the locket had to be hidden under the hearthstone in front of the fire, and remain there until Uri was sixteen. At that time Alma should give Uri the locket and tell him about his parents

Alma still refused to take the locket so Dinara lifted the hearthstone and buried the locket herself. Knowing that Alma was superstitious, as most peasants were, Dinara told Alma that she had put a spell on the locket to keep it safe.

Two days later, with leaden skies hovering over a light dusting of snow, Fedor heard shouts in the village. Picking up Uri, and taking Dinara by the hand the family raced for the protection of the woods, but the soldiers were waiting for them. Dinara was shot in the back, and as she lay dying, more snow started to fall covering this gentle woman with a feather-light blanket of white that began to stain scarlet from her blood. Fedor was clubbed on the head with a rifle, but before he lost consciousness he saw the terror in his son's eyes as the soldiers wrenched the screaming child from his arms. The last memory Uri had of his father was seeing soldiers holding Fedor's feet as they dragged him through the snow, his head bumping over the frozen ruts.

As soon as the villagers heard shouts they ran for the protection of their homes. They knew better than to be seen watching as someone was arrested. After the soldiers left, Alma's husband looked cautiously outside. Seeing the weeping child sitting in the snow beside his mother, the man gently picked him up and carried him into Fedor's house. Stripping off

Uri's wet clothes, he dressed him in dry garments then wrapped warm blankets around him. Covering the boy's face so that he didn't have to look at his mother for a second time, they walked past her body to reach the man's home.

When Alma's husband walked into the house carrying Uri, Alma smiled a sad weary smile. She had seen too much pain in her life for the smile to reach her eyes. It was as Dinara had predicted. The man sat the boy down beside a rickety wooden table and Alma put a steaming bowl of soup in front of him. It was only two small potatoes in thin liquid but it was hot and it was all they had.

That night, while the family slept, wolves crept silently into the village. They dragged Dinara into the forest and devoured her body.

Alma hadn't told her husband about Dinara's visit but knowing that her husband was a generous man, she was happy when he said that they should care for Uri. They embraced the traumatized child and raised him as their own.

On Uri's sixteenth birthday, Alma removed the hearthstone, but told Uri to dig up the locket; she still didn't want to touch it. Showing Uri how to open the locket, he gazed at the incandescent image of his mother as Alma told the boy about his parents and the family's history.

When Uri was eighteen he heard that Fedor had been taken to a Gulag and had died in the labor camps.

Uri had been courting a young woman for almost a year, and upon hearing the news of his father's death, he realized that life is fragile and that he had to embrace whatever happiness he could find in this wasteland he called home. He married the young woman and they had a daughter whom they named Vida. Uri prophesied that this extraordinary child would continue the Alexandrian line of Priestesses. And so it was.

After she told Athos her family's history, Vida removed the silver locket from around her neck and pressed it into Athos's hand. He opened it and looked at the photograph of her grandparents. The man was in shadow but the woman's smile was radiant.

She almost glows, Athos thought, *no wonder Vida is an extraordinary young woman, and I'm never going to let her go.*

Holding the locket, Athos tried to hide his shaking hands by turning away from Vida. Vida thought she might faint from the pain in her chest as she wondered if she had lost the man that she loved. Turning back to her, she could see the tears in his eyes. As he fastened the locket back around Vida's neck, he kissed her cheek and told her that he was saddened and shocked by her violent past, but that it didn't matter where she came from or who her family was as long as she loved him, and he promised to protect her forever.

Athos's family generously gave them a traditional Greek wedding and welcomed Vida, treating her like a daughter.

Because Vida loved Athos so much, there was always a small pain in her heart. This hard little lump in her chest reminded her of what she could have lost by confessing her past, but her new husband was completely besotted by his young wife with hypnotic violet eyes who was descended from mystics.

Once married, her Russian soul was pulling on her. When she suggested that they move to the countryside, and Athos agreed, Vida knew that her wonderful husband would do anything to make her happy. The family business was thriving and Athos could do much of his work from home, only needing to go to San Francisco once a month.

Wanting to start a family they bought an old farmhouse, large enough for many children, in the village of Finchfield in Humboldt County, 230 miles north of San Francisco. They called it "Pippin House" because of the apple tree in the garden called the "Coxy's Orange Pippin," a special British apple that reminded Vida of her Scottish heritage.

Vida immediately felt at home in the village. The villagers, although wary of this young woman from Russia, welcomed her and in time grew to rely on her expertise as an herbalist and midwife.

Although they'd hoped for more, Vida and Athos had only one child, a daughter whom they named Eve. Vida passionately loved the farmhouse, but she and Athos decided that when their daughter married they would give her Pippin House as a wedding present, and so they did.

Vida, now twenty-one-years old, was excited when her Scottish grandmother manifested herself. Vida had been dreaming about Dinara and was thrilled when she realized that she could actually see her.

On the afternoons, when Athos was out of the house and baby Eve was down for her nap, Dinara would visit Vida. Over a four-year period she taught her the rites and rituals of a Priestess of the Egyptian order, telling her that she was descended from Alexandrian Druids. Dinara told Vida that she had inherited great abilities and that one day she would teach her own granddaughter the sacred rites that would be used in a great battle.

Vida had been dreaming about a being with wings, whom she assumed was an angel. When she asked her grandmother about the dream and described the angelic being, Dinara was astonished and concerned. The angelic energy she was describing was Metatron, the highest of all the angels, considered the celestial scribe, the one who recorded all of history. If the angelic forces were involved, this was going to be a very great battle indeed.

Chapter 3

Leaving her small home on Maple Lane, Vida silently makes her way to Pippin House. Sensing that she is being watched she stops to listen for footsteps, and inhales deeply. She loves the smell of the earth and her acute senses tell her what animals, or humans, have just passed by.

As she waits, her breath forms a white cloud in the cold night air; but hearing nothing she hurries on. There is a lot to fear, but there is caution, not fear, in the way she walks. Her body language and footsteps are those of a stately woman who exudes confidence. She is a Priestess and a warrior and she's teaching her granddaughter everything she knows. At the moment, she just happens to be in a hurry.

Vida is being watched, but the watchers are billions of miles away in the infinite darkness of deep space. She is unable to see who is watching, but they can see her. The constellations have been watching her and the family for some time.

She slows her pace as she hears voices. Moving through the wall of trees that frame and protect the garden, she hears her son-in-law speaking to Maya.

"It's past your bedtime, Maya," Philip says. His voice is kind but firm.

Vida stops to watch. She knows how willful her granddaughter is, a trait the girl inherited from her. And at fifteen years old, this willfulness has only gotten stronger.

"Five minutes," Maya says, "just five more."

"Now," says Philip without taking his eyes from the sky. "You should have been in bed thirty minutes ago. Your mother is going to be mad at me for letting you stay out this long."

Maya, shivering from the cold, wipes her nose with the back of her hand. In the darkness she is barely visible. She's wearing sweat pants and her favorite old navy hoody and has pulled the cord so tightly around her face that her grandmother can see only her eyes and runny nose. Usually Maya is asleep by now, but Vida realizes that the girl must have been watching her father photographing the stars. She knows that her granddaughter loves looking at the night sky even though she can't see her favorite constellation, the Monoceros or Unicorn Constellation, without a telescope.

Vida hears Maya's protests. It sounds as if she is trying to bargain with her father, but he appears resolute and Vida sees her granddaughter's shoulders slump in resignation. Turning, Maya makes her way back to the farmhouse and, stamping up the porch steps, slams the front door behind her.

Knowing that it will take some time for Maya to settle down, particularly if she is in one of her moods, Vida decides to stay and watch Philip.

There's a heavy frost tonight and Vida can see that he's wearing his thick parka and is blowing on his

fingers and rubbing his cold hands together.   Vida
knows that he needs to keep his fingers warm, because
he can't use his camera with frozen fingers, and gloves
just get in the way.   In an effort to keep his equipment
dry, Philip is lying on an old blue plastic tarp that is
frayed at the edges; but it is glistening in the darkness
and he seems frustrated by the reflection, and pounds
the ground.   Cradling his camera as he tries to get the
perfect shot of the Milky Way, Philip is unaware that
the Milky Way is returning his gaze as if posing for his
lens.

The night is cold and clear and a thin sliver of
new moon is pushing its way to Earth, lighting up the
darkness.   Vida would love to help him capture the
explosion of stars that arc across the cosmos; wishing
she could pull the black velvet backdrop a little to the
left and cover the light, or just switch off the moon; but
there are some things that even she can't do, and
besides, she has more important things on her mind.

The frost-covered lawn gives the impression
that the frozen blades of grass are standing at attention
as they reflect what light there is back to the universe.
The pungent aroma of skunk wafts through the cold
night air.   Has something scared the animal?   Vida
turns as she hears a soft crunching sound that
announces the arrival of an opossum as it starts to
make its way through the frozen garden looking for its
evening meal.   Stopping abruptly, its glistening eyes
that glow in the moonlight are fixed on something dark
in the distance.   The opossum momentarily pauses,
then turns and scurries away from the farmhouse. Two
barn owls call a warning to each other and a fox barks,

but most of the other animals appear to be hiding in their burrows. Perhaps they too are becoming aware that the evil energy is gaining ground.

Philip makes a sound, somewhere between a sigh and a groan, and Vida can understand Philip's frustration. She saw him last night when the clouds wouldn't cooperate and she's glad that he's trying again. If he can't get the shot tonight he'll have to wait another month for the dark of the moon. He's so engrossed with his task that he doesn't notice her. But even if he could tear himself away from the magnificent night sky and look in her direction, he wouldn't be able to see her; at the moment she's invisible.

The night sky, as magnificent as it is, bears little resemblance to the sky of her childhood but it brings back memories of a vast expanse of stars that were so close you could almost touch them. Tonight's chill is practically balmy compared to the deep snows and freezing slush of the harsh Russian winters, but it reminds Vida of that moment in time when her life changed forever. The moment when her father had told her the family history.

As she does nightly, Vida slips into her sleeping grandchild's small bedroom and is greeted by Maya's pets, Mango, a big orange cat and a shaggy wolfhound named Frederick. Vida is still invisible but the animals can see her. Mango jumps into her lap and Frederick stretches out on the rug and puts his head on her feet.

Annoyed with herself for wasting valuable time watching Philip, Vida gently moves Frederick aside and puts Mango on the floor. She stacks crystals at Maya's crown chakra and feet, then projects fire into them from her fingertips. As the crystals heat up there is a faint smell of burning as the tiny hairs on Maya's body are singed. Then holding her hands over her granddaughter's body she directs the energy back and forth between the crystals to strip any negativity from Maya. Surrounding her with candles and lavender Vida wraps Maya in bright rainbows, but the evil energy no longer seems to be afraid of the light.

Vida watches with concern as her grand-daughter thrashes in bed, gasping for air. It pains her to see the fear on the girl's face as she flails her arms at the enemy while it tries to take control of her dreams and visions, and she wishes that Maya could have a normal life, but she knows that her grandchild's destiny is going to be far from normal.

As she looks into the child's dreams she sees that Maya is fighting the snakes. This is a dream she's been experiencing since she was six years old. Sitting at her bedside, Vida is afraid that the snakes are becoming bigger and more powerful. Tonight they are wrapping themselves around her neck, trying to strangle her. The evil energy has found its way into her mind and is trying to eliminate her. Vida watches as the girl tries to climb beyond the reach of the vipers that, in her dream, are covering the floor. There are piles of them, slithering and hissing at each other as they wind their way onto her bed. Covered in sweat, her wet hair plastered to her head, Maya tries to run, but an unknown force holds her down.

Vida watches as Mango hisses and Frederick growls. Mango jumps onto the bed and tries to wake Maya by pawing her face and gently biting her eyelids, but she is in another world and the animals are powerless to help.

Nighttime is when the evil energy is the strongest and most aggressive. This black mist slips into the girl's bedroom smothering everything in its path. It slides through the window across the sill and down the wall and its tentacles glide silently across the wooden floor, mimicking the snakes in her dream. It slips through the crack under the door, and what used to be a black mist is now as sticky as heavy black syrup.

Vida, still invisible, wishes she could comfort her grandchild. Every night is a battle for Maya's survival and, as painful as it is to watch, this is a battle that will only make her stronger and, ultimately, Maya is the only one who can defeat the snakes.

As the sun rises, the snakes retreat and Vida watches Maya as she awakens, covered in sweat and exhausted. For several months the child has been waking more tired than when she went to bed, and the fear and fatigue on her face is alarming. Reluctant to let her out of her sight even for a moment, Vida hovers as Maya, her drained body shaking, drags the damp sheets off the bed and dumps them onto the floor and makes her way, unsteadily, to the bathroom. Turning the water on full blast, Maya braces herself against the cold tiled wall as she lets the hot water pour over her head and down her tortured body.

Vida knew when Maya was conceived that her daughter, Eve, was going to have a very special child. She had looked into her womb and discerned a range of colors in patterns that she had never seen before. The fetus was surrounded by indigo light but there was also light blue, pink, green, and white spiraling around the infant. Vida helped Eve through her pregnancy, making sure that she ate only the organic produce that came from their own garden, and used the herbs that Athos, had shown them how to use. Vida didn't tell her daughter that she had seen the child's destiny; she didn't want to frighten her.

Vida knew that Eve was going to give birth to an Indigo Child. A few are being born around the planet, and more will follow. They will grow into adults who will guide Earth in a new direction: a direction of peace and inclusion. Vida knew that the baby needed to grow and take risks, so she kept the secret; she didn't want Eve to become overprotective.

Today is Maya's fifteenth birthday and, after tonight's birthday festivities, Vida plans to explain to the child what is in store for her. There are great dangers ahead for Maya, but Vida knows her grandchild will succeed, she must succeed; the fate of the world rests on her small shoulders.

Chapter 4

The Constellations are watching the drama unfolding on Earth.

"Hydra, why are the snakes attacking the young girl?" asks Leo. He is developing a fondness for Maya because of the way she treats Mango.

"It seems that the enemy is controlling the snakes," replies Hydra, the Snake Constellation, sounding bored.

"Can't you stop the snakes from attacking?" asks Leo, nervously. Hydra is so big and has such a sharp tongue, that he is a little afraid of her.

"Don't you think that I would if I could?" snaps Hydra. "Stop looking at me like that, it's not my fault."

Leo persists, his voice quivering. "Magnus, is there any way that Hydra can help Maya?"

Magnus sighs. He doesn't want to be pulled into the middle of an argument. "Leo, I know you are concerned and are anxious to help; we all are, but it's a little too early to get involved."

"But what if Grandmother can't help Maya, the snakes might kill her," says Leo, starting to choke up.

"Try not to get so emotional," replies Magnus gently. "If you watch carefully you'll see that Grandmother believes that this is a problem for Maya to solve, that this is part of her education."

Hydra flicks her tongue at Leo. He looks crestfallen and backs away. Sirius, the Dog Star, says, "I'm with you Leo. I've never liked snakes." Hydra hisses at him.

Chapter 5

The animals seem to be aware that when Maya is meditating she needs to be alone and they keep their distance; but as soon as she opens her eyes Mango jumps onto her lap and rubs the side of his mouth along her chin. This is part of their morning ritual, Mango announcing to the world, "She's Mine." Getting up from the chair Maya puts Mango onto the floor as Frederick nuzzles her, patiently waiting to be scratched behind his ears.

The family found Frederick at the local animal shelter. He was only six months old, but was growing so fast that his former owners were afraid they wouldn't be able to manage him, completely unaware of how gentle this puppy with huge paws was going to be.

Mango, on the other hand, adopted Maya.

The sun had been hot that day and Maya had been working hard in the garden. Her mother, afraid that she might get sunstroke, insisted that she rest in one of the lawn chairs. As Maya relaxed, sipping from a tall glass of water containing thin cucumber slices and baby wild strawberries, she saw a small orange face peering at her through the long grass. She called softly to the animal. It came a little closer. She called again and a little orange cat moved cautiously towards her. Maya called a third time and a flash of orange light ran at her, jumping into her lap and knocking her backwards in the chair. The water glass went flying and the cucumber slices and strawberries landed in the grass. As Maya lay back in the chair, trying not to laugh in case she frightened the animal, it stretched itself across her chest, put its front legs around her neck and drooled all over her. From that moment on, this little orange cat, which Maya called Mango, was reluctant to leave her side.

This morning, she rubs her beautiful feline on the top of his head as she says, "Sorry, Mango, I don't have time for a cuddle this morning, but as it's my birthday, you can sleep with me tonight." Mango purrs loudly, gazing at her with his big yellow eyes. Maya is aware that her grandmother doesn't like Mango sleeping with her; she had told her that their energy fields could become entangled, especially when she is having so many violent dreams. But tonight, as it's her birthday, Maya is looking forward to breaking the rules; she's going to let Mango sleep with her.

Sometimes, when Maya is too exhausted to sleep, it soothes her to watch the colors that dance around the animals, and she loves to see the sparks fly when they are dreaming.

This morning she doesn't feel like doing Yoga, but she does the Sun Salutation and some stretches, telling herself that she'll do more later.

Taking fresh sheets from the closet Maya holds them to her face and breathes in their healing fragrance before making the bed. Her mother always places bags of home-grown lavender between the sheets in the linen closet, the energy of the herbs penetrates Maya's core and helps her feel grounded and regenerated.

Maya has a critical look on her face as she studies herself in the bathroom mirror. There are dark circles under her eyes and she thinks she is starting to look like an old woman. Her green eyes are framed by long thick lashes, and she smiles when she thinks of the girls at school who accuse her of using mascara. She studies her mouth. Her full lips and slightly lopsided smile give more interest to her almost symmetrical face. Maya has her maternal grandfather's Mediterranean complexion, and never seems to get burned by the sun. This is a great irritation to her best friend Rose, who is blond and has pale English skin, courtesy of her father. Trying to tuck the frizzy locks of her curly auburn hair into place, Maya gives an exasperated sigh as they spring back, and she gives up.

This morning, Maya is going to break another rule. She puts her Minoan gold bee necklace on a long black cord and, placing it around her neck, tucks it into her clothing so that her teachers can't see it. It was a gift from grandfather Athos, and it's one of her most treasured possessions. She misses him and always wears it on weekends and usually puts it on when she gets home from school; but today is different, this is her special day.

Athos, who was born in Greece, gave Maya the necklace when she was twelve years old, and told her that it was a replica of an almost four-thousand-year-old piece of jewelry found in a cemetery near the town of Heraklion, close to the Palace of Knossos on the island of Crete. He also told her that the Minoan Cretans were the first people to domesticate bees, building hives and harvesting the honey.

Maya thinks this necklace symbolizes life; it shows two bees holding a small globe between them. Some people think it might be a drop of honey or some pollen, but Maya thinks that it's the sun. The sun, water, and bees are essential to life. Without the bees to pollinate the blossoms, and the sun and rain to help them grow, there would be no food, no crops of any kind, just a wasteland.

Maya's other treasure is a gift that Grandpa Athos gave her for her tenth birthday. It's a statuette that is a reproduction of a Snake Goddess from the Minoan period. It shows a beautiful bare-breasted woman in a long skirt with snakes wrapped around her arms. At the top of the Goddess's headdress sits a golden cat, and Maya thinks he looks just like Mango. It is strange that Maya, who has such a fear of snakes, loves this statuette.

Athos was a great storyteller and Maya loved to hear about Goddesses and Amazons. He told her that during the Minoan period the Palace at Knossos was, at that time, the largest and most advanced building in Europe. She took some books from the library that showed the palace's red columns that are narrower at the bottom and wider at the top; it doesn't make sense, but apparently worked because, thousands of years later, parts of the Palace are still standing. But her favorite picture is that of the bull dancers. She would listen, enthralled, as her grandfather told her tales of a labyrinth under the Palace of Knossos and the Snake Goddesses who cared for an enormous bull, and she visualized the bull dancers vaulting over this huge animal. Athos told her that, at the time of the Snake Goddesses, Crete was a matriarchal society, and that Crete was one of the most advanced civilizations in the world. They had their own navy, with warships that could repel anyone who tried to invade them, and they traded with Egypt, Greece, Turkey, and many of the islands in the Mediterranean.

Looking at herself in the mirror, Maya wishes that grandfather Athos were here for her fifteenth birthday. *Not that he would notice a huge change,* thinks Maya, *I still have the body of a twelve-year old boy.*

Maya is small for her age, only five feet two inches tall and is almost flat chested. Rose, who is the same age as Maya, is two inches taller and has developed quite a figure. *It's just not fair! All the boys are attracted to Rose.*

Maya wonders if Amul, her friend since kindergarten, is attracted to Rose. With Rose's light skin and blond hair and Amul's dark skin and hair they would make a cute couple. While she's having this thought she realizes that she's feeling a tinge of jealousy and secretly hopes that Amul is interested in her instead of Rose. Although he was born in America his Indian parents gave him the Hindi name Amul, which means "Priceless."

Why can't I look more like a woman, she wonders as she carries the damp sheets downstairs.

Maya inhales the aroma of freshly baked bread wafting from the kitchen as she walks into the laundry room. Dropping the sheets into the basket on top of the washing machine, she tells her mother that she'll take care of the laundry when she gets home. She doesn't mention the bad dream; she has them so often that they are beginning to feel normal to her, and she doesn't want to worry her mother unnecessarily.

Eve receives her daughter's morning kiss with a smile. "Happy birthday Darling," she says and quickly turns back to the stove; she doesn't want Maya to see the concern in her eyes. Her daughter is looking so tired, almost haggard. Where is the beautiful child who always used to wake smiling? Eve thinks that she has to talk to Vida; something's not right. *Why is Maya waking in damp sheets? Is she having nightmares that nobody is telling her about? She's too old to be wetting the bed.* This is more than growing pains. Teenage girls can get moody, and she certainly was a handful when she was younger, and sometimes she still is, but it's as if her daughter and Vida have a secret that they aren't sharing with her.

Eve puts Maya's favorite mushroom omelet on a plate, surrounding it with homegrown tomatoes and sprigs of parsley. Slicing a large piece off the loaf that's fresh from the oven, she adds it to the plate; then spreads the warm bread with butter and drizzles honey all over it.

"Just the way you like it," she says, putting the plate in front of her daughter.

Almost everything is from the garden. The house is on four acres so Eve has plenty of room for her beehives, the apple trees, vegetable and flower gardens, milkweed for the butterflies, and the lavender. There's also a large barn for the animals. They have chickens, ducks, their own cow, and goats, so the eggs, honey, and butter are as fresh as they can be. The chickens and ducks are wonderful at eating the snails and slugs that plague the vegetable garden. Everything is natural, with no need for pesticides.

Eve is not as tall as her mother and definitely doesn't have Vida's stately bearing but she's never happier than when she is on her knees digging in the well-fertilized soil. She has a lovely singing voice and, while she works in the garden, she serenades her plants and they reward her with a rich bounty of flowers, vegetables, and herbs.

Eve loves the farmhouse, but when she married Philip they were both reluctant to accept her parents' generous gift of Pippin House. Vida assured them that she and Athos would be close by and that the grounds needed Eve's gardening skills, insisting that the young couple accept the farmhouse. Once Eve got over her guilt she embraced the magnificent gift. She was thrilled because of her many childhood memories, and the knowledge that she had been born at Pippin House. She really wanted her children to be born there too. Eve had put her heart and soul into the land and it would take years to recreate the wonderful flower garden elsewhere, even if that were possible.

Vida makes herself visible and arrives just as Philip walks into the kitchen. Birthday wishes and kisses from everyone, but Philip has a breakfast meeting with a client and has to leave.

On his way out of the door he calls back to Maya, "Sweetheart, I don't want you opening any of your gifts until this evening, I want the family to be together, and Rose and Amul will be hurt if you don't wait for them." Desperately wanting to open her gifts now, Maya reluctantly agrees.

Maya loves her grandmother dearly but has always been a little frightened and awed by her power. As Maya finishes her breakfast she wonders if tonight, on her fifteenth birthday, she will finally have the courage to ask her grandmother about her fears. What makes this woman so powerful?

Chapter 6

Vida is going to retire from The Sisterhood and, for the last two years, she has been transporting herself beyond time and space to sit beside the girl, gently teaching her while she sleeps. Normally initiates do not start their training until they are eighteen, but these are not normal times. Tomorrow Vida will start the girl's formal training. She had wanted to wait until Maya was sixteen because the girl is young for her age and Vida still thinks of her as a child, but the situation is becoming critical. She has to empower the girl now, and she prays that Maya is strong enough for the rigorous tests and intense challenges ahead.

As High Priestess of The Sisterhood, it is Vida's duty to train her granddaughter to take her place as Priestess of the Egyptian Order. The title of High Priestess will not go to Maya but will pass to Artemis, Vida's second in command and a very experienced member of The Sisterhood.

The Sisterhood spans the globe with many Priestesses teaching students to eventually replace them. The tests are so rigorous that many initiates fail, some even die; but Vida is determined that her granddaughter will be initiated and take her place as Priestess. Once she has passed all the initiatory rites,

Vida can share the sacred knowledge with her. Maya will have access to the deepest secrets and rituals of The Sisterhood and have the help of her guardians and guides in order to cut through the darkness and bring back the light. Maya will wear the breastplate of the Priestess and have unparalleled protection, and she will need it; the evil energy is getting stronger every day and Vida is worried that her granddaughter might not survive long enough to fulfill her destiny.

Vida has watched this evil energy, or what she is now calling the "Dark Menace," gathering strength. It slides out of its hiding place and weaves its black tentacles around the delusional, and encourages those seeking revenge. She has seen it engender chaos around the world and knows that its fuel is blood. As countries get pulled deeper into conflict the stronger the enemy becomes. It stokes the fires that cause the atrocities that are increasing around the globe: mass beheadings, people being burned alive, and tyrants gassing their own people. It's as if some countries have reverted back to the Dark Ages, and that's exactly what the enemy wants. This vile energy revels in chaos and sucks the blood out of the earth, the blood it needs to survive.

The Dark Menace has existed for thousands of years in one form or another and Vida knows that it can adjust its shape to fit the current landscape. It wraps itself around the weak and frail. Its poison penetrates the brains of the superstitious and self-righteous and it feeds off the blood of its victims. And it is growing.

Vida knows that in its current manifestation the Dark Menace is a monstrous vampire whose only purpose is to cause misery; and without blood to feed on, it will shrivel up and lose all power. She also knows that this evil energy is unpredictable. At the moment it is a mist that is hiding in the cracks and crevices of the world, but its poison is spreading. It is taking lies and manifests them as truths, corrupting the gullible.

Maya isn't aware of it yet, but she threatens the Dark Menace, and Vida is determined that this evil energy will not harm her grandchild. When Maya meditates, Vida knows that the enemy can see the light radiating from the girl. Even the constellations can see it. Maya frightens the enemy, and a frightened enemy is an unpredictable enemy.

Vida, as midwife, brought Maya into the world. Her daughter Eve is slender and small-boned, and this baby with a mission fought so hard to be born that Vida was worried that Eve might not survive. Vida knew that Eve would refuse to have a Cesarean; she felt strongly that the infant had to make its own way into this world or not at all. Vida empathized with Philip as he pleaded with his wife to let him take her to the hospital, but Vida knew that her daughter was as stubborn as she is.

Once Maya arrived, healthy and unharmed, Vida told her daughter that she might not live through another birth; so, instead of siblings, the family provided Maya with a puppy and kittens, something that she could cuddle and love. As she grew older and worked with the farm animals she treated them with a firm but loving hand, and they rewarded her tenfold.

Chapter 7

Vida is conflicted. She adores her fifteen-year-old grandchild and would love her to stay young forever, but worries that she isn't mature enough to understand the gravity of what she is about to tell her. Vida strokes Maya's hair absentmindedly, while thinking that this will be her last birthday as a child. Tomorrow Maya will have to take up the mantle of a warrior, and Vida is fearful that she isn't ready for the enormous task. She's also afraid that the Dark Menace is not only trying to attack Maya, but is targeting the village; she has seen the black mist hovering over the houses.

"What do you think Dad got me?" Maya asks her grandmother.

"Darling, you've not exactly been subtle," replies Vida. "I'm pretty sure he got the message. I know you want to open your gifts now but it's very important that you learn how to control your emotions, you have to be patient."

Maya gives an exasperated sigh.

"Maya, I'm serious. One day, your life and the lives of others may depend on how well you master your emotions."

Maya gives her a startled look, but is so excited by the possibility of getting the gift that she's been longing for, that the enormity of what she has just been told doesn't seem to register.

Philip, an amateur astronomer, has two powerful telescopes, but Maya wants her own. She wants to follow the Unicorn Constellation. Her father had pointed it out to her when she was very small and she feels a special connection with the unicorns. In fact she has been dreaming about them.

One morning, Maya awoke and saw two unicorns, standing on either side of her bed, and she knew, or thought she knew, that it wasn't a dream. The unicorns were white, unusually large and thickly muscled, and had energy spiraling around their horns.

"Why are you here?" Maya asked. "What are you here to teach me?"

The unicorns did not speak, but a voice in her head told her that she would get that information when the time was right.

Maya gobbles down her breakfast, grabs her jacket, slips her arms through her heavy backpack, and dashes off. Today she has a science test and she's looking forward to it. She has an aptitude for science and math, and some of her classmates harass her. She laughs it off, realizing that they are just frustrated because they have to struggle to get passing grades, while Maya seems to breeze through with little effort. The day feels infinitely long, so, when the final bell finally rings, Maya quickly confirms with Rose and

Amul that they are going to join the family for dinner, and she runs along Maple Lane.

Maple Lane is a misnomer, lined as it is with Horse Chestnut trees. This is one of the charming peculiarities of the village. In fact all of the streets that are named after trees, are lined with a different species of tree. This spring day the branches are leafless, but small buds are starting to show themselves, and Maya can't wait until the trees are in full bloom. Running beneath the canopy of branches, Maya thinks of Amul and how they used to play Conkers together in the fall. Rose had shown her how to play the game; something she learned from her English father. The Conker is the brown nut or seed of the Horse Chestnut tree. You drill a hole through the center of it and thread a long string through the hole and knot it at one end. Each person has the Conker on a long string and you whack your opponent's Conker until it breaks. Amul always managed to win but would be very upset if he hit Maya's arm by mistake. Maya always ended up with bruises, but it was such a fun game, and they both got covered with dirt when they buried each other in piles of crimson and gold leaves. She can still remember the smell of the damp earth and that it took forever to get the small leaves and twigs out of her curly hair.

Vida had told Maya that there wouldn't be any lesson today but as she reaches her grandmother's house she goes inside to see if she can help, or at least that's what she tells herself. What she really wants is to see if there are any clues as to the gift that her grandmother is giving her.

Finding her grandmother's house empty, and knowing that the farrier's wife is about to give birth, means just one thing; Maya's birthday celebration is going to be a little late. A baby is on its way and the only birthday this baby is interested in is its own. Maya runs to the Phelps's house, and finds Jim Phelps sitting on the porch.

He smiles nervously at Maya as she walks up the steps. This is his second child. Vida delivered the couple's first baby, a son, and he and his wife feel very comfortable with Vida taking care of the delivery. Maya has known Jim all her life. When she was younger, sometimes, as a special treat, he would let her ride in the truck with him when he visited the local ranches to shoe the horses.

Maya gives Jim an encouraging pat on the shoulder, and then looks up at the sky. A large dark cloud covers the sun that was shining brightly just moments ago. It briefly registers that there are no other clouds in the sky, before she quickly enters the house. As she slips quietly into the bedroom her grandmother acknowledges her with a smile. Vida is in charge, but something feels different. Maya can't tell what the difference is, but her grandmother has been teaching her how to feel energy and she knows that something is wrong.

There's a lot of activity, bowls of hot water and towels are carried into the bedroom, and the tension is palpable. Maya's excitement grows as she watches from the shadows; it's as if there's a rainbow over the small room and the space is filled with light. A large green flare shoots out of her grandmother's side and the room is filled with a green glow as Maya sees the colors dancing around her grandmother's hands, but now the colors are fading. There is definitely something wrong. Maya looks at her grandmother and she has never seen such grim determination etched into her beautiful face.

Vida has been watching the Dark Menace and knows that it can smell blood. She senses that this bloodsucker not only wants the baby but also wants to take the mother. Calling on The Sisterhood for help, Vida uses all of her power to drive it from the house. Abruptly, the colors around her hands become stronger and Maya watches the tension flow from her grandmother's face. Maya can now see the colors of the rainbow envelop the infant as a new life is brought into the world. As soon as she sees the baby, Maya lets out a sigh. She'd been holding her breath, but now that she sees the colors around the child, she can relax.

"Well, that was an unexpected lesson," says Vida. "I'm glad you were here to see the power of The Sisterhood. I'll tell you more about it later, but I need to stay here a little longer."

"But everything's okay?" asks Maya, a little anxiously.

"Yes, my sweet, everything is fine, in fact, more than fine. Look at this beautiful child. Tell Jim he can come in."

Maya bends down and whispers to the tiny infant, "Happy birthday, little one," and quietly leaves the room.

Grandmother has been teaching Maya how to see auras, and there have been a couple of births recently when the newborn looked grey and the baby had lived only a short while. Maya had been very distressed when this happened, but Vida had explained that, sometimes when babies are born, the experience of this world is so traumatic that they want to return to the Spirit world they came from, and they make the decision to go back to the "Source." She said that there are many reasons that someone chooses to leave this earthly life. Sometimes a baby comes into this world to teach its parents about grief and loss, before it makes its journey home.

"Is 'Source' the same as God?" Maya had asked.

Her grandmother said that different people have different names for it. Many native peoples call it "Great Spirit," some call it "Yahweh," but it doesn't matter what you call it, it really has no name, it's just all that there is.

Walking onto the porch Maya says, "Jim, you can go in now, you have a beautiful, healthy daughter."

Jim beams at Maya as she runs down the steps; she must get home to help her mother prepare her birthday dinner.

Walking into the house Maya hears music. Eve loves to sing and play the piano, so music is an important part of their lives. Eve is quite talented; she can play classical music and even tries a little jazz, but with less success. Entering the kitchen, she can hear that Eve has her Bose speakers on full blast playing her favorite folk music. This is one of Eve's little indulgences; if you are going to listen to recorded music it should be on the best machine that you can afford. Maya picks up the colander filled with snap peas and, holding it in an embrace, dances around the kitchen, making her mother laugh. Putting down the colander Maya starts to trim the brussels sprouts while her mother puts the finishing touches to the ducks and the roasted potatoes.

Maya always feels a pang of regret when one of her animals is killed, but she realizes that they have lived a free life and have been killed in the most humane way. She had recently taken some live rabbits to the market but when she heard how some people killed the rabbits, she was horrified. Now she kills them herself.

Rose and Amul are the honored guests and, for the celebration, Eve has filled the house with flowers from the garden. Eve always has flowers in the house, but tonight, even though it's cold outside, it almost feels as if they are sitting in the garden surrounded by a riot of color and texture. There are Peonies, Maya's favorite, brilliant yellow Daffodils, multicolored Tulips, pretty little Crocuses, and Hyacinths whose perfume is so delicious you can almost taste it. Rose doesn't say anything about the cut flowers, but everybody knows that it's painful for her. She is so sensitive that she can hear their cries when they are cut.

The dinner table is set with the finest china, crystal glasses, and beautiful linens, and the Hyacinth centerpiece is spectacular.

Philip's father, Grandpa Joe, made the dining table and chairs, and at a glance it is clear that a man who loved wood and working with his hands had created them. The Cherry wood boat-shaped trestle table has a dark stained oak base with matching chairs. It is a work of art; the contrasting colors of the woods are quite dramatic but it's a simple design that fits the lifestyle of the family and is enjoyed by them all daily. Two bottles of Eve's Elderberry wine are on the table, placed on small, round, beautifully etched, silver trays. The trays were a wedding present from Philip's parents.

When everyone is seated Philip pours wine into all the glasses. The children feel very grown up, this is the first year that they've been allowed to taste wine. Philip holds up his glass to make a toast. "To Grandpa Athos, Grandma Fergie, Grandpa Joe, and all absent friends."

Everyone holds up their glasses and repeats, "Absent friends."

Eve has cooked two ducks so there is plenty for everyone to have seconds, with leftovers for sandwiches tomorrow. The birthday dinner is a great success, and Maya gets her special chocolate cake for dessert.

Maya opens her grandmother's beautifully wrapped gift first. She gasps when she sees the Garnet stud earrings and runs to a mirror to put them on. She had her ears pierced two years ago on her thirteenth birthday and always wears earrings when she isn't in school. Maya throws her arms around her grandmother.

"I love them, thank you so much. I've wanted Garnets for a long time."

"I know you have, Darling, and they are a wonderful stone for protection."

"I'm never going to take them off," exclaims Maya.

"Mom," says Eve, "can't earrings just be earrings?"

"No they can't," replies Vida. "Every stone has its own unique power."

"Whatever you say, Mom."

"Ladies, let's not do this," says Philip. "Tonight is a celebration for my special girl."

Everyone can feel the tension in the room but Rose takes a deep breath and gives Maya her gift. Knowing that Maya loves unicorns, Rose has chosen a journal with a magnificent unicorn on the cover and Amul gives her a statue of Ganesha, the Hindu God with the elephant head. Maya knows that Ganesha is the God of new beginnings and the remover of obstacles, and she says she is going to put it on her altar. She gives Rose and Amul big hugs and kisses and notices that Amul's cheeks flush, but Rose is pale and seems distracted.

Maya's excitement is building but she almost doesn't want to open the gift from her parents in case she is disappointed.

When Maya finally tears the wrapping from her parent's gift, she is speechless. They have given her a very powerful telescope, far more than she could have hoped for. She runs to her father and, on the verge of tears, gives him a big hug. Then she takes her mother's hands, pulls her out of her chair, gives her a big kiss, and twirls her around the room until Eve laughingly protests, saying that she's getting dizzy. Maya is so excited that she wants to set up her telescope now and the one constellation she wants to see is the unicorn, the Monoceros.

Chapter 8

When the guests leave, Maya is still on a high. She's thrilled with her gifts but she's also had too much chocolate cake, and the sugar is giving her the shakes. A little unsteadily, Maya follows as Vida leads her up the stairs and into her bedroom. Vida is always beautiful to Maya but, tonight, she's resplendent in a deep blue velvet gown embroidered with silver thread that twinkles as if it were drawing light directly from the stars. Her thick dark hair, with the broad silver streak in the front, is pulled back with silver combs that sparkle and reflect the light.

Stroking the silky softness of the velvet dress, Maya has a pleading look on her face as she asks her grandmother if she can borrow her combs someday. She adores her grandmother and wants to look just like her. The combs would look wonderful holding back her unruly hair. Vida replies, with a smile, that she will give them to Maya on her sixteenth birthday.

A shadow dulls Vida's stunning violet eyes and she has a grave expression on her face as she takes Maya's hands. She doesn't want to tell Maya what's in store for her, but she has to prepare her granddaughter for the dangers ahead.

"Grandmother, have I done something wrong?" asks Maya, concerned by the look on Vida's face. She is sitting cross-legged on her bed so that her grandmother can have the rocking chair.

"Maya, you know that I have been watching you at night, and I told you that it was so that I could continue your instruction while you were sleeping, but it's a lot more complicated than that. You are a very special young girl and now I feel you are old enough to learn the truth."

Maya leans forward, eager and fearful at the same time. She wants to hear what Vida has to say but is concerned by her grandmother's ominous tone. She had felt so light and happy during the party, but now all the joy is draining out of her. Vida leans forward in the chair. Her grandmother's eyes, that have always been so full of love and understanding, now have a hard steely look to them.

Vida is speaking gently, softly, trying not to frighten her granddaughter. She knows that Maya has only felt love and compassion from her, and it's tearing her apart to tell her what the future holds.

"I know that your dreams are becoming more violent, because I can see into them," Vida whispers. "Remember that I told you that where there is light there is darkness. There are always opposing forces, like a positive force and a negative force. We all have light and dark within us; learning how to integrate the two is a challenge that we all face. Science shows that if there is a shift of energy in one part of the world, however minute, it could be the flutter of a butterfly's wings, this shift is felt in another part of the world.

Compared to the size of the Cosmos, which is far bigger than our little brains can comprehend, we live on a very small planet and everything we do affects everything, and everyone else. We are all connected."

If we are all the same, how can we tell the good from the bad? Maya wonders.

As if reading her mind Vida says, "Sweetheart, you intuitively know good from bad, and you see and hear things that others don't. This is the reason your dreams are becoming so frightening; the evil energy is threatened by you, it sees you as a beacon of light and it is trying to attack you."

Vida sees that Maya is trying to make sense of her grandmother's words.

"I'm not going to let anything happen to you, Darling, but I want you to understand why you are having so many nightmares and sleepless nights."

"Why is this evil energy threatened by me?" asks Maya, feeling as if she is about to faint, as the color drains from her face.

"You have a very special destiny and this evil energy wants to stop you from reaching your goal," replies Vida

"What is my goal?" asks Maya, alarmed by the expression on her grandmother's face.

Vida walks over to Maya and sits on the bed next to her. Taking her hands she kisses Maya's fingers.

"My darling, you are going to stop this evil energy, I call it the 'Dark Menace,' from destroying the world."

Maya's mouth falls open.

Vida is afraid that Maya might be going into shock.

"Are you alright, Maya? Can you still hear me? We can stop and continue this tomorrow."

Maya closes her mouth, she's having trouble swallowing, but she manages to shake her head and in a croaking voice says that she wants to continue.

"I want to ask your permission to get some additional help to protect you," Vida says.

"What sort of protection?"

"You know that to take my place as Priestess, I was planning on starting your formal education when you were sixteen and hoped to complete it by the time you were eighteen."

Nodding her head, Maya has the feeling that she has been lifted up out of her body and is looking down at two complete strangers.

"The situation has changed and we have to accelerate the process."

Maya has definitely left her body now, and feels as if she might float away.

"If it's alright with you, I want to start your training early tomorrow morning."

Maya knows that she is nodding her head but she's not sure why; she's just a young girl who loves her family and animals. What is happening?

"Do you remember your reaction, I think you were about six years old, when your dad first let you look through his telescope and you saw the Unicorn Constellation?"

"Yes," says Maya. She hears her voice but it's as if someone else is talking, someone who is far, far away.

"I remember, too," Vida says. "You fell in love with the unicorn for a reason; it is going to be very important in your future."

Taking a small bottle out of a pocket, Vida rubs some lavender oil onto her palms and then, without touching Maya, passes her hands around the outside of her granddaughter's body. The room is infused with a wonderful fragrance as Vida passes Maya a glass of water.

"Now, I know I'm asking a lot, because you want to escape, but I want you to come back into your body. Will you do that for me?" A flickering light returns to Maya's eyes as she blinks, struggling to regain her focus.

"I want you to take three deep breaths and focus on me, only me; don't look at anything else in the room."

Mango jumps onto the bed, bringing Maya back to the present with a jolt.

That's one way to do it, thinks Vida.

Vida takes her granddaughter's shaking hands and tells her that she wants her permission to ask for help from Draco, the Dragon Constellation. Seeing the question in Maya's eyes, Vida continues.

"I need your permission because this is your journey," says Vida, "and I have been communicating with the constellations for some time, I just have to think the question and the answer pops into my head.

"I will give my life to protect you, and The Sisterhood is very powerful, but if Draco agrees it will give you another layer of protection, and you are going to need it, the Dark Menace is getting stronger all the time."

"But what is Draco going to do?" asks Maya.

"I'll get into that in a moment, but first I have to ask him if he is willing to help."

"I'm sure he will agree, Grandmother. You can persuade anyone to do anything. I have complete faith in you." Maya is trying to sound positive but she is frightened by the concern she sees in her grand-mother's beautiful eyes.

"Your initiations will be very difficult," says Vida, "very few students are able to complete the course, but I have faith that you will be able to accomplish all that will be asked of you. The problem is that, in order to complete the initiatory rites, you have to make yourself very vulnerable, and that is an ideal situation for the Dark Menace to penetrate your defenses."

"But, Grandmother, what is Draco going to do?" Maya repeats.

"Draco is one of the biggest constellations in the Milky Way, comprising many dragons; but there are also dragons already here on Earth.

"When you were a little girl you were fascinated by the unicorn constellation and your Dad told you a story about the unicorns not being allowed onto the Ark so they had to start swimming; well, some of the unicorns became dragons. They have been hiding in the forests waiting until planet Earth needs their help. Draco can call on them at any time to defend the world from evil. If Draco agrees, I hope that the dragons will breathe fire on the Dark Menace and burn up the darkness so that your light can shine through. But their abilities are limited, they are here to help you, not take over."

"Will I be able to see them?" asks Maya.

"No," replies her grandmother, "you won't see them, but I will, and I can guide them, so that you will have the maximum amount of protection."

"I would love to see the dragons, could I just get a glimpse of them?" pleads Maya.

"Not now, but they will be very important in your future. They will help, along with the unicorns."

"I'm going to work with unicorns?"

"Yes, Sweetheart, they have already contacted you, you have seen them standing next to your bed."

"I thought that it was just a dream; oh, how wonderful," says Maya "I will feel very safe with the unicorns protecting me."

Chapter 9

The constellations are fascinated by the interaction between Grandmother and Maya and they can see how important it is for Maya to defeat the Dark Menace. They realize that she is the one who is going to stop the evil energy that is trying to destroy Earth, and ultimately affect the Cosmos. They all vow to stop their bickering and work together to help this special young girl.

They also want to continue to watch Maya's progress, and ask the elderly unicorn's permission to do so.

"Draco, I need your help."

"Yes, Magnus, what may I do for you."

Draco already knows what is required of him because, from his corner of the Cosmos, he's been watching Maya and Grandmother, but out of respect for the elderly unicorn he pretends that he doesn't know what Magnus wants.

"Draco, I need you to assemble several dragons to act as protectors for this young Earthling called Maya."

"Of course, Magnus, what exactly do you want them to do?"

"They need to constantly watch the young girl, and protect her from the Dark Menace that is trying to destroy her."

"Of course, Magnus, we will breathe fire on the dark energy so that it doesn't have a chance to reach the girl."

"Thank you, Draco," says the elderly unicorn, "and I'll need your brothers and sisters to protect her in the future, but we will talk about that later."

"Ask for help any time, Magnus, we will be honored to help as long as you need us."

"Thank you, Draco, your protection is more important than you realize. This young Earthling, Maya, is in greater danger than even her grandmother realizes."

Chapter 10

Relieved that Maya has the help of Draco, Vida plans the next day's activities. It's the weekend and, as Maya doesn't have to go to school, Vida wants her to start her education with something fun, and she decides on shape shifting. It's something that Maya has already had some experience with, so it should be easy for her.

Waking to the bird's beautiful morning songs as they greet the new day, and smelling the earthy aromas of the garden wafting through the window, Maya feels refreshed, well rested and hasn't had any frightening dreams. *Oh, the Dragons must have been working hard during the night to protect me. I'm so grateful I must ask Grandmother how I may thank them.*

Maya looks forward to spending the day with her grandmother and lets Mango and Frederick get onto the bed. This is a special treat for them all and they luxuriate in each other's company, but Frederick is big and heavy so Maya gently pulls his ears and rubs his back and tells him to get onto the floor.

She kneels at the side of her four-poster bed and says her morning prayers out loud. Grandmother had told her that saying them out loud is more powerful than just thinking them, that the energy goes further, especially when she is asking for all people to be blessed.

Mango stays snuggled in the covers, his golden eyes watching his mistress intently. Maya loves Mango's eyes because they are the color of the Sun.

Maya wraps grandma Fergie's comforter around her and sits in her rocking chair to meditate. It's in the Windsor style with a rounded back and arms that fly out to the sides like wings. When Maya sits in the chair, she feels as if she is an angel and can take flight at any moment, which can be a problem. Her grandmother has stressed that when she meditates she has to stay completely grounded. Vida wants Maya to visualize her legs as the roots of a great tree that go deep into the earth, keeping her well anchored; she doesn't want her floating off somewhere.

Finishing her meditation, Maya focuses on her crown chakra and asks the light to remove the darkness, to send hope, love, and peace to all beings around the world. Vida had told her that when she does this, the Spirits and Guides can see the light shooting into the sky like fireworks, and falling in sprinkles around the world, seeking out those who need help the most. Vida also said that, if enough people would do this simple practice, it would create a positive energy shift that would change the way people think.

Rubbing the comforter against her cheek, Maya can see her paternal grandmother's beautiful smile. Smoothing out the wrinkles in the fabric she folds the comforter, and hangs it over the back of the chair. After doing her yoga stretches, Maya gets dressed and goes down for breakfast.

Eve is relieved that her daughter is smiling as she walks into the kitchen. She can tell that her child has slept well.

"Your grandmother tells me that you are going to the woods today. I wish I could join you but I have to take some things to the market."

Maya is torn. She wants to go to the woods with Vida but she knows that her mother is unhappy and she wants to spend time with her.

"I should help you," offers Maya.

"Thank you, Darling, but it's more important that you study with your grandmother. I shall be just fine, although I appreciate the offer," replies Eve. "Rose is going to help me. She loves the garden almost as much as I do, and she's wonderful with the people in the market."

I'm wonderful with the people in the market, thinks Maya, feeling a little jealous. *I'm even more wonderful than Rose, and everyone loves my eggs and chickens.*

"Liam will be here at 8:00, and he'll be staying all day," says Eve.

Eve tries not to show it but she feels left out and is resentful. She's not happy that Vida seems to be utilizing all of Maya's time.

This is a really busy time in the garden and there are more and more needy people in the village who rely on Eve to help them feed their families. Eve gives away as much produce as she sells, and she needs help to keep up with the demand.

Thank goodness for Liam Sorensen. Liam had bought Eve's honey for years, and when he asked her for a job it was a perfect fit. He loves the physical labor and is wonderful with the animals.

Vida meets Maya after breakfast and they walk to the woods that back up to their property.

To the townspeople they are just woods; but when the family, including Rose and Amul, walk into the woods, the landscape changes to a magical forest, thick, dense, and protective. The townspeople think that the family is a little different, and they are only partly correct. The family is *very* different.

The sun is strong and its warmth is pushing its way between the trees, casting shadows that dance in the light. The trees thicken as Vida and Maya walk into the forest, and Vida explains to her granddaughter what she has in mind.

"We are going to work on several levels. I want today to be fun, so we will do some shape shifting, something you are already familiar with; then tonight, after dinner, I want to hypnotize you so that I can take you through some of the challenges that are frightening you."

"What are you planning to do?" asks Maya, with some trepidation.

"The snake situation is something you have been dealing with for years, and it's time to confront your fears, because one of the initiations involves snakes."

Maya's heart starts to pound. Snakes are the creatures she is most afraid of and she's had enough of them in her dreams.

"Don't worry," says Vida, "we will work very slowly and eventually you will feel so comfortable with a snake that you will be able to communicate with it."

Maya thinks that becoming comfortable with snakes is highly unlikely, but doesn't want to contradict her grandmother. She had talked to her grandmother about her fears and had been told that what she was experiencing was an event from a past life, and at the moment she just wasn't ready to accept the power that the snakes represented. In time she would feel more comfortable with snakes and their power, the power that she was destined to have.

The forest opens up and they see a magnificent clearing in front of them. Vida tells Maya to take off her shoes so she can have a better connection with the earth. Picking up the shoes, Vida tells Maya to focus on the beautiful day, the green grass, and the nature around her, and wait for a spontaneous shift. Or, if she prefers, she can focus on an animal and see if she is able to become that creature.

Maya isn't focusing on any particular animal; she wants the shift to be spontaneous. Walking through dappled sunlight, Maya tries to identify the birds from their songs and she wiggles her toes as she enjoys the sensuous feel of the soft grass under her feet. Inhaling the delicious perfume of the wildflowers growing in the lush green meadow, Maya realizes that she is starting to roll from side to side. Looking down at her feet, she sees, with a shock, that they are big and hairy and she has large claws.

She is starting to lumber, and Maya realizes that she has become a bear. Maya is feeling invigorated.

As they continue to walk through the meadow, Maya is aware of the reactions of the other animals and, at the same time, she is analyzing the situation. She is aware that she is a bear, but another part of her is watching the bear. Some of the forest animals are afraid of the bear, and some are just curious, as they watch them arrive at a lake.

As the sun glistens on the water the bear prowls around the edges of the lake, then walks down the bank to the lake and drinks, causing small ripples on the surface.

Seeing the ripples makes Maya want to pick up a stone and skip it across the water, but knows that, as a bear, she can't.

Still aware that she is both herself and the bear she senses the bear's reluctance to move farther into the water. Apparently he doesn't want to swim. She has become a brown bear, and although brown bears wade into rivers to catch fish, they stay close to shore; only polar bears enjoy swimming.

The bear starts to turn around as if he is going back home, so Maya decides to change into a tiger.

Vida says nothing, waiting to see what her granddaughter will do.

Visualizing a beautiful big cat with striped fur, Maya transforms herself from the bear into a tiger and splashes into the cool water. Swimming with powerful strokes, the water streaming over the magnificent animal's coat, the tiger revels in the experience. Maya hears her grandmother say that she will see her on the other side.

But something is wrong.   Maya is a good swimmer and tigers swim well, but Maya feels as if she is being pushed down. The powerful animal is struggling to stay afloat, but Maya's legs feel like lead and she is swallowing water.

Within moments, Vida is hovering over her, shooting fire from her fingertips into the water. The tiger roars as it sinks towards the bottom of the lake and Maya feels herself drowning just as Vida reaches into the water and separates her granddaughter from the animal. Gathering Maya in her arms, Vida lifts her above the water and skims across the surface of the lake to the shore.

Carrying Maya up the bank, Vida gently places her on the ground and turns her on her side while pressing on her back.   Throwing up a considerable amount of water, Maya, coughing and spluttering, asks, "What just happened?"

"What just happened, my precious girl, is that the Dark Menace has learned to shape-shift.   The enemy is becoming more powerful and inventive than I realized. We have a formidable foe. When you gave up part of yourself to become the tiger you became more vulnerable. It took control of the tiger and therefore of you.   How do you feel, Darling?   Do you want to continue? There is something really special I want to show you."

"Give me a few more moments to catch my breath," replies Maya, "but I want to keep going. I really felt as if I was drowning but I'm not going to let the Dark Menace ruin my day. And how were you able to shoot fire from your fingers? Will you teach me how to do that?"

"Of course I will, Sweetheart, it will become an important weapon that we can include in your arsenal, but take all the time you need to recover, that was a violent attack. We've got a long day ahead and I don't want you to get too tired," says Vida.

"I'm feeling okay now," says Maya. "I want to shift into another animal and it will be good to get out of these wet clothes."

"Wonderful, Darling, what do you want to become," asks Vida.

"I want to shift into a deer, in fact a young doe," replies Maya.

"Go ahead, Maya, you can become anything you want," says her grandmother. "I'm proud of you."

Maya makes the shift with Vida keeping a close eye on her, she doesn't want another attack. As they walk deeper into the forest the trees are getting thicker with very little light making its way through the dense canopy of branches. They continue to push their way through the trees, stepping around thick brush and over fallen branches while walking on soft mounds of pine needles.

Never having walked this far into the forest, Maya is a little concerned, but she is still a doe, and has complete confidence in her grandmother.

As they cautiously step over rocks, the trees become even thicker. It is so overgrown that Maya starts to wonder if her delicate doe's legs will be able to get through the branches.

Vida is still pushing ahead, as if on a mission.

Trying not to trip on roots that thrust their way up out of the earth, or slip on the lichen-covered rocks, they look in wonder at the soft green moss that's climbing the trunks of the trees, and wild mushrooms that explode from the crevices between the rotting vegetation.

"Grandmother, why don't you just open a path for us to walk through? This is exhausting."

"Darling, some things are better if you have to work for them," replies Vida.

As they listen to the hum of insects, the air starts to feel heavy, almost as if it's holding its breath.

Suddenly a green dragonfly hits the doe on the snout and Maya snaps back into herself. Maya claps her hands in delight and looks at her grandmother for approval. The dense canopy has lifted and they see a pale sky as they walk into the clearing. Vida is pointing at the trees that fringe the clearing in front of them. But these don't look like any trees that Maya has seen before. Shafts of sunlight push their way between fluffy white clouds to spotlight what looks like constantly moving tiny orange and black triangles hanging in huge clumps. The clumps resemble giant piñatas suspended from arms that are attached to trunks of orange and black trees. The trees are quivering, a kaleidoscopic swarm of orange, yellow, and black.

Suddenly this vibrating mass of color erupts, as if a child has struck the piñata with a stick. But instead of its contents falling to the ground, it explodes upwards towards the sky like a volcano erupting. It is butterflies seeking the warmth of the sun.

"Sweetheart, these are Monarch butterflies. They usually only roost in trees on the coast; Santa Barbara has a large colony, also San Francisco; but this is the first year that I've seen them here. Floods devastated their home in the mountains of Mexico and it disrupted their migration route. Maybe this is a renegade group who's trying to find an alternate roosting site in order for the species to survive. There are people who have been studying them for years. Some scientists think that the Monarchs have been migrating from their home in the Mexican mountains for thousands of years."

"They fly all the way here from Mexico?" questions Maya, astonished.

"Darling, they fly farther than that; they fly all the way to Canada. One butterfly doesn't make the entire trip they do it in stages. After leaving Mexico, the first group looks for Milkweed upon which to lay their eggs and when those butterflies hatch, they pick up the baton, so to speak, and set out on another leg of the journey and lay more eggs. I almost said, 'leg of the race' because it is a race, it's a race against time. Milkweed is essential to the butterfly's survival but it is poisonous. That's why birds don't eat the Monarchs, and I wouldn't suggest that you eat them either," says Vida, smiling. "Unfortunately, farmers are spraying the Milkweed with poison because they are afraid that their cattle will eat it and get sick, and the drought is killing off much of what's left. It's all because of climate change; on the west coast we are suffering from drought while rain and floods are deluging other coasts."

"We have Milkweed in the garden, Mom plants it specifically for the butterflies; I frequently see Monarchs, but not in numbers like this."

"Your mother is aware of the problems that are happening around the globe. She is very concerned about the increase in the earth's temperature. All creatures are affected, the Polar Bears might not survive unless we are able to stop the ice from melting; and many other species are on the verge of extinction."

Maya has heard the dire reports about global warming, they've even talked about it in school, but it was all very abstract, something that happens somewhere else; but seeing the Monarchs and hearing her grandmother voice her concerns makes it a reality. This information crashes down on Maya as she tries to hold back tears.

"This is supposed to be a happy day," says Vida. "I assure you, Darling, there are people and forces who are working very hard to keep the earth from overheating."

"Will they really be able to save all the animals?" asks Maya, her voice quivering.

Vida strokes her granddaughter's cheek. "Unfortunately, many species have already become extinct and many more are doomed, even if we make some major changes in the way we live. It seems as if people have gone crazy, completely ignorant of the fact that they are destroying their own home and we have the Dark Menace to thank for that."

Tears are streaming down Maya's face.

"Can't you call it something else," says Maya. "The Dark Menace is such a frightening name."

"What would you like me to call it?" asks Vida.

"I don't know, but Dark Menace sounds as if it's something that's going to suffocate me and it scares me."

Vida doesn't say that she had been thinking the same thing, and she is determined that Maya isn't going to be devoured by this monster. Instead she says, "It's late and your mother may be getting worried, and you need some hot food. Hold my hand, Sweetheart, we're going home and I promise I will do everything in my power to take care of you."

Vida is beginning to realize that as Priestess and grandmother she is walking a tightrope of sorts. Actually more like walking on a knife's edge. She has to prepare Maya for what is to come, but she can't push too hard. She knows that Maya is stubborn but also frightened. If she pushes too hard she might lose her. She has to find a way to make Maya want to succeed and want to become a warrior, not just go through the motions to please her.

Chapter 11

There are wonderful smells coming from the kitchen and Eve smiles at the pair as they walk into the room, but her face darkens when she sees that her daughter's grimy face shows traces of tears.

"You look as if you were caught in a cyclone! Go and wash your hands and face while I put dinner on the table."

Although Maya is nauseated from the information her grandmother has just given her, the growls emanating from her stomach are telling her that she needs to eat. Shape-shifting burns up a lot of calories, and, for now, she pushes aside all thought of the Dark Menace.

After Maya leaves the room Eve turns to Vida. "Mother, what happened in the forest today? Maya has obviously been upset."

"Oh, she was upset when we talked about some of the animals who are endangered, and then she had a little trouble shifting into a tiger, but I put it right. She's just frustrated and disappointed in herself. She'll get better with practice," replies Vida.

"Shifting into a tiger! Mother, really. If that's what you were planning to do today, you might have told me." Eve says, a little petulantly. But then a thought occurs to her: "Maya already knows how to shape-shift. Mother, what aren't you telling me?"

"Everything is fine, she just had a little problem today, there's nothing for you to worry about," says Vida. "Maya's using more energy than she needs to; with practice, shape-shifting will become as easy as breathing."

Eve gives her mother a penetrating look. "Please don't keep anything from me, okay?"

Eve watches with pleasure as Maya attacks her dinner, she knows that her daughter needs fuel to keep up her strength.

The family has a quiet dinner together with some unanswered questions hanging in the air, but Eve, knowing that her daughter has had a stressful day, allows Maya to clear the dishes and then tells her that she will take care of everything else herself.

"Darling, go to your room; I want to talk to your grandmother for a moment," says Eve.

Eve knows that Maya is being groomed to take Vida's place as Priestess, but still doesn't understand what that entails. When she asked Vida for details her mother told her that she couldn't divulge that information, it can only be given to the student.

"Mother, you know that I love you and I know that you adore Maya and you will give your life to keep her safe, but I don't know if I can handle the stress," says Eve, on the verge of tears.

Vida knew when Eve was born that her daughter wasn't going to take her place as Priestess. She wasn't disappointed; she had expected it. Her father had told her that Dinara, Vida's grandmother, had rare abilities and he prophesied that one day Vida would pass these gifts onto her granddaughter. It's not uncommon for psychic powers, including clairvoyance, telepathy, or the ability to use universal energy for healing, to skip a generation. Usually, if someone is gifted, they might only have one ability; if they are especially talented, they might have two. It's very rare for someone to have multiple abilities, but Maya is one of those rare individuals. She doesn't know it yet, but she has even more extraordinary powers waiting to be unlocked.

Vida tells Eve that Maya still has a couple of hours of instruction ahead of her. Even though she is concerned that Maya is being pushed too hard, Eve reluctantly agrees and Maya smiles as her grandmother enters her bedroom.

Maya hopes her grandmother is going to hypnotize her. She trusts Vida implicitly and their hypnosis sessions are always wonderful adventures.

Vida is concerned. If the Dark Menace is so close, putting her granddaughter into a hypnotic state is risky; the enemy could take over her body like a giant parasite, but she has to risk it. She tells Maya to sit in the rocking chair while she sits on the bed. Mango is curled up in the bed covers and, as usual, Frederick is stretched out on the rug, snoring.

Vida tells Maya to close her eyes, relax, and count backwards from one hundred. Almost immediately she can see from the movements of her eyeballs that Maya is in a state of hypnosis.

"Maya, I want you to see me standing in front of you. We are in a beautiful green meadow, the sun is shining and we are surrounded by wildflowers. There is a gentle breeze blowing and you can hear the rustle of the leaves in the trees. I'm holding something in my hands, but you can't see what it is, so you come a little closer.

"You are completely relaxed, aware that what I'm holding is moving. As you get closer you realize that I'm holding a small snake, it's a very pretty, almost iridescent, shade of blue. It is so pretty that you want to touch it, and you slowly stretch out one hand. You hold out your other hand and gently take the snake from me. It feels good as it slides between your fingers and you play with it, moving it from one hand to the other. You are doing wonderfully, Sweetheart. Give the snake back to me, slowly and gently, and I want you to move away as I bend down and release it. Now watch it as it slithers into a patch of wildflowers."

Vida realizes with alarm that the flowers are turning grey and the snake is moving into a black mist, but Maya doesn't seem to have noticed.

Covering her concern, Vida says, "Sweetheart, I want you to slowly come back to your bedroom and know that you are sitting in your rocking chair, and, when you feel ready, I want you to open your eyes."

Maya is smiling as she looks at her grand-mother. "The snake was so pretty, I didn't want to give it back to you."

"That's what I was hoping to hear, Darling. That was a wonderful start and we'll keep repeating this exercise until you feel comfortable holding a real snake."

But Vida is angry. *If the Dark Menace is able to penetrate their hypnosis sessions, it's going to be a lot more difficult to educate Maya,* thinks Vida, *and I have to prepare her for a great battle.*

Chapter 12

"Hydra, are you watching this?" asks Leo.

"Of course I am, I wouldn't have missed it for the world," replies the Snake Constellation.

"Interesting choice of phrase," snorts Taurus sarcastically. "I wonder how much longer there will be a world that can be inhabited by Earthlings."

"Taurus, you can snort all you want, but I can hear you; and remember, I'm the biggest constellation up here, so watch it!" says Hydra.

"Magnus," says Leo, "thank you so much for letting us watch the Earthlings, I'm learning so much."

"Suck-up," sneers Scorpius,

The elderly unicorn is starting to get irritated. "I'm not going to tell you again, if we want to survive, we can't fight amongst ourselves. We have to work as a team to help Maya, her grandmother, the dragons, and the unicorns."

Everyone agrees that there will be no more squabbling, and apologizing to Magnus, say they do understand how important it is to defeat the Dark Menace.

"Well, act like it," snaps Magnus. This rebuke is a shock to all the constellations; no one has heard the old man talk like this before. He must really be worried.

"We are on the edge of a precipice," says Magnus. "Aren't you watching and listening to what they are saying? The Dark Menace is getting stronger. It almost drowned the girl when she was shape-shifting. The grandmother and the girl are aware of what is happening on Earth and are trying to help, but the majority of Earthlings seem oblivious to the dire consequences of their actions. Our universe, as we know it, might not exist much longer. This young Earthling might be our last hope."

"How can we help?" ask the constellations.

"You can come up with some positive suggestions instead of bickering amongst yourselves, or you might find that an overheated Earth is going to destroy us."

Chapter 13

Christopher, the crow, pecks at Maya's window and wakes her from a wonderful dream.

It must have been the shape-shifting we were doing yesterday. I can't wait to tell grandmother about it, she thinks.

In her dream, Maya looks at a small wooden door, about two feet tall with a rounded top. She has no sense that she is big and the door is small, so she pulls on the handle and, as it opens, she steps into radiant, golden light; light brighter than a thousand suns.

Slipping out of her skin, Maya adjusts her balance on feet that are now sinewy claws. As she admires the graceful curve of her powerful beak, she spreads her wings and is lifted into deep space.

Flying through the cosmos she sees Earth below; it is a pulsating, living, breathing planet. This magnificent globe radiates energy, and the shining lines around it make it look as if it is held in a net of silver light.

Maya slides down the seven stars of the Big Dipper, floats on her back in the ladle bowl, and then dances with the Great Bear.

Caught in Earth's magnetic embrace, she hurtles towards a shimmering ocean. Slowing her descent, she spirals lazily through clouds of white lace as she enters Earth's atmosphere.

Finding herself flying over a vast desert, her powerful hawk's eyes can see the smallest of creatures as they burrow in the shifting sands.

The sun is setting as she heads back towards the ocean. She can see the curvature of Earth, and finds herself wrapped in brilliant shades of pink, red, and orange light.

Longing for the all-encompassing radiance, Maya catches an updraft and flies back to the Cosmos. Soaring amongst the stars she wishes she could stay, but knows that she must return to Earth.

Maya hasn't told her mother about last night's dream, she doesn't tell her everything. Eve keeps pressing her daughter for information and Maya is tired of being stuck in the middle. Gobbling down her breakfast, Maya heads for the door.

"Where are you going? I thought we had planned some time together this morning," says Eve, frowning.

"Sorry, but I've got to talk to Grandmother," replies Maya.

"Can't it wait? I want you to work in the garden with me."

Eve gives an exasperated sigh as her daughter clatters down the porch steps.

Maya runs down Maple Lane to Vida's house, but stops as a cold shiver slides down her back.

Looking up at an ominous sky she feels anxious and exposed and runs faster. She has to get to her grandmother's house, and quickly.

"Sweetheart, why are you so out of breath?" asks Vida

"I don't know. I was feeling happy when I left the house, and I was looking forward to telling you about my dream but then a black cloud seemed to settle over me."

Vida sits her granddaughter down at the kitchen table and hands her a mug of steaming herb tea. Wrapping her hands around the mug, Maya sips the tea. It warms and soothes her, and she relaxes as she starts to describe the dream.

When she finished, Vida says, "Darling, you had quite an adventure last night."

"Yes I did, it was fantastic. Then while I was brushing my teeth I looked out of my bathroom window and I saw a murder of crows flying in single file across a sky mottled with white clouds, and a thin blue line seemed to be drawn under the birds accentuating them. It was so beautiful I wanted to paint it but it disappeared almost instantly. This has to be telling me something."

"Yes, Darling, it is, and next time you see something that seems to have significance, like the crows, take a photograph or better yet, sketch it. You have a pad and watercolor pencils in your bedroom. Scenes like the one you just described are a gift. Take a moment to record them; that way you are honoring the image and thanking the universe for its amazing diversity. Remember that I told you that there are no coincidences. It's interesting that Christopher the crow seems to have adopted you and then showed you this amazing sight. I think you are being told that you have a greater connection to the stars and nature than you realize."

"In what way?" questions Maya.

"Remember when I told you that everything is connected, that our Earth is very small in comparison to everything else in the Universe? When I said that, I was talking from a metaphysical viewpoint, although scientists believe that they can prove this theory. We are, in fact, just a small speck in the Milky Way."

"I know," replies Maya; "even though kids learn the basics of astronomy in school, many people can't comprehend how big the sun and the moon are."

"When we look up at the sky, the sun and the moon appear to be the same size," says Vida. "Most people have no idea how huge the sun is in comparison to our little Earth or how far away it is. Astronomers estimate that the sun is approximately 93,000,000 miles from Earth."

"And it's good that it's so far away," says Vida. "If it were any closer we would all fry. Not a pleasant thought."

"No, not a pleasant thought at all," says Maya with a shudder.

"But getting back to your exquisite image of the crows, I think you are being told that the other planets and constellations are aware of you and what you are destined to do. I think it means that you are going to get help on several different levels, not just from the dragons and unicorns."

"How exciting, what are they going to do?" asks Maya, her eyes shining with anticipation.

"Sweetheart, I don't know yet, but it's obvious that they are watching and, when they are ready, they will offer us their help. I definitely think that you should sketch the morning sky," she continues. "This might be another way to understand what the Universe is telling us."

Filling Maya's mug with more tea and putting some oatmeal cookies on a plate, Vida says, "Tell me more about this dark feeling you had. Do you remember exactly where you were when you had this feeling?"

Maya thinks for a moment and says, "I was close to the stump of the horse chestnut tree that blew down in the storm a couple of years ago."

Vida frowns as she ponders the best way to handle the problem.

"Darling, you know that I can shoot fire from my fingertips, you saw me destroy the Dark Menace when it was trying to drown you and the tiger, and I told you that I would teach you how to use fire. It's a very destructive force and consumes a lot of your energy and should only be used in extreme circumstances. When I used fire at the lake, we were alone, but this is a public place and you know how important it is not to draw attention to ourselves."

Vida fetches herself some tea and seems to be having a conversation with herself as she walks around the kitchen.

"Unfortunately, my requests to have the stump removed have been ignored and it's possible that the

Dark Menace is using the stump as a place to hide, so I'm going to burn it up. I will put the fire out immediately and surround it with a wall of light hoping that nobody else can see it, but it is still a risk."

Vida sits down and takes Maya's hands. "I'd like you to come with me so that you can see just how destructive this force can be. This will help you see that this is not a game, and why I'm pushing you to strengthen your body and focus your mind. We will have help from many different levels, but ultimately you are the chosen one, you are the one person who can defeat the Dark Menace."

Maya's body starts to tremble as the enormity of the situation sinks in. *Why have I been chosen for this fight? I don't have the strength or skill for any kind of battle. I'm just a kid. What if I can't perform and let everyone down?* Beads of sweat are forming on Maya's forehead and she feels as if her head is spinning.

Walking down the lane Vida can feel the energy changing, confirming her concerns. Maya can feel it too, and she is starting to get depressed; a dark weight is pressing on her. When they get to within ten feet of the stump, Vida tells Maya to stand behind her. Stretching out her arms, Vida points at the base of the stump. Speaking quietly, as if talking to herself, she shoots fire from her fingertips into the root of the tree. The rotting trunk explodes and a high pitched scream mingles with the crackling wood, and black smoke shoots sideways, knocking Maya flat on her back. Picking up her granddaughter's limp body Vida transports herself to Maya's bedroom. Gently placing her grandchild on the bed Vida can see that she's still not breathing, her face is white and her lips are turning blue. Vida calls in The Sisterhood and then lies on top of Maya so that her granddaughter's body can absorb her own energy.

Thirty seconds later, Maya takes a deep breath and coughs. Vida moves to the side of the bed and kneels with her hands on Maya's heart chakra. Slowly the color returns to the child's face and she opens her eyes.

Relief floods Vida's body and she connects to the universal energy field to recharge her own depleted body.

Vida takes Maya's hand. "How are you feeling, Sweetheart?"

Maya struggles to speak, "I have a cracking headache."

"I'm delighted to hear that, it means that you're still alive."

Vida reaches into her pocket and pulls out a small paper packet. Opening it she pours the powder into a glass of water and urges her granddaughter to drink. Maya drifts into a light sleep and the first thing she sees when she opens her eyes is Vida's serene, loving face.

"Darling, how do you feel now?"

"My headache's gone, but I feel a little wobbly," replies Maya. "What happened at the stump? I had this image of a wide open mouth with sharp teeth and it was going to devour me," and then Maya whispers, "it was Rose's face."

Vida's serene face darkens. "The Dark Menace attacked you and has either corrupted Rose or is using her image to frighten you. You've had quite a wallop; perhaps it wasn't such a good idea for me to take you along."

Maya feels a surge of anger with heat rising from her belly, and her face is flushed. Looking directly into Vida's amazing violet eyes she coolly says, "No, Grandmother, you did the right thing. I need to see what I am up against. I'm not going to let this evil energy intimidate me. If I am the chosen one, I plan to win."

"I'm so glad to hear you say that, Sweetheart. You've just experienced the power of the Dark Menace. You were able to feel its strength and see its destruction, and you've also experienced, firsthand, that magic has a price; don't ever forget that. Do you feel that you can hear more or would you like to sleep?"

"I want to keep going, I have a lot to learn. I want you to teach me everything I need to know about how to defeat this vile opponent."

Maya is putting on a brave face for her grandmother, but wonders what would have happened if Vida had been the one struck down by the Dark Menace. *Would I have been able to save Grandmother?* She shivers at the thought. *If Grandmother is injured or killed, how will I defeat this evil energy?*

Vida is reading Maya's mind and diverts her attention by changing the subject.

"The dream you had about the hawk was amazing but it was particularly special because you were able to see the energy around the earth."

"I did? How did I do that?" questions Maya.

"Sweetheart, it was the silver net that you saw holding the earth. Those lines are energy lines called 'Ley Lines.' In Russia, where I was born, there are many people who are able to sense energy lines in the earth. These lines can be traced through Romania, Hungary, France, and into England. In fact Ley Lines circle the globe, but the energy is stronger in some parts of the world than others, and some people are more aware of this energy than others. I'm telling you this because you are very sensitive to the energy around you, whether it's in the earth or in a person. You know if a particular area makes you feel good, or if someone you are talking to makes you feel bad."

Maya nods her head slowly, then asks, "Are there times when I can feel bad for no particular reason?"

"There's always a reason; the more you become aware of how you feel in a particular situation, the easier it will be for you to make decisions that could become lifesaving." Vida rolls her shoulders and stretches her neck. *I hope I'm not getting too old for this,* she thinks.

She smiles at Maya as she continues. "Other people are attracted to you because you radiate light. They aren't aware of why they feel this attraction, but sometimes, unknowingly, they feed off your energy. They don't mean you any harm, but everyone has drama in their lives and they like to be around people who make them feel better. If you are around someone who has a lower, slower vibration, it can drain you."

Vida pauses and stretches again. *That attack took more out of me than I realized,* she thinks.

She continues, "It's really important that you become aware of negative energy, whether it's in the ground, in a building, or in a person. If you feel it, move to somewhere that feels more positive. You will know when you are in a more harmonious location."

"You mean like now, here with you?"

Vida smiles, and searching her granddaughter's pretty face her eyes land on Maya's. She sees not just the love that Maya holds for her, but also the trust. Her trust is infinite and Vida understands the enormity of her responsibility to Maya. She must teach her well, she must give her everything she has to give.

"The Ley Lines," she adds, for she has to make sure that Maya understands this complicated principle, "connect the sacred sites around the world. These lines also connect important natural monuments that many consider hallowed ground. The Catholic Church knew that the pagan places of ceremony and worship were probably built on a Ley Line, so they built their churches and magnificent cathedrals on this sacred ground. They knew that this was the best way to convert the so-called heathens, because people felt comfortable on land that was familiar to them.

"Sweetheart, numbers are also important."

"I see the number 8 all the time," says Maya.

"I'll give you a book so you can read about it," says Vida. "Pythagoras came up with some fascinating theories about numerology. Some sensitive people see numbers in ways that are different to the way others see them."

"But what does it mean?" asks Maya.

"At this point it just means that when you see the number 8, pay attention to what is going on around you; the Universe is just giving you a 'heads up'," replies Vida.

"Do you have a special number?" asks Maya.

"Yes, Darling, I do, but I don't tell anyone what it is, and you shouldn't either, some things are best kept to yourself. Remember, you are not like other people. Some people are frightened by things they don't understand, and frightened people react unpredictably."

Chapter 14

While the family is having breakfast, Eve reminds her daughter about the funeral at 4:00 o'clock that afternoon.

Eve has several beekeeper friends, and one of them, Fred Kern, died earlier in the week. Maya really liked Fred. He had been working with bees since she can remember. In fact, it was Fred who taught Eve everything she knows about beekeeping, and they all want to be at the graveside ceremony.

Maya is helping her mother clean up the breakfast dishes and, hearing Rose arrive, turns and gives her friend a stiff hug.

She looks the same, thinks Maya, but she can still see Rose's bloated face and those needle-sharp teeth coming towards her, and she tries to conceal a shiver.

Eve wants Rose to work with her in the garden; and later they are all going to the funeral.

Glad to get away from Rose, Maya says, "See you," over her shoulder, as she heads to her grandmother's house.

Vida knows that the Dark Menace is getting stronger; she can see it as it hovers over the village.

She is frustrated because every day she has to balance between preparing everyone for the battle and not giving away too much information. It's too soon to tell Amul and Rose about the life and death struggle that they will have to undergo, and she is teetering on the edge, undecided about how much she can tell Maya. She needs to strengthen their bodies and minds and increase their workouts, but knows that Eve will resist, and she doesn't want to get into an altercation with her daughter.

"I've asked Amul to join us today and he's going to give you a workout," says Vida.

"Oh, are we going to wrestle?" asks Maya.

Amul is a very good wrestler and has been on the school team, but unbeknownst to Maya, he has been studying martial arts with Vida, specifically working with Filipino Fighting Sticks, these are rattan sticks called "Kali" sticks.

"Yes, you are going to wrestle," says Vida, "but there is something else we are going to work with. It's going to be fun."

"What time will he be here?" asks Maya. "Remember, we have to go to Fred's funeral this afternoon."

"He's on his way," says Vida, "and we have plenty of time."

Amul arrives almost immediately.

How does she do that? I want Grandmother to teach me everything she knows.

It's a beautiful day with a gentle breeze whispering through the tall grass as they walk towards the forest. Amul is completely unaware that the Dark

Menace within the tree stump had attacked Maya. He is carrying four sticks with him and Maya asks him what they are going to do with the sticks, Amul just smiles and says, "You'll see."

"Amul, just tell me what we are going to do. It's really irritating when you treat me like a child. Just because you're a boy you think you're superior, but I know a lot more than you do," huffs Maya.

Amul just smirks as they walk to their favorite clearing. It has thick green moss covering the ground, which will make a nice soft cushion for their workout. Amul puts the sticks on the ground.

"Amul, I want you to warm up Maya with some simple wrestling throws."

"But, Grandmother, we've been walking for a while, I'm already warmed up," says Maya.

"Not the way you need to be," says Amul, as he throws her to the ground.

Damn it; I should have known he'd trick me. Maya is small, but she is quite agile and she manages to dodge Amul's next move.

"Okay, kids, let's mix it up," says Vida. "Maya, I want you to anticipate Amul's moves, not just get out of his way; I want you to fight back. It doesn't matter that you don't know the finer points of wrestling, I'm not interested in rules here, I want you to hold him down."

They wrestle for a while and Maya does the best she can, but she is no match for Amul. He is six feet tall, still growing and has a powerful physique.

"I think it's time for a break," says Vida, "and then we are going to use the sticks."

They open their water bottles and find a tree to sit against as they munch on dried fruit and nuts.

"Maya, the sticks don't need physical strength," says Vida; "it serves you better to relax your muscles and stay completely focused so you can anticipate what Amul is going to do."

"Yeah, listen to your grandma," Amul says with a wicked grin.

Because Amul was able to throw her around like a rag doll, Maya is already bruised, in body and ego, but she realizes that she doesn't have the strength or coordination that she will need to fight the Dark Menace.

Maya is angry, not at Amul, but because of the attack at the tree stump. She has been pushing her feelings aside, but now that she's seen what the enemy can do, she is ready for a fight.

Getting up, Amul strips off his shirt and hands Maya two sticks, each of them about two feet long. Her throat catches as she looks at his glistening bronze skin and muscular body. Confused by her body's response, Maya tries to cover her reaction with a cough.

"Amul, I want you to stand in front of Maya and show her how to hold her sticks," Vida instructs. "Maya, take a minute to see how the sticks feel, this could mean the difference between life and death."

Maya passes the sticks from one hand to the other, feeling the smooth wood, and deciding which she will hold in her right hand and which in the left. She tosses them around to gage their weight and feel their balance.

"Are you ready, Sweetheart?" asks Vida. "Amul, I want you to strike her sticks. Slide one stick down the other in the one, two, three, progression I showed you. Always remember, right, left, right, then switch, left, right, left. Relax your muscles and let the movements flow. Start slowly, until Maya gets into the rhythm. I could give you foam covers for the sticks but I think you need to see what damage these sticks can do," says Vida.

Great! Thinks the already bruised Maya; *I'm going to Fred's funeral black and blue.*

Maya and Amul work together slowly, and then, as Maya gets the hang of it, Amul speeds up. Maya is starting to get into the rhythm when Amul changes tactics, causing Maya to drop a stick. He steps back as Maya spins, inadvertently striking one of his sticks while reaching for the stick on the ground. Amul instinctively hits back and his stick slides up hers bashing Maya on the nose. With blood streaming over her chin she leaps at him, flailing. Shocked, Amul blocks her blows, then drops his sticks, so he can grab her around the waist, and pins her arms to her sides. She starts to kick him, screaming as she tries to wriggle free.

Vida doesn't interfere as the bewildered young man holds Maya in his arms. As Maya starts to sob he pulls her to the ground and begins to rock her while wiping the blood from her chin with the back of his hand.

"What the hell just happened?" he demands, as he glares at Vida.

"Amul, I'm sorry," says Vida. "I should have told you earlier; but I've been holding back not wanting to give you too much information too soon."

"Told me what?" he yells.

"I'm not just preparing Maya for her initiations, I'm preparing her for a battle with a formidable opponent."

"And you're only getting around to telling me this now?" Amul shouts at Vida, his face red with anger.

"She was attacked yesterday by an evil energy that I'm calling the Dark Menace, and this is a delayed reaction. She needed to release her fear," replies Vida. "Rose doesn't know anything about the Dark Menace, and I'm not ready to tell you more at the moment. You know I love Maya, I ask you that you trust me."

This new information causes Amul's jaw to tighten, and the muscles in his cheek twitch as he tries to suppress his anger. He continues to stroke Maya's hair, trying to soothe her. Vida pulls a white cloth out of her pocket, pours some of the bottled water over it and cleans Maya's face.

Then the delicious aroma of lavender fills the air as Vida rubs Maya's hands with oil and then sweeps her hands around the outside of the child's body, removing the negative energy from her aura.

"Darling, do you still want to say goodbye to Fred, or would you rather rest at the house?" asks Vida.

"I want to go with you to the funeral," replies Maya. "Fred was a very special man and, although I know that he's already started his journey home, I want to be there to celebrate his life and put flowers on his coffin."

"It is good to celebrate Fred's life and even though I've told you that when you die, it's just like changing out of your old clothes into new garments, you also need to take the time to grieve. Not for Fred, he is just fine, but you need to acknowledge that you have lost a friend and that you will miss him. You don't want to stuff your feelings. They will only come back to bite you."

They walk back to the house in silence. As Amul reaches to take Maya's hand she pulls back slightly and then relaxes in his firm grip.

Rose and Eve are waiting for them. The blood on Maya's clothing and the bruise that's developing on her face shocks Eve and she looks pointedly at Vida.

"What were you doing in the forest and why is my daughter injured?" Eve demands. "You're supposed to protect Maya," *but you're obviously not doing a very good job of it,* she thinks. Eve tries to hold back because she thinks that she is about to explode but then she says, "Mother, Maya is my daughter and I demand to know exactly what is going on."

"I'm alright, Mom. I fell and then I got a nosebleed," says Maya over her shoulder as she runs upstairs to wash her face and change into something more appropriate.

Maya isn't just physically hurt she's confused and frustrated and feels as if she is on a roller coaster. One minute she feels strong enough to fight this evil energy, the next minute she's frightened and the tension between her mother and grandmother isn't helping things. She feels caught in the middle, as the two women she loves the most in the world seem to be fighting over her.

As they walk to the village cemetery Eve is angry. She's angry that Maya was hurt, but also angry with herself for her outburst. She knows that Vida will protect Maya and that there will be many more bumps and bruises on her daughter's journey, but her heart breaks at the thought of her child having to assume the mantle of the Priestess. *She is so young, why is Vida pushing her so hard?* It's as if her mother has taken complete control of the child, she hardly sees her daughter anymore.

Rose is in a chatty mood and recounts her morning working in the garden with Eve and then their trip to the market. It doesn't take long to drive to Thaxton, it's only about eighteen miles from Finchfield; but loading and unloading their van takes time and organization, but once there they sell out quickly. "As soon as we set up the stall, customers swarmed us. Everyone said that they had never eaten eggs with such rich yellow yolks and that they felt nourished knowing that the produce was organic."

Those were my eggs, thinks Maya resentfully; *you did nothing to produce them.*

Rose prattles on, "We couldn't bag the fruits and vegetables quickly enough, and Eve told the customers that they were buying happy produce, that the fruits and vegetables were serenaded, and the chickens were cherished, each having its own name, and were praised for every egg it produced."

A couple of Eve's customers told her that they wanted the organic produce because they were worried about the local water. Apparently several people in town had become sick; in fact, it was being called a "cluster," and they wondered if it had anything to do with the sawmill that had closed a few years ago. Had the mill polluted the ground water? Was it poisoning the town? They were alarmed by the possibility.

Eve has been keeping tabs on the companies around the country who were suspected of polluting the water, but this was the first time that she had heard concerns about a local business.

As they continued to walk, Eve's anger at her mother grows. She wants to protect and support her daughter and wishes that she were the one going through the initiations. She becomes irritated with Rose's incessant chatter and tries to tune her out. On the verge of snapping at Rose, Eve realizes that she has to take responsibility for what she is feeling. Nobody can irritate her unless she allows it.

Immediately Eve feels better when she accepts the fact that she has no control over the situation. Maya is the one chosen to defeat the Dark Menace, and who is she to challenge a higher power?

While Rose prattles on, Amul and Vida have dropped behind and are deep in conversation, and Maya wonders what they are talking about.

Eve has calmed down and she talks with Rose about the beekeeper and his hives. Eve knows the man who is going to assume the care of Fred's bees. He has already tied black ribbons around each of the white boxes and has talked to the bees, explaining that their former beekeeper and protector has died, and that now he is the person who is going to take care of them.

Maya is carrying the flowers she wants to place on Fred's coffin and has drifted to the other side of the road, away from the others. She knows that Rose gets upset when flowers are cut, but, too bad; she's not happy with Rose at the moment and she's going to place these flowers on Fred's coffin. As she walks she wonders if we ever really know what a person is thinking or who they really are.

Rose, her best friend, seems to be in another world with no idea of the enormity of the situation, or does she? *Is this all in my imagination or has Rose been corrupted by the Dark Menace?* But then Maya has to admit to herself that she's not being fair, Rose hasn't really been told of the seriousness of the situation. But she can still see that open mouth and all those teeth.

Then Maya's mind wanders to her response towards Amul. She was surprised by the intensity of her feelings towards him. If we don't know ourselves, how can we really know others?

Maya looks up and blushes as she sees her grandmother looking at her and realizes that Vida is listening to her thoughts.

When they reach the cemetery they are pleased to see how many of the townspeople have come to pay their respects.

Standing at the graveside Maya thinks back to her discussion with her grandmother about how some things are better kept to yourself, and she wonders about Fred. She hadn't been aware that he was sick and she feels sad that she hadn't been more conscious of his situation. He was unmarried, and his only children were his bees. Did he talk to the bees and tell them all of his secrets?

When the Pastor finishes his sermon everyone throws dirt onto the coffin and Maya places her flowers on top.

Having just said goodbye to their friend they hear a strange noise, far off, but it's getting louder. The mourners look alarmed, wondering what is happening. As they all look towards the noise they see a black cloud, which almost blocks out the setting sun. Maya wishes that she had her fighting sticks with her, thinking it might be the Dark Menace.

The noise gets louder but the black cloud breaks up into a thin black line. The line comes straight at them; some people run, while others hide behind the tombstones. A few seem to realize that it's the bees coming to honor Fred, their friend and protector. The group becomes very quiet as the bees circle the gravesite; they circle three times before flying back to their hives.

As the family walks back to the house, completely awed by the power of nature, Maya talks about her Grandfather Athos, who had given her the Minoan bee necklace, and about the statue of the Goddess Artemis and how she has bees carved down the sides of her gown, showing how important bees were to ancient cultures. Athos had also told her of bees that were found in the tombs of Merovingian Kings, and that Napoleon pinned gold bees to his ermine robs for his coronation.

They are within sight of the house when they see Philip running towards them.

"I've been trying to reach you for hours. Something terrible has happened in Thaxton," says Philip, "and I was so afraid that you might still be there."

Chapter 15

"Tell us what has happened," says Eve.

Looking at her dad's concerned expression, Maya is alarmed. Her dad is usually so easygoing; this has to be something really bad.

"Honey, you're frightening us, what happened in Thaxton?" Eve repeats, as they hurry into the house.

Keeping one eye on the family, Eve fills the kettle to make herb tea for the kids, and passes Philip a glass of Elderberry wine.

Philip takes a deep breath and holds his glass with two hands as he tries to control his shaking.

Wagging his tail, Frederick pads into the kitchen to greet them, while Mango rubs up against Maya, but the animals only get a passing pat on the head as the family focuses on Philip.

Gazing at the beautiful faces of his family, Philip relaxes and starts to talk. "A man with a machete ran through the market slashing at people; he had a wild look in his eyes. A couple of women were cut, but, fortunately, no one was trampled in the melee. A cop arrived and held his fire in case he hit bystanders. Back-up arrived and they were able to arrest him."

"How do you know all this?" questions Eve.

"Liam called me. His cousin still lives in Thaxton, and apparently he saw the whole thing; he even took a photo."

Philip takes out his phone.

"Look, you can see for yourselves. I knew you were going to the funeral, but I was afraid you might still be at the market. This happened about 3:30, I think the world is going crazy. They don't seem to think that it's terrorism, just someone with mental problems, but it's very frightening for something like this to happen in a small town."

Vida has been listening with great concern. She knows that the world is going crazy and she knows what is causing it. The threat is accelerating and moving into the small village and she has to prepare Maya for the fight of her life.

It's been a long day and Rose calls her mom to tell her that she's on her way home, and her mother didn't express any concern. Apparently she hadn't heard the news yet.

Amul decides to wait until he gets home. His parents knew that he was going to be late, and if they had heard the news he's sure they would have called Eve.

Eve invites her mother to stay for dinner. She knows that Vida was planning on working with Maya tonight, but with everything that has happened, surely she can give Maya the night off. Eve has calmed down a little but still isn't happy with her mother. Not wanting to get into a fight with her mother tonight, Eve decides to bide her time before saying any more. There's been enough grief for one day.

Over dinner the family explains the events at the graveside. Philip is quiet as they tell him the story.

Expecting her mother to leave after dinner, Eve is surprised when Vida asks Maya to follow her upstairs. Eve is about to protest when she sees the look of resolve in her mother's eyes. This is definitely not the time to pick a fight.

It's been a very long day and Vida wants to distract Maya from the horrific events at the market. She knows that the Dark Menace is using these small acts of terrorism to intimidate Maya, and she has to ensure that Maya feels safe and stays focused.

Vida sits cross-legged on the bed telling Maya to sit in her rocking chair. Philip's father had made the chair for her and Vida knows that her granddaughter feels comforted while sitting in it.

"Sweetheart, I want you to tell me what you understand about the chakras," says Vida, "and I want to do some more work on opening your heart chakra. Your pure spirit is the reason you're a threat to the Dark Menace; I want to open your heart chakra to its fullest extent. The more open you are, the more powerful you become."

Maya looks alarmed; the thought of completely opening her heart chakra makes her shiver, and she's already feeling vulnerable after two skirmishes with the Dark Menace; but seeing her grandmother's expectant face she explains what she understands about chakras.

"Once, when I came home from school with dust in my eyes, you showed me that I have very powerful chakras in the palms of my hands, and I was able to stop my eyes from watering by just cupping my hands over my eyes. And you've told me that the main chakras start at the base of the spine and go all the way up to the top of the head."

"Yes," says Vida, "but it's a lot more complicated than that. I have a full length chart of the body with all the chakra points on it," says Vida, "and I want you to study it.

"The seven main chakras are represented by colors. The first of the seven starts at the base of the spine, or root chakra, and it is red. The next is at the level of the abdomen; it is orange and represents sexual energy and creativity. Then you move up to the solar plexus, and this chakra symbolizes power and mental energy, and is yellow. Next is the heart chakra, it is green and is the seat of compassion and balance; then blue for the throat, which depicts self-expression. The third eye is Indigo, and the crown chakra is violet. When you look at the chart, you'll see that there is also a chakra above the head and a second heart chakra, which is depicted at the level of the heart but in or behind the back.

"It's quite complicated and we don't have time to go over everything now, but I want you to memorize the chart, then you'll get a better understanding of how energy works in the body," says Vida. "Once you understand how this energy works you can use it for healing, yourself and others," Vida adds.

"Opening your heart chakra will be critical in one of your initiations, if you are not able to open it fully you will fail. And, remember, you have to pass all the tests to become a Priestess and have the protection of The Sisterhood.

Maya shudders. *What if I can't pass all the tests? Who will fight the Dark Menace? What happens if we don't win? Are people going to die?*

Chapter 16

The constellations have been listening to Vida and Maya talk about chakras. Aquila, the Eagle Constellation, is confused and asks, "Anyone know what chakras are?"

"I can tell you about chakras," says Virgo, speaking softly.

"Earthlings have this outer layer called 'skin' that covers all the stuff inside. Inside are bones, organs, muscles, fat, veins, arteries, and a long strand of kinked up tubing that takes what is put in at the top end, or mouth, and pushes out at the bottom end."

"Why do they do that?" asks Aquila.

"It's what keeps them alive," replies Virgo. "But when you interrupt me, I lose my train of thought."

"Sorry," mutters Aquila. Aquila thinks Virgo is very beautiful and doesn't want to annoy her.

"So these Earthlings are made up of all this stuff, covered by this skin coating, and sometimes the skin breaks open and some of the stuff oozes out."

"Sounds messy," clicks Cancer.

Virgo gives him a withering look.

I've got a hard shell, thinks Cancer, *you can't hurt me with a look like that.*

Virgo continues.   "It can get messy; in fact if they can't stop the ooze, the Earthlings die. There are, however, some Earthlings who don't mind dealing with the ooze."

Cancer's feelers twitch at the thought.

"These Earthlings are called 'doctors,' and it's their job to push back in what slips out," says Virgo.

The nostrils in Aquila's beak flare and Centaurus wrinkles his nose.

"I'm starting to feel nauseous," says Scorpius, "and we haven't got to the chakras yet."

"Sorry," says Virgo, "I got sidetracked. Running through all of this messy stuff are lines of energy, which intersect at certain points; by the way, this messy package is called 'The Body', and one of the important intersecting points is in the hands; so when Grandmother helps birth a new Earthling, the chakras in her hands are activated, and this helps give energy to this small body that they call a 'Baby'."

"Are the chakras just in the hands?" asks Aquila.

"No," replies Virgo.   "The main ones are in a line that runs up the body from the base of the spine to the top of the head. The spine is all those little bone segments that sit on top of cach other, and it's what helps Earthlings stand up straight.

"You've heard Grandmother talk about the seven chakras, or wheels of energy; but there are actually a lot more. There are some outside the body, and above the head, but not many Earthlings know how to turn them on."

"What happens when they are turned on?" asks Taurus.

"Humans have this artificial starlight they call 'electricity'," replies Virgo. "You've seen Maya turn on a switch in her bedroom so that she can read books at night? Well, activating the chakras is a little like turning on an electric switch."

"Why do they want to activate them?" asks Aquila.

"They think that by turning on the energy, it will bring them closer to the source of all energy."

Virgo is looking at some astonished faces.

"You mean, 'The Source'," says Aquila.

"Yes, the Source that is within and beyond our Galaxy; the Source that we all came from billions of years ago. The Source that everything came from," says Virgo, quietly.

There is complete silence for a moment and then Scorpius can't contain himself. "I didn't realize that Earthlings were so presumptuous," he says.

"It's what they are here for," says Magnus.

The others turn in surprise; they hadn't known that the elderly unicorn was listening.

"They are on Earth to reach beyond themselves, to gain a deeper connection to everything that is in the Universe."

Chapter 17

"Maya," says Vida, "normally when a student starts doing advanced meditation and working on the chakras, they start slowly until they learn how much energy their body can handle. Unfortunately, on this plane, we don't have the luxury of time so we are going to be working in a parallel universe. It is a risk, but I will be with you every step of the way to make sure you don't overload your body. Be sure to tell me if you start to feel uncomfortable, and always follow my instructions. You are literally being re-wired, being stripped of old energy patterns and replacing them; but when you do this, always request that the work you are doing is for your highest good.

"We aren't going to work on the chakras tonight, I need you to get a good night's sleep, but we will work on them tomorrow."

Watching the fear move across Maya's face, Vida continues. "I will ask for additional help from the dragons and call in The Sisterhood. I will keep you as safe as I possibly can."

Despite her fear at the thought of her heart chakra being wide open, Maya had a peaceful night and she's bursting to tell her grandmother about her dreams.

Maya loves her classes, and this makes her an oddity among her fellow students and she senses that they are getting resentful.

Today is her favorite class, astronomy. Maya's teacher is very impressed with his student, who seems to know almost more than he does. She asks probing questions about the universe; which shows that she has a greater understanding of the Cosmos than many of his older students.

Please don't pick me; don't make me different from the others. I've got to keep quiet and stop asking questions, thinks Maya.

Maya has lunch with Amul and Rose and they compare notes on the previous day's activities. They talk about their amazing experience at the funeral and how beautifully poignant it was to see the bees saying goodbye to Fred, and how important it is to be in touch with nature.

Maya is having great difficulty trying to appear normal around Rose, and Amul has picked up on it. He pulls Maya aside. "Is there a problem between you and Rose?" asks Amul. "Is there something I don't know about?"

Maya explains her experience when the Dark Menace attacked her at the tree stump and that she had seen Rose's face. "I'm sure it's my imagination, but I don't feel safe around Rose and it makes me very sad."

"What does Grandmother say?" asks Amul.

"She thinks that the enemy is using Rose's image to frighten me, that she might not have been corrupted by the Dark Menace, but that we have to watch her."

While Maya and Amul are talking, Rose breaks into the conversation. "Guys, I'm sure it's not intentional, but I'm feeling left out."

Maya has to switch gears for a moment as Amul stares at Rose. Now Amul has doubts about Rose and he has to admit to himself that he loves Maya and will do anything to protect her.

"Amul," says Rose, "I know that Grandmother wants you to spend more time with Maya, but would you teach me stick fighting? It really sounds like fun."

"I think that's a great idea," replies Amul, the muscles in his jaw tightening. "I'll talk to Grandmother about it."

"I'm so sorry you feel left out and I'm glad you spoke up. We'll make sure that you're included in everything we do from now on," says Maya, thinking that it would be better to keep an eye on Rose rather than running away from her.

The afternoon classes are basic and boring and Maya counts the minutes before she can escape. She wants to get away from the classes that don't seem to be teaching her anything new, but she's starting to get nervous about her visits with her grandmother. Telling Amul about her experience with Rose has made her fears more real, and she tries to push away her anxiety as she walks slowly to Vida's house.

What will Grandmother want me to do next? It's not easy to say no to her. What will I do if it's something that frightens me? thinks Maya.

It's a hot day and Maya is sweating as she walks up the porch steps and flops down onto the padded bench. She picks up the glass of lemonade that's sitting on the old wicker table in front of her and gulps it down.

"Sweetheart, did you have any interesting dreams last night?" asks Vida.

Vida already knows about Maya's dreams because she's been watching her all night. In spite of Draco's help, Vida has to remain vigilant; she can see the Dark Menace lurking in the shadows but she is particularly interested in hearing Maya's version of the first dream.

Maya tells her about the swan dream. "It is a beautiful day, the sun is shining, but there's a brisk breeze. There's a large body of water that seems bigger than a lake and the water is quite choppy, because I can see small white caps. There are floating islands with very tall grass, maybe six or ten feet high, and the smell of the grass is intoxicating. Gliding between these islands are enormous white swans. I'm sitting on the back of one of the swans, which is almost the size of the islands. Everything is so beautiful, and I feel so safe tucked into the soft white feathers of this great bird as we glide silently between the islands. When I woke I just lay in bed recreating this magnificent dream, I didn't want to let it go and I can still remember the smell of the grass.

"I finally go back to sleep and see myself in an old vehicle that is traveling over a rough mountain road, I think it's in another country. I'm wearing some sort of black mesh garment. I feel someone behind me pull up the back of my mesh top. I'm saying that I'm not sure if I'm ready and try to push the person away, but the person persists and pulls up my top. I'm not feeling naked or exposed; it's not as if I'm being physically attacked. My concern was on a much deeper level. It was as if I was being propelled to a deeper level of consciousness.

"Now, here's the interesting part. Because I'm facing forward, you wouldn't think that I could see what's on my back once my garment is lifted; but I can, and what I see, set into my back, at about the level of my heart, is a large emerald cut ruby. It's at least two inches by three inches. What on earth does this mean? This was one very big ruby and what is the significance of the black mesh?"

Vida gets up and refills Maya's glass with lemonade.

"Your dreams are very helpful," says Vida looking thoughtful.

"In what way?" asks Maya.

"I think that Cygnus, the Swan Constellation, is offering to help you."

"How exciting, but how is Cygnus going to help me?" asks Maya.

"I think we need to get farther along with your education before I can reveal what is going to happen," replies her grandmother.

Vida's certainly not going to tell her granddaughter her concern that if more of the constellations are offering to help it means that they are getting worried and think that Maya requires more protection. Vida needs Maya to focus on completing her initiations and not get distracted by the constellations' fears.

"Oh, Grandmother, you know that I'm not very good at waiting, can't you tell me now?"

"No," says Vida smiling. "One of the most important emotions you have to control is your impatience, and that can only be done over time."

"What about the dream with the ruby?" asks Maya.

"This is showing us how well protected you are and what a big generous heart you have," says Vida. "This ruby is set at the level of your heart chakra, and nothing is going to get past that big beautiful jewel; and regarding the mesh, many people have described the veil between the worlds as an open-weave material, just like the mesh you describe. You are absolutely correct; you were being taken to another level, the level that enabled you to see the ruby.

"I've asked Amul to come over and bring his snake," says Vida.

Maya inhales sharply. Amul has a pet snake at home but he keeps it out of sight because he's aware of Maya's snake phobia.

"What is he going to do with it," whispers Maya.

"I've asked him to bring it so that you can look at a real snake."

"I won't have to touch it, will I?" croaks Maya.

"No, Sweetheart," says her grandmother, "but you did so well under hypnosis, I think that you might be surprised by your reaction."

I doubt it, thinks Maya. "When will Amul be here?" she asks.

"Any minute now," says Vida.

I've got to learn how she does that, Maya thinks.

"You will, Sweetheart, it's one of the things we are going to work on next."

Of course, Grandmother can read my thoughts; I can't get away with anything.

"That's right, my darling, you can't," says Vida.

Darn it, thinks Maya.

"I'm still tuned into you, Sweetheart."

Amul walks onto the porch and, smiling at them both, asks, "Is this going to be the big day?"

Not if I can help it, thinks Maya, and then blushes because she can see that her grandmother is still reading her thoughts.

"Let's go into the kitchen," says Vida.

Amul places a small cloth bag on the floor by his chair. Maya eyes it suspiciously and walks around to the other side of the table before placing a glass of lemonade in front of Amul. Maya refills her glass and sits as far away from Amul as possible. A plate of Maya's favorite oatmeal cookies are on the kitchen table, and she grabs one, and then another—as if she hasn't eaten all day. Vida waits patiently, giving Maya time to calm down.

"Amul, I want you to take the snake out of the bag and just hold if for a few moments."

Maya shuts her eyes tightly; she doesn't want to see what is happening.

"Maya, I want you to open your eyes and look at the snake, see how pretty it is, and know that it is quite harmless."

"I don't want to," says Maya.

Vida had thought that this might be her reaction and she's reluctant to use hypnosis because she's sure that the enemy had slipped into their last session, but they are running out of time, so she takes a breath and smiles.

"Alright, Sweetheart, then I'd like to hypnotize you so that you feel more relaxed. Is that okay with you?" Maya nods her head. Vida puts her granddaughter into a hypnotic state and then tells her to open her eyes. Maya opens her eyes and sees Amul sitting across from her with the snake in his hands.

"Darling, you need to let go of the fear," says Vida. "Amul, I want you to stay where you are; and, Maya, I want you to move your chair and sit a little closer to him. When dealing with animals, you have to get onto their wavelength, and slow down your vibration. Do you remember how we talked about the fight-or-flight response, and how the primitive part of your brain works?"

Maya nods her head but she's closed her eyes again.

"Amul, what is your snake's name?" asks Vida.

"William," replies Amul.

"Maya, I want you to slow your breathing and your heart rate, and move into your reptilian brain so that William doesn't feel threatened."

Still with her eyes closed, Maya takes a deep breath. She exhales slowly and her muscles start to relax.

"When you feel ready, you can open your eyes," says Vida.

Maya looks at her grandmother and then at William.

"Sweetheart, you are doing wonderfully, I want you to move even closer to Amul. It's alright, you don't have to touch the snake," says Vida. "I just want you to look at William for a couple of minutes more, and then we will be through for the day."

Maya does as she's told, even lowering her head and tilting it to one side as she tries to hear what William is saying.

Maya is familiar with Parseltongue, the language of serpents.

When she dreamed about the snakes that were trying to strangle her, she could hear them saying to each other, "Kill her, kill her."

William is different; he has a positive energy field and almost feels like a friend.

"Thank you, Amul, you may put William back into the bag," says Vida.

Vida brings Maya out of hypnosis and is happy to see that she is smiling.

"I did pretty well, didn't I," says Maya.

"You certainly did," replies her grandmother.

Vida sees the pride in Amul's eyes. She's been watching him and has seen his affection for Maya growing. Vida thinks that if she weren't there he might even have swept Maya up and twirled her around the room. But she can't let her granddaughter get distracted by the love of this young man; Maya's life is at stake. Gently, Vida breaks the spell.

"Amul, I know you're aware that I'm preparing Maya for some important tests," says Vida, "and this means that I have to spend a lot more time with her. If you are willing, I want both you and Rose to be involved with our project. I think that it's a great idea that you teach Rose stick fighting, and when you add it to the Tai Chi you already practice, your physical, mental, and spiritual balance will improve immeasurably."

As he leaves, he gives Vida a kiss on the cheek and says, "Thank you, Grandmother."

When Amul was quite small his mother had told him that he had to be polite to older people and use their last names, but Vida had quickly told him, "Just call me Grandmother."

"Thank you, Amul," says Vida, "your help is going to be invaluable."

Walking down the porch steps, Amul wonders if Vida can read his mind. Maya had told him that her grandmother always knows what she is thinking and he feels that this is too intrusive. Everyone is entitled to their own private thoughts. He was astonished when Maya, in tears, had told him that she has to fight the Dark Menace, and that she is supposed to save the world.

It's cold and Amul rubs his hands together but, he also is starting to sweat at the thought of Maya getting hurt. *I wonder if I can talk Maya out of it, or maybe Vida will let me take her place. I couldn't live with myself if Maya is injured or killed. I'll talk to Vida tomorrow.*

Chapter 18

A baby is due at any moment; so Vida, as midwife, is on call and won't be able to work with Maya this evening, but her grandmother tells Maya that she will open her heart chakra tonight while she sleeps. She says that it will be safer this way because Maya won't be fearful. Fear is the easiest way for the Dark Menace to penetrate her defenses.

Maya tells Rose and Amul that she isn't going to her grandmother's house after school, but is going into the forest to talk to the wild bees, and she asks them if they want to come along.

The kids are concerned about what is happening to the domestic bees. Not their own hives, their bees are healthy; but there's a strange event called "colony collapse," where bees in other parts of the country are dying, and nobody seems to know why. It's quite alarming. There are many theories; but if the problem can't be solved it's going to have a major effect on agriculture. Bees are needed to pollinate the crops.

Rose and Amul are anxious to help in any way they can, and are eager to go with Maya and watch her talk to the bees.

The morning sky had been tinged with pink, a good sign if you want rain. It's been cool all day with strong winds pushing clouds across an almost grey sky. The forecast had predicted rain, but the kids don't hold out much hope.

Zipping up their jackets against the chill, they walk towards Maya's house so that they can collect Frederick and tell Eve where they are going.

Maya has walked along Maple Lane several times since she was attacked, but as they get closer to the burned stump, Maya has the sensation of darkness closing around her and an overwhelming feeling of dread. As Rose and Amul are talking to each other, Maya realizes that this is the first time since she was attacked that she has passed this spot with both of them.

Rose lets out a yelp and swats at her ear.

"I think I've just been bitten by a mosquito," says Rose. "I've been hearing this pesky insect buzzing around me for several days. I know it's much too early for mosquitos but it feels as if something is boring into my ear."

Maya looks over at Rose and sees a dark mist surrounding her, but, as soon as she sees it, the mist disappears.

Rose and Amul don't notice that Maya isn't joining their conversation as they proceed to the house.

Maya is deep in thought about Rose and can still see the gaping mouth trying to devour her. *Is the Dark Menace just trying to frighten me or has it somehow infected Rose? I'm sure that she wouldn't willingly try to harm me, but I know that I didn't imagine the black mist.*

That wedge of fear is getting bigger.

Frederick runs out to greet them and, when they tell Eve that they are going to the forest, she invites the children to join the family for dinner on their return.

As they move from the woods into the forest, the trees become denser and are starting to block out the light. The air is damp, but, despite the trees, they can still feel a brisk breeze, and they cinch up their jackets.

Frederick startles a young doe with her fawn and, scolding him, Maya calls him back to the group. He has so much energy; if Maya would let him, he would race after every animal he could find.

Completely focused on the bees, Maya has pushed aside her earlier concerns on Maple Lane, but Amul is watching Rose closely.

Maya is very comfortable around bees, and feels a special connection to them. She's been helping her mother with their own hives since she was quite small; and Eve would reward her with a piece of honeycomb, which she would hold up above her face and let the golden liquid drip into her mouth. She knows that happy bees work in harmony together and produce superior honey. She's never afraid of being stung, and only covers herself when moving the queen to another hive. There had been times when she used a smoker, but that was rare, she knew that the soldier bees were only protecting their queen.

As they walk deeper into the forest they feel it close around them. They are all perfectly relaxed and feel that the forest is protecting them from prying eyes. Many people in the village think that the three kids are strange, and some don't want their own children associating with them.

They can hear a faint humming sound that gets louder as the trees open up and they enter a big clearing. They have reached the old tree where the bees have made their home. The hive is very active but nobody is afraid of getting stung.

Maya walks up to the tree, takes off her jacket and sits on the soft layer of dried grass and leaves at its base. Then she presses her back against the trunk and moves her body in an almost sensual way, as she rubs herself against the rough bark. It's still cool, but a thin sun is shining into the clearing, creating a little pocket of warmth. A warm breeze is dancing around her; it almost feels as if giants are breathing on her.

She motions to Rose and Amul to move farther away and Amul calls Frederick to his side. When she feels that her friends are at a safe distance, she closes her eyes and begins to hum a very soft melody, nothing that Rose or Amul has heard before.

Maya is tuning into the bee's vibration and they start to swarm around her. She is completely relaxed as their wings brush against her bare arms. They land on her, almost as if she is the queen at the center of the hive. They land on her hair and her face and, when her entire body is covered with bees, she changes her tone and starts to croon.

Maya is having a conversation with the bees. She asks them if they will mate with the domestic bees to make them stronger and more adaptable to change. The domestic bees need to be able to fight off what is killing them.

Some people think that there's a mite that is getting to the queen, others say that it's the pesticides that are being sprayed on the crops. Other theories are that the large numbers of bees that are being moved around the country, in an effort to pollinate the crops, is disorienting them and they don't know how to get back to their hives. Whatever the reason, it's becoming a serious problem.

Unbeknownst to Maya, that serious problem is the Dark Menace. It is trying to disrupt all aspects of human life and one of its goals is to create famine. If the bees don't pollinate the crops, people will starve, and starving people will fight to survive. There will be many deaths, which means more blood for the Dark Menace upon which to gorge.

After about ten minutes, Maya changes her song to a different tone and the bees start to leave and fly back to their hive in the tree. When they have all left, she waits, without moving, for about twenty minutes. Her skin is pink and smooth and the dark circles under her eyes have disappeared. She looks as if she has emerged from a long deep sleep and is radiating energy.

"Well," asks Rose, "what did the bees say?"

"They are going to talk to the queen. They realize that their food source is going to dwindle if the crops fail, and it's to their advantage to keep the domestic bees alive. I'm sure they are going to help."

Amul is looking at Maya in awe, as if he'd never seen anyone look more beautiful.

At that moment, Amul vows to give his life to protect Maya and is determined to convince Vida to let him take Maya's place to defeat the Dark Menace.

It is getting colder but there are still pockets of light shining through the trees, and Maya asks Rose and Amul if they want to go home or walk deeper into the forest.

They choose to keep going. After a while Maya realizes that this is the farthest she has penetrated the forest and looks for a clearing where they can sit and enjoy the beauty around them.

Suddenly everything becomes very quiet. The birds stop singing. The hairs on the back of Maya's neck stand up; worried, she looks around for the Dark Menace. Rose and Amul seem unconcerned as they try to see what might have disturbed the birds.

As they strain to look through the trees they see some movement and, moments later, three horses emerge from the forest and walk towards them. The biggest one is black, and the other two are white and a little smaller. Maya is holding her breath looking at these beautiful creatures, when she lets out a little cry, and then covers her mouth. As the animals come closer, Rose and Amul simultaneously become aware of what they are looking at. The kids are looking at three magnificent unicorns. The animal in the center is black and there is a white unicorn on either side of him. All three have golden horns.

Rose and Amul both freeze in disbelief as the unicorns walk up to them. The two white unicorns stop but the black one continues to walk towards the kids.

The black unicorn looks very powerful with a glistening coat and rippling muscles, and all three animals have energy spiraling around their golden horns. He stops about ten feet in front of Maya, and puts his head down as if bowing to her.

Maya stands, hoping that her shaking legs won't buckle under her. She walks slowly up to the black unicorn and gently puts her hand on his nose. She asks him what his name is and hears a voice in her head saying: *Gustav.*

"Thank you, Gustav, for visiting us," says Maya. "We are most grateful, and truly honored by your presence."

Gustav paws the ground then rears up and tosses his beautiful head. He turns and trots away followed by the white unicorns.

Amul and Rose seem mesmerized, but are able to stand, barely, and the color has drained from Rose's face. They look at Maya and both say, "What just happened?"

"I think that we were just visited by the unicorns who are going to be very important in our future," replies Maya.

"Our future," say Rose and Amul in unison.

"Yes," says Maya. "I don't know what role the unicorns will play, but it's something important, and it seems that the three of us are going to be working together. You can ask Grandmother to give you more information. I'm sure she'll tell you what she can, but even I don't know the whole story yet. It's late and we need to get home. I want each of you to hold my hand.

This is something I've been working on with Grandmother; I'm going to show you a shortcut."

They slip into the adjoining realm and instantly are back in Eve's kitchen. Maya smiles at the astonishment on the faces of Rose and Amul.

The children stay for dinner, and they excitedly tell Eve that the wild bees are going to mate with the domestic bees so that they can get stronger and become healthier.

After telling Eve about the bees the three children are unusually quiet and look nervous.

"Maya, what else happened in the forest?" Eve asks.

"What forest?" says Rose. Then confused and embarrassed, blushes bright scarlet as she feels the heat in her face.

"Is that the best you can do, Rose?" Amul says, laughing.

Maya, trying to make light of the awkward situation, joins him, but her laughter has a sharp edge to it.

Eve does not laugh. Her eyes cloud over with concern. "What aren't you telling me? Is there a conspiracy I'm not privy to?"

"Mom, there's no conspiracy. It's just that Grandmother is teaching me things that I can't talk about. Perhaps she can give you some more information. I don't want to hurt you, but I also don't want to be put in the middle."

Eve takes a deep breath, stands up, and starts clearing the table. Maya feels terrible. She doesn't like keeping things from her mother, knowing that her mother only wants to protect her.

Walking along Maple Lane to her mother's house, Eve passes the remnants of the tree stump and, seeing the burned wood, she wonders what happened. She doesn't remember anyone saying anything about a fire.

Vida is waiting for her as she walks through the door and gives her daughter a hug.

"Mother, I've just had a frustrating conversation with Maya. I know you are grooming her to take your place as Priestess and that there is information that can only be shared with the initiate, but it seems that Amul and Rose are in on it. I also get the feeling that there is something much bigger, something that might endanger Maya. What is going on?"

"Eve, I'm sorry that you're feeling left out, and yes, Amul and Rose are being given just enough information to help me keep Maya safe. I assure you that I will do everything in my power to protect Maya.

"I've told you that the initiations are difficult and that the laws of The Sisterhood prevent me from sharing information with you. I need you to trust me. You know that I adore Maya and I believe that she will pass all her initiations so that she can take my place as Priestess. Maya needs your love and support. This is the way it's been done for hundreds of years and I can't change it.

"I don't want to frighten you, but, yes, what is at stake is much bigger than Maya becoming a Priestess. Sometimes I wish it were you going through the initiations; Maya is so young, but neither you nor I have any choice in the matter. This is Maya's destiny. I cannot predict whether she will live or die and I don't have the power to change the outcome."

The color drained from Eve's face. "I'm not saying that you have to make a prediction," argues Eve. "I'm asking if there is a way to ensure that my daughter will be alive a year from now."

"That is in the hands of a higher power," replies Vida.

"Don't give me platitudes," says Eve, looking frantic. "I'm not a child and you are pushing my daughter into something that might kill her."

Vida smiles sadly at her daughter. "Eve, I really wish I had the power to prevent this battle. I adore Maya and it will destroy me if she comes to harm, but, unfortunately, I am powerless to change Maya's destiny."

Chapter 19

Walking down the porch steps on her way to school, Maya sees a red-tail hawk flying overhead with a snake in its beak. As Maya watches the dangling snake, she softens her focus, just as Vida has taught her to do, and she can see the snake's aura. The hawk drops the snake and then dives to the ground after it. Running into the house Maya grabs a pair of binoculars and runs up to her bedroom so that she can watch from her window. From this vantage point she can see exactly what is happening. The hawk is pecking at the snake and she can see its aura fading as it dies.

Although Maya is now late for school she doesn't hurry; she wants to process what she has just seen. As she thinks about the snake, a creature that is apparently going to be pivotal in her education, she remembers a dream that she had a few days ago.

In her dream, Merlin, the magician, asks her if he can come and live in her kitchen. She replied that she would love him to move in with her, and that he could live wherever he wanted.

She hasn't told her grandmother about the dream yet, and wonders if she has started receiving information that she is supposed to interpret on her own. Maybe she shouldn't rely on her grandmother to tell her what things mean.

Thinking about Merlin and his request to live in the kitchen, Maya realizes that the kitchen is a place of alchemy. You take food and, when you cook it, it changes. Sometimes the change is subtle, but it changes. Is this what she is supposed to learn? Then she thinks about how most people look but don't see, as if they have tunnel vision. They have blinders on, like a horse where the rider doesn't want the animal to be distracted by what is happening around him. All you have to do is shift your perspective a little to the side and a whole new world opens up. Is this how she is going to work with her grandmother in the alternate reality? And what was she supposed to learn from seeing the snake's aura?

School is over for the day and Maya is sitting next to Vida in the kitchen, she is excited but also a little nervous as she waits to find out what they are going to do next.

"My sweet," says Vida, "do you remember when you were about ten years old and you were having dreams that were overwhelming you?"

"Yes," replies Maya, "and you told me to ask my Spirit Guides to stop giving me information until I was strong enough to receive it."

"That's right," says Vida. "Your guides were so excited by your potential that they forgot how fragile mortals are in comparison to themselves. Also, they have a completely different understanding of time.

What seems like years to us is like a blink of an eye to them."

At that moment they hear a cracking sound in the kitchen cabinet. Maya jumps and Vida smiles. Maya has heard this sound before, and asks her grandmother about it.

"It's the Spirit World confirming our conversation. I think that they are telling you that you are ready to receive more information from them."

Vida gets up and makes them both some tea.

"They? Who are 'they' Grandmother?" asks Maya.

"Well," replies Vida, "I think of the Spirit World as beings of light, the very opposite of the Dark Menace that is threatening us. These beings of light want to help, so you must tell them how grateful you are, and that you feel truly blessed that they are interested in you. Now that the dragons are burning through the dark energy at night, you will be able to receive the information that Spirit wants to give you."

Maya looks thoughtful. "I have heard this cracking noise in a corner of my bedroom at night. I thought it was just the house shifting."

"When you hear that crack," says Vida, "make note of what you were just thinking, because they are confirming that thought."

"Why is it a cracking noise?" asks Maya.

"Sweetheart, remember when I explained to you that everything is just energy?"

"Yes," replies Maya.

"The sound you hear is a concentration of energy that the Spirit World is using to get your attention. Darling, I don't want you to feel overwhelmed by all this attention but the Dark Menace is gathering strength and gaining ground, so we can't slow down."

Maya wonders if she is strong enough to do what will be asked of her, and she still doesn't really know what that is, apart from the fact that she is supposed to save the world!

Vida takes Maya's hand. "You know that the constellations are anxious to help; what happens here on Earth will affect them," says Vida, "but they also have a different concept of time. The stars have a history of billions of years and they don't want to hurt you by giving you information that your body isn't ready to accept. The problem is that we are running out of time. It is vital that they learn how to slow down their vibration so that we can communicate with them more fully. It's a lot easier for them to slow down than for us to speed up. In fact, unless you are highly evolved you can easily fry your brain and nervous system if you try to do more than your body is prepared for; but this is a chance we will have to take."

Maya's face drains of color at the thought of her brain being fried.

"I will talk to Magnus and explain the problem and ask him if he can recalibrate the energy that he is sending us. He is very wise and resourceful and he knows that the fate of the constellations depends on defeating the Dark Menace.

"Also, you have a completely different level of energy now than you had five years ago," says Vida. "In fact we all do; more powerful energy is being streamed to us through the Cosmos from Spirit, but that's a story for another time.

"Getting back to your energy, you are already getting dreams that show your connection to the constellations, and it seems that you are going to be combining the spiritual work necessary for you to take my place as Priestess with an almost unbelievable connection to the Universe. It's only because of you that I'm able to communicate with the Great Unicorn; and, without his help, I'm not sure that we would be able to overcome the Dark Menace."

Maya's thoughts are spinning. *This is over-whelming. I'm not sure if I can handle the pressure, I don't want to die. Maybe I can take a break for a while. Grandmother did tell me to let her know if I can't handle the pressure. Is it too late to tell her that I want to call it quits?* When Maya looks up, Vida is staring at her; *When will I remember that Grand-mother can read my every thought!*

Vida moves her chair so that she can look directly into Maya's eyes.

"Darling," says Vida gently, "I want you to tell me what you remember of the unicorn story that your dad told you when you were little."

"Oh, that was such a lovely story," says Maya, and she smiles at the thought.

"Tell it to me as if you are your dad, and I'm you," says Vida.

"Alright," says Maya, "I'll do my best.

"It had rained for forty days and nights and there was a big flood. Noah had been told by God to build an Ark and take two of every animal on board. As

Noah was putting all the animals into the Ark he blocked the unicorns and wouldn't allow them to get on board," says Maya.

"Now you have to remember that Noah was only allowing two of each animal on board, so even if two unicorns were allowed onto the Ark there would still be a great many unicorns left behind."

"Why wouldn't Noah let them onto the Ark?" asks Vida.

"They were too independent, and Noah only wanted animals who would do exactly what he wanted them to do," replies Maya.

"So what happened next?" asks Vida.

"They joined their brothers and sisters and started swimming. They swam for hundreds of years and, during that time, some developed wings and joined the dragons. Some who grew wings joined Pegasus. Others grew a long thin horn and became Narwhals, and the rest kept swimming until they came to the island of Atlantis.

"Long, long ago, the island of Atlantis had been colonized by aliens from a galaxy beyond Andromeda, now called M33. They had arrived in their flying machines and were welcomed by the native peoples. They merged with the natives and created a new race of people. The original colonists knew how to manipulate time and space. For them, time and space was not something that was fixed, an obstacle to overcome, twenty-four hours in a day, an exact distance from here to there, but it was fluid and mutable; something that they could manipulate in any way they saw fit.

"Because they were able to manipulate time they never grew old, they had knowledge far beyond what we can comprehend today. They also knew how to harness energy using the crystals that they had brought with them. They built atomic reactors and created a power grid, using the crystals in ways we are only discovering today, and everyone was happy.

"All was well for hundreds of years. It was the land of milk and honey. They built magnificent golden temples, and enormous flying machines. The island had beautiful lakes and towering mountains. Anything that was planted grew to magical heights; the berries were sweeter, the oranges juicier, and the colors of the flowers were brighter. It was never too hot or too cold and the beautiful people lived a beautiful life.

"The problem was that the people got bored; they were not honoring the land, and the more they got, the more they wanted. They started to squabble with their neighbors, everyone trying to outdo the other. The people weren't respecting their neighbors, but how could they? They didn't respect themselves.

"The Elders were getting worried. In their quest to get more, the new generation had increased the energy output of the reactors. As the reactors neared their limit, the Elders came to the unicorns and told them that they were going back to the planet from whence they came. But before they left they gave the unicorns their secrets about how to manipulate time, and showed the animals how to use their horns as lasers, using crystal energy.

"Just as the Elders were leaving in their flying machines, the reactors blew and the volcanoes spewed molten lava into the sky. The island started to sink and the ocean washed over the island with all the greedy people on it.

"The unicorns started to swim and wondered if they would ever be able to find land again; but as one last gift the Elders had the ocean floor rise up and create a land bridge, and the unicorns were able to walk to their new home.

"How did I do?" asks Maya.

"You told the story beautifully, Darling," says Vida, "and there's a reason I wanted you to remember as much detail as possible."

"It's a fun story," says Maya, "but why is it important?"

"It is important," replies Vida, "because it's more than a fun story, it's a prophecy."

"I don't understand," says Maya.

"I don't want to go into detail at the moment, but the three unicorns who visited you in the forest are going to help you," says Vida, "and I will be with you, riding Pegasus."

Maya claps her hands. "Dragons, Unicorns, and Pegasus, what an exciting adventure, I can hardly wait."

Vida has a serious look on her face. "Darling, I don't want to frighten you, but this is not a game; it is deadly serious, and it will be on us before you know it."

There is a loud cracking sound in the kitchen. In fact it was coming from several directions.

"Wow," says Maya, "the Spirit World really wants to get our attention. Grandmother, it's agreeing with you. We don't have any time to waste!"

Chapter 20

The constellations are in a tizzy. They have been listening to Maya tell the unicorn story and they are as excited as she is.

"Did you hear that?" says Pegasus. "Grandmother is going to ride one of my brothers."

"Don't let it go to your head," says Cygnus, the Swan Constellation, "several of my siblings are going to accompany the young woman on her final ride."

"I hadn't heard about that," cuts in Orion.

"It's something that Grandmother requested after Maya's dream about the swans," replies Cygnus.

"Why aren't I included?" asks Leo? "Maya is in love with me and my heart star Regulus."

"You are all going to be included," says Magnus, "and I do wish that you'd stop fighting amongst yourselves; save your energy for the final battle."

"How am I going to be included," demands Leo.

The elderly unicorn lets out a big sigh. "I will give you the details later, but I assure you that you will be represented."

"What about me?" asks Lupus, the Wolf Constellation.

"You are going to be represented by Grandmother. You are her totem because wolves devoured her grandmother, Dinara. The wolves are impregnated with her spirit; that's why Grandmother will be wearing wolf pelts. But I don't have time for this, you all have to let go of your selfish interests, and sort it out amongst yourselves. I have more important problems to deal with."

"Magnus," says Virgo, softly. "I might be able to help."

"In what way?" asks Magnus.

However irritated he becomes with the other constellations he always makes time for Virgo, he loves her gentle energy.

"Hydra and I have been talking about the Earthlings called Rose and Amul, and we'd like your permission to watch over them. Because of his interest in snakes, Hydra would like to watch over Amul, and I would like to watch over Rose, if that's all right with you."

"Of course, Virgo; they will both need all the protection they can get. I think it's a wonderful idea, and thank you for offering. If anyone else has anything constructive to offer, please let me know."

"Thank you, Magnus, I know that Hydra and I can help keep them safe," replies Virgo.

Chapter 21

It's time for Maya to go home to help her mother with dinner and, as she is leaving, Vida says, "Darling, I'll be over later, we have to do some more work on your fear of snakes. I can't stress how important it is that you feel comfortable with them. A critical initiation involves snakes and, at the moment, the way you feel about them, you would not be able to pass the test."

Maya goes home with a heavy heart. She doesn't want to disappoint her grandmother. She knows how important it is that she be initiated so that she can complete her mission. Maya groans at the thought, and once again thinks, *Why me?*

Maya is feeling anxious. She doesn't want to work with snakes. Her stomach is upset and she has difficulty eating her dinner. She knows that her mother is angry with Vida and, not wanting to be caught in the middle, she doesn't eat her dessert and hurries to her room.

As Vida arrives, Eve glowers at her mother and says, "Maya didn't finish her dinner, you must have put a spell on her." Bile rises to Eve's throat. "Mother, I think that you are using Maya as a pawn to achieve your own goals."

Vida ignores her daughter and goes upstairs.

"Hello, Sweetheart," says Vida. "I know that you have homework to do, but if you put your books on the desk, I'll make sure it gets done by morning."

Maya sets down her books and kisses Vida on the cheek, but her hands are trembling.

"Sweetheart, you are going to have to overcome your fear of snakes so I'm going to hypnotize you again. You did so well the last time."

Maya nods and Vida taps her granddaughter on the forehead, putting her into a deep hypnotic state.

"I want you to see me holding a snake and, when I hand it to you, you are completely relaxed and have no fear. You take the snake and play with it. Now what are you going to do?"

Maya is smiling, as Vida waits for her to answer.

"Maya, what are you doing?" she repeats.

Vida already knows what Maya has done, but wants Maya to put it into words to reinforce her actions.

"I play with the snake, and then I bite its head off and swallow it," Maya replies.

"How does that make you feel?" asks Vida.

"It makes me feel wonderful, I'm empowered, I'm no longer afraid, I have taken the snake's energy, it's essence, into the very core of my being."

Vida looks relieved and smiles. "I am so happy for you, Darling. I have been waiting for you to accept your power; snake power is the power of the Priestess, the power of the Goddess."

After Vida leaves, Maya looks at her books and, seeing that her homework has been completed, tucks them under her pillow so that she can absorb the knowledge while she sleeps.

Maya knows that she didn't really bite the head off a snake, that it was just in her imagination, but she is still wired from the sense of exhilaration and power that she felt after her experience. She's also exhausted and as soon as her head touches the pillow she falls into a deep sleep.

Tonight Maya dreams of an enormous white bull in a stadium. She is sitting four rows above the stadium wall, which looks approximately ten feet tall.

There are athletes, bull dancers vaulting on the back of the bull, but when the animal sees Maya it shakes off the dancers and trots to where Maya is sitting. This huge bull paws the ground, then stands on its hind legs and stretches out its head and neck towards her. The bull is so big that Maya can reach out and touch his snout. She has the feeling that he is acknowledging her, that he is adding his power to hers. As she wakes, Maya's fingers can still feel the prick of his wiry whiskers.

Christopher is tapping on the window. *Go away, I want to sleep.* But Christopher is relentless. She opens her eyes and sees a woman with dark curly hair and startlingly blue eyes smiling at her. Her mind is muddled from sleep but she realizes that she has seen this woman before. It takes a moment for her brain to focus. Maya gasps. This is the woman in the photograph that Vida wears in the silver locket around her neck. This woman is her Great, Great, Grand-mother Dinara.

It's Saturday and Vida has suggested that the kids go into the forest alone and try to contact the unicorns. Rose and Amul meet Maya at her house. As much as Maya wants to contact the unicorns she can't wait to see Vida and take another look at the locket and ask her grandmother about Dinara.

Mango follows them to the edge of their property and will be waiting for them when they return.

Frederick zigzags ahead as he leads the way into the forest.

They stop to watch a line of ants moving a large piece of dung closer to their anthill, but Frederick touches the anthill with his nose and yelps when they bite him. As the ants start to swarm over him, the kids frantically brush off the insects, while Frederick yelps at every sting.

They come to a clearing and sit, silently enjoying the stillness around them. Maya focuses her attention on the unicorns, visualizing the animals walking towards them.

Insects are buzzing all around them and, as they watch a large tarantula being dragged into the tarantula wasp's den, they hear a noise in the brush.

Frederick is alert, looking for danger, but moves behind Maya as Gustav and the two white females walk towards them. Maya holds her breath, overwhelmed by the beauty of these magnificent creatures.

The females stand back as Gustav walks up to Maya.

Amul and Rose watch as Maya stands. She reaches out and touches the black unicorn on the nose. He paws the ground and Maya looks directly into his eyes. She asks him if she may get onto his back, and he lifts his head then kneels before her.

Walking to his left side she grasps his mane and carefully throws her right leg over his back, then, holding tightly onto his mane, commands the unicorn to stand. He neighs and the two females walk up to Rose and Amul and get down on their knees allowing Rose and Amul to mount them.

Turning to Frederick, Maya tells him to stay, then she says something in Gustav's ear and he starts to walk out of the clearing and into the forest. Rose and Amul follow on the white unicorns. As they walk, a path opens up for them so they don't have to worry about ducking under branches as the unicorns start to trot, and then shift into a canter.

All three hold tightly to the animal's manes, giving them a combined feeling of disbelief and exhilaration. Gustav moves to a full gallop and the trees rush by. Maya has never ridden an animal with such a smooth gait, and, with the wind in her face, it almost feels as if she is flying.

Looking over her shoulder Maya can see that Amul is no horseman. His lanky frame is all over the place and she can see the tension in his hands as he grips the unicorn's mane. Rose, on the other hand, is riding effortlessly and she is glowing.

Maya bends forward and whispers something in Gustav's ear; he slows until he comes to a trot. Unable to see through the thick trees, Maya hadn't realized that they were riding in a circle until Gustav re-enters the clearing.

When the animals come to a stop, Maya rubs Gustav between the ears and jumps down. Rose and Amul do the same. Maya is about to stroke Gustav's neck to thank him, when the unicorns lift their heads in unison. Energy spirals around their golden horns, sending sparks into the clearing. Maya looks in wonder as the unicorns shoot energy from their horns, bathing the group in a circle of light and power.

When the light subsides, Maya asks Gustav the names of the two females that Rose and Amul are riding, and he tells her.

Throwing up his head Gustav stares deeply into Maya's eyes through his long dark lashes, then turns, and the three animals walk into the forest.

The kids throw their arms around one another and, laughing, collapse in a heap on the ground. Frederick, his tail whipping back and forth, barks loudly as he dances around them.

Maya can hardly get the words out but tells Rose that she was riding "Blanca" and that Amul was riding "Simone."

As Maya lies on her back, stunned, and wondering if she's been dreaming, Vida appears in the clearing.

"Well done," says Vida. "The unicorns have accepted you and are completely committed to protecting you. We are truly blessed to have their help. I'll talk to Magnus and tell him how grateful we are."

Maya pulls Vida aside. "Grandmother, I need to talk to you. I think I just saw Great, Great, Grandmother Dinara."

Vida inhales sharply. If Dinara is here, things are worse than she thought.

Chapter 22

Maya's been so busy that the seasons seem to have merged into one another, and the only way she knows what day it is, is because of the homework she had completed the previous night. She shivers and realizes that she should have worn a warmer jacket. Looking up she sees dark, fierce clouds jostling one another, and wonders if it's going to rain. When Maya arrives at her grandmother's house, Vida tells her that Rose and Amul are joining them.

"Oh, they didn't tell me," says Maya.

"No, Darling, I just asked them."

Maya doesn't ask how her grandmother contacted them. There's a lot about her grandmother that she still doesn't understand, but Maya is determined to learn all that she can.

Amul and Rose arrive at the same time.

Vida welcomes them with her radiant smile. "I know you've had some exciting experiences lately, and I want you to believe me when I say that your involvement is very important. Although I can't give you the details now, when you know what is at stake you will be grateful to be included."

Rose and Amul look at each other expectantly.

"I know I'm asking a lot from you," says Vida, "but I want you to help Maya as she prepares for the tests that she's going to take."

"I'll do anything you want me to," says Amul.

"Me, too," adds Rose.

"What I'd like you to do right now," says Vida, "is to go with Maya into the forest and help her dig her grave."

Maya gasps, and Vida looks at Amul as his eyes widen.

"It's alright, she's not going to die, right?" says Rose.

"Of course not. This is just a practice run. Being buried alive is one of the initiatory tests that she will have to undergo, and it will help if her friends are there with her."

"Well, this is a first," says Amul forcing a smile. "I never thought I'd be digging Maya's grave. Are we going to throw dirt on her too? And this will be a great workout for Rose, she really needs the exercise."

"Don't pick on me," protests Rose. Her voice is strong and indignant. Vida is glad that these exercises are not only making Maya stronger, they are having a positive effect on Rose as well.

"Amul, I know you are in great shape," says Vida, "but you need to be even stronger, you both do."

Vida sees Rose give Amul a look, as if to say, "Take that."

Maya is pleased and relieved that her friends are going to help her; the idea of being buried alive is quite frightening.

"Maya I have told your mother that you will be gone for the night," says Vida.

Maya has to stop the panic that is creeping into her throat. The words "gone for the night" emphasize that this is reality, not a game.

"Sweetheart, it will only be for one night, but it's important that you are able to do this; when you go through the actual initiation you won't have your friends to help you."

Amul, Rose, and Maya are silent as they walk into the forest carrying shovels, the only sound is the crunch of their footsteps on dry leaves, and the occasional snapping of a twig.

The birds have stopped singing as if they know that something very important is about to happen, and Maya's racing heart is also swelling with gratitude knowing that her friends are going to be with her.

They reach a clearing and Maya tells them that this is a good spot to start digging. Maya lies on the ground so that they can measure how big they want the trench to be. Only two can work at a time without hitting each other; so Amul starts at one end of the trench and Maya at the other. Rose steps in when Maya starts to tire; she works hard with strength that is astonishing to both Maya and Amul. After removing the soft top layer, the ground is harder than Maya had anticipated, and she wishes that they'd brought a pickax.

They dig in silence.

This is going to take a while, thinks Maya, as all three start to sweat.

When they have dug a hole that Maya can fit into, they start looking for branches to cover the trench. Maya crawls into the space and Rose and Amul cover the top with branches, and then pile leaves on top.

"Are you alright?" shouts Amul. "Is it big enough? We can keep digging, there's no need for you to be cramped."

"I'm alright," replies Maya, but then has a coughing fit from the dust created by the pile of dry leaves. "Thank you both. I wish you could spend the night with me, but I know that I have to do this alone."

Amul is reluctant to leave, but Maya hears Rose say, "She will be fine and I'm hungry, let's go home." Then Rose says even louder, "I saw a snake a little while ago, but I doubt that it would jump into the hole with Maya." Rose grins when she hears a shriek.

Maya's already shivering, partly from fear but also because the earth is cold and hard and she wishes that she was anywhere else but in this hole in the ground.

Maya will have to spend the night alone in the darkness, not knowing what animals might be prowling around, but she holds onto the thought that this is just the first test. Nothing is going to happen to her tonight, there is too much at stake. She knows that she has many obstacles to overcome before the final test. *I can get through the night, this is just one little test*, thinks Maya. *I wonder where Rose saw the snake? Or was she just being mean?*

Amul and Rose leave Maya, sure that Vida is looking over her granddaughter; she wouldn't let anything happen to her, would she?

Maya is slowing her breathing, the way Vida has taught her, because she knows that in the actual initiation she will be in a sealed coffin, with only a finite amount of air.

Here there is plenty of air because she is only covered by branches and leaves; but one of her concerns is that a large animal might step onto the leaves and fall on top of her. It could be a fox or, worse, a bear.

As it gets darker she hears the rustling of small animals as they scurry by, out for their nightly hunt. She stiffens as a large animal comes snuffling around the leaves and, when it steps on one of the branches, Maya screams, sending the animal running. With no more interruptions Maya relaxes as she hears two owls hooting. Maya loves the sound of owls calling to each other at night. Sometimes, when she's in bed, she imagines that she is flying with them as they hunt, gliding silently over a field, looking for prey.

As she starts to shiver in the damp cold Maya wonders how Mango and Frederick are. She isn't separated from them very often, and she knows that they have to be wondering where she is. *I'm sure Mom is giving them some extra attention, she's probably letting them sleep on my bed, and I bet they are warmer than I am.*

As she drifts off to sleep she sees a beautiful falcon. Maya had noticed a falcon watching her as she walked in the forest a few days ago and had hoped that it would come a little closer. In her dream this falcon not only comes close, it's huge and she realizes that it's more than a falcon, it's Horus, the Egyptian Sun God, the falcon who is the son of Isis and Osiris.

Maya has several books on Egypt and is quite familiar with the Pharaohs, the gods and goddesses, and their mythology. She's always wanted to go to Egypt, and her mother had told her that one-day she would.

"Aquila, it's Virgo, did you just hear that the falcon visited Maya?"

"Yes, I did," says the Eagle Constellation. He fluffs up his feathers and starts to preen, pleased that the virgin has singled him out. He has a crush on Virgo but is afraid that the other constellations will make fun of him if they find out.

But Scorpius has been watching and is annoyed that Virgo seems to favor Aquila over him.

His voice dripping with distain, Scorpius says to Aquila. "Why are you so puffed up? Horus is a falcon and you are just an eagle."

Virgo is really annoyed by this comment. "Firstly, Aquila is a spectacular constellation, and secondly the falcon is his cousin. You really are vicious sometimes."

Scorpius realizes that his criticism has backfired. "I apologize to you both; sometimes my sting gets away from me."

"Well," says Magnus, "you'd better find a way to control it; you're causing problems and I'm starting to get angry."

The birds wake Maya and she sees a little light through the canopy of leaves and branches covering her. *I wonder when they will come to get me?*

Vida hadn't told her how long she was going to be buried because, in the parallel universe, time is flexible, and she didn't want Maya to count the hours or minutes. Even Maya's bones feel cold; she is cramped, and wishes that they had dug a larger hole. Thirsty and hungry, her stomach starts to rumble and Maya knows that it's past breakfast time.

Even when the sun filters through the leaves she is still shivering. Now her stomach is really starting to growl and she has completely forgotten about slowing her breathing.

Okay, I'm going to meditate and put myself into a state where I'm not hungry, thirsty, or frightened. I'm going to relax and wait until they come and get me.

But other thoughts start to creep in. *If this is the easy test, will I be able to pass the real thing? I don't think I'm strong enough to do this. Don't be such a wimp! This is nothing compared to what I'm going to have to go through. Rose didn't seem too concerned about my being alone. How can I find out if she is still on my side?*

Even though her body is starting to warm a little, the thought of what is to come turns her blood to ice.

Maya hears voices in the distance. It might be anyone, a couple of hunters perhaps; but then she hears Frederick's woof, and she knows that they are coming to get her.

Relief floods her body and brain as she longs to be back with her family and friends.

Walking up to the gravesite, Vida, Rose, and Amul call out to her to tell her that they have arrived, and they start to pull the leaves and branches off her. Frederick is beside himself, sniffing and digging to help get his mistress out.

With the branches and leaves out of the way, Amul and Rose reach down and pull Maya out of the hole.

Maya can see the concern on Amul's face, but Rose has a vacant stare. Maya looks at them both and, with a wry smile, says, "I'm okay, I think." But when she sits on the ground her legs are so stiff and cramped that they go into spasms.

Maya is shivering uncontrollably as Vida puts a blanket around her shoulders and another one around her legs, and then she starts to rub Maya's entire body.

Vida has brought a flask of her special herb tea and pours some into a cup. Handing it to Maya's shaking hands she tells her to sip slowly.

"Darling, why did you allow yourself to get so cold?"

Vida already knows why, because she has been constantly watching her granddaughter. "Did you forget what I taught you about how the Tibetan monks are able to dry wet sheets draped around them just by increasing the heat from their bodies. We practiced this, and you were doing so well."

"Yes, I did forget," sobs Maya, her tears making dark little channels as the rivulets flow down her dirty cheeks. "And when it got dark I forgot to slow my breathing. I guess I'd be dead by now if I was in a sealed box. Maybe this whole thing is too much for me to handle."

Vida takes the cup from Maya, and puts her arms around her. "Sweetheart, you are just beginning the process, and you'll be making a lot more mistakes; but this is why we will keep practicing until you feel completely comfortable. I promise that I won't let anything bad happen to you."

As she warms up, and her circulation improves, the color starts to come back into her cheeks. She looks at Vida and her friends and says, smiling, "That was quite a night, can't wait to do it again!"

As Maya relaxes in Vida's arms, Amul asks if he should fill up the hole; he doesn't want any animals falling in by mistake.

"Thank you, Amul," says Vida, "and Rose, will you help him please."

As the two get to work, Maya asks, "What is the time?"

"It's eight o'clock," replies Vida.

"Then I've been in the hole for fourteen hours, no wonder I'm stiff."

"I'm very proud of you, Darling, you did wonderfully."

"We could take the shortcut home, but I want Maya to walk to regain the use of her muscles and get her circulation back," says Vida.

"Fine with us," say Rose and Amul.

Frederick is in ecstasy as he leads the way, he's with his mistress and surrounded by the exciting smells of the forest.

When they get home, Eve gives her daughter a big hug and says, "It's time for breakfast, but first a hot bath. I hope Rose and Amul can eat with us."

Everyone is hungry, especially Amul, but he's always hungry. Amul is growing fast and needs new pants because his socks are showing. He's over six feet now and, although he is muscular, he's looking a little lanky and needs to put on weight.

Vida goes up to Maya's bedroom to prepare the next lesson while Maya walks into the garden. The warmth of the sun on her skin feels wonderful as she does some Yoga stretches.

Maya is anxious to talk to Vida about her time in the forest and she wants some more information about her Great, Great, Grandmother Dinara; and she walks thoughtfully to her bedroom.

"Grandmother, I want to ask you about your grandmother Dinara. May I look at the photo in your locket?"

Vida unclasps the chain around her neck and hands the locket to Maya.

Even though Maya is looking at an old black and white photo she can see that the woman's face is glowing and has no doubt that the face she saw at her window was Dinara, Vida's grandmother.

Previously Vida had talked to Maya about reincarnation and had told her that she believed that she herself had lived many lifetimes, and that several religions base their beliefs on reincarnation. When Maya had asked if she had been born before, Vida smiled and said that she was sure that her granddaughter had lived many lives, and in several of them she had been a warrior. Vida also told Maya that, just because she is a woman, in this life it doesn't mean that she has always been a woman; previously she might have been a man.

Maya had been intrigued by their conversation and wondered if she had known Amul in a previous life and what their connection might have been.

"Does seeing Dinara have anything to do with reincarnation?" asks Maya.

"Not really, Sweetheart, although you probably knew Dinara in a previous life. I believe that the image you saw at the window is Dinara's spirit coming to visit you."

"But why is Dinara visiting me now?" questions Maya.

Vida had been hoping that Maya wouldn't ask about Dinara, but she replied, "My grandmother was a remarkable woman with talents that you have inherited, and I believe that she is here to watch over you."

"Oh, that's wonderful," says Maya, but then she stops and thinks for a moment as a chill runs through her. "Does this mean that she thinks that I'm in a lot of danger?"

Vida thinks for a moment and then chooses her words carefully. "I think that she sees some of her traits in you, and is curious," replies Vida.

Trying to steer the conversation away from Dinara, Vida says, "Sweetheart, I want to hear all about your adventures last night; but first, I want you to practice moving objects with your mind. This will be an important skill during one of your initiations. Stare at the little statue on the table and, with your mind, push it towards me."

Maya concentrates very hard and it starts to move.

"Wonderful," says Vida. "I want you to practice this every day, and you'll be astonished at how easy it becomes. Now tell me about last night."

"I had a dream about this huge falcon, I think it was Horus, I could almost touch him."

"I'm constantly in awe of how you are connecting with the entities who are going to help you; yes I'm sure it was Horus."

"You mean that Horus is going to help me?" Maya is thrilled at the thought, but all this is starting to feel perfectly normal.

"Yes, Darling, it seems that way; so I want to take advantage of this opportunity. I was going to wait awhile before having you take this next test, but it seems that we are being told that you are ready to do this now."

"What test?" asks Maya, hardly daring to breathe.

"You are going to work with lions, Sweetheart," replies Vida, as she watches Maya's eyes widen with fear.

"Lions?" she whispers.

"Yes, Darling, just think of them as bigger versions of Mango."

Chapter 23

"Take my hand, Sweetheart, as we step into the adjoining world," says Vida.

Holding tightly onto her grandmother, Maya finds herself in an arena that is surrounded by magnificent statues of Sekhmet, the lion-headed Goddess.

Maya is alone now but aware that her grandmother is nearby. She can hear Vida's voice in her head. *Remember, Darling, the lions are just bigger versions of Mango. You must tune into their vibration so that they don't feel threatened. Slow your breathing and relax, you don't want to show any fear.*

A large gate in the wall of the arena swings open, and three lionesses walk in. Maya is grateful for the gentle breeze because she's starting to sweat and knows that animals can smell fear.

The lionesses start to pace slowly back and forth, with their eyes fixed on Maya. They don't look as if they're about attack, but they are swishing their tails and watching her intently as they move towards her.

There's a sudden gust of wind and Maya's vision is blurring. It's more than dust in her eyes, the walls of the arena seem to be moving, fading in and out, almost rippling, shimmering like a mirage. A dust devil has whipped up the sand, stinging her bare arms; and she can taste it in her mouth. Her long white gown is already stained with sweat, and she's starting to feel lightheaded.

As she tries to slow her breathing and fight the panic that has already reached her throat, she visualizes a cold wet blanket wrapped around her. It momentarily stops her from sweating, and she starts to relax. Then she envisions her sweet, gentle Mango, and feels a soft warmth run through her body.

Without realizing what she is doing, she starts talking to the lionesses as they move closer to her. They seem a little more relaxed because their tails have stopped twitching. They move closer still, and then lie down in front of her.

The animals are stretched out on the ground, but now they are floating in and out of her vision, something has changed.

I know I'm in another reality, thinks Maya, *but this is very strange.*

She can see the animals' bodies tense and then they become agitated. One gets up and walks towards her, growling through bared teeth, and the other lionesses follow. Maya backs away, but now she is surrounded and they are slashing at her with their tails. They knock her facedown in the sand, and Maya closes her eyes as she feels her scalp scraped by teeth that grab at her hair.

Maya hears her grandmother's voice. *"You have to get control of the animals."*

Holding her breath, Maya struggles to her feet thinking that at any moment one of them is going to sink its teeth into her throat. She backs away and stumbles as she bumps into something solid. Keeping her eyes fixed on the animals she turns her head slightly. She has collided with a large seat. It looks like a high-backed chair, or throne, on a raised platform. Still focused on the animals she puts her shaking hands out behind her and feels for the armrests. Grasping the cold hard stone she steps up and back and sits on the seat while trying to get control of her shaking body. Taking a deep breath she speaks to them again, softly, but with more authority. One lies down in front of her and one lies down on each side while she tries to regulate her breathing.

As Maya sits, watching the animals, she realizes what has just happened. Her hands are in her lap and she strokes the beautiful fabric of the long gown that has replaced her soiled and torn dress. Then she runs her hands to her face, to confirm her belief. She feels the soft fur and knows that she has the head of a lioness. She has become Sekhmet, the Goddess of War.

The door to the arena opens. The lionesses stand, turn to look at Maya, then stroll to the opening, and the door closes behind them. Maya now sees that she is standing alone in the arena and hears Vida's voice in her head: *That was close, Darling; I wasn't sure if you were going to be able to get control of the animals. Something slipped into the arena and disturbed them, it must have been the Dark Menace, but I wasn't able to see it. This is worrying; I didn't know that the enemy was able to become invisible, but it's time to come home and I'm coming to get you.*

There's a whoosh, and Maya is in her mother's kitchen with Vida sitting opposite her.

Maya looks at her grandmother and says, "Did I really have the head of a lioness?"

"Yes, you did, Darling, and you were magnificent."

"Grandmother, what would have happened if I hadn't been able to get control of the animals?"

Vida has a grim look on her face. "I would have had to pull you out of the other dimension, and that's not something that should be done suddenly. Maya, I don't want to frighten you, but everything we do has a risk. Sometimes it might seem like a game, but it's deadly serious and the Dark Menace appears to have abilities that I wasn't aware of. I'm glad your mother is in Thaxton. I would not have wanted to explain to her what happened. Let's keep this to ourselves.

"Sweetheart, go upstairs and get started on your homework, I'll be up in a moment."

Vida needs to be alone to think for a moment. It seems that the so-called "natural disasters" are increasing. More earthquakes in Italy and Asia and blocks of cities erased by fires caused by breaking gas lines. At the same time, arsonists are setting fires in the Smoky Mountains, burning thousands of acres, destroying two towns and killing many people. The fire department called it "apocalyptic," and she doesn't even want to think about what is happening to the refugees in Syria.

The Dark Menace is making a large part of the world homeless, and desperate. People are building shelters; stocking them with food, water, and guns.   If they turn against each other, anything can happen.

Chapter 24

"Leo, did you see that?" asks Taurus. "Did you see how Maya worked with the lions?"

"Yes I did," replies Leo, hardly able to get the words out, he's so choked up.

"Forget the lions!" explodes Ursa Major. "Have you seen that Earthlings are using ships to break the ice so that they can take tourists to see the polar bears? Magnus have you seen what is happening?"

"Yes, I have," says Magnus. "It is so irresponsible I can hardly believe it."

Leo is indignant. "'Forget the lions'? How can you say that? You know that Maya is being trained to help us fight the Dark Menace."

"I don't mean to belabor the point," says Ursa Major, "but my brothers are starving. The sea ice is shrinking and the seals are moving farther away from shore, so the bears have to swim great distances, sometimes ten or twelve Earth days, to find solid ice. If they have cubs, the cubs drown; a yearling can't swim that far and the bears are so hungry that they aren't able to conceive. In a few Earth years they will no longer exist. I'm so distressed, I'm overwhelmed."

"Magnus, I'm sorry for interrupting; and, Leo, I apologize," says Ursa Major. "I didn't mean to hurt your feelings. Maya did a wonderful job with the lions but I can't believe the Earthlings' stupidity."

"Ursa Major, you don't have to apologize," replies Magnus, "we are all distressed, but I hold onto the hope that Maya will defeat the Dark Menace and stop global warming. The ice will come back and your brothers will thrive."

Chapter 25

Maya had a dream that night; it was so simple and obvious that she almost forgot to tell her grandmother about it. In her dream she was cutting out some paper dolls. She held them up and they formed a circle. Maya could feel the weight of someone sitting on the side of her bed. Then she heard a man's voice speaking into her ear. He was so close that she could feel his breath on her cheek, and the hairs in her ears vibrated.

The man said, "We are all cut out with the same pair of scissors."

Of course, thinks Maya, why can't we all get along?

Later, while sitting in Vida's kitchen, Maya told her grandmother about the scissors dream.

Vida had never looked so nervous.

This is bigger than getting control of the lions; thinks Maya, *Grandmother is almost wringing her hands.*

Vida has read Maya's mind. "We are not getting along because the Dark Menace has found a way to inject its poison into large numbers of mosquitos in Florida. These mosquitos are infecting pregnant women; their babies are being born with deformities and people are starting to panic.

"Trying to control the epidemic, vast quantities of chemicals are being sprayed on entire towns. The bees are dying from the toxins and people are moving to parts of the country that aren't infected; but it's spreading. The Dark Menace has found a way to destroy an entire generation." As a midwife, Vida is taking this very personally.

"And there have been more horrific bombings in Germany and France; families celebrating in the streets have been mowed down by a crazy man driving a truck, and it's all because of the Dark Menace." Vida is becoming breathless she's so upset.

"Grandmother, I'm sorry I screwed up with the lions. It's all my fault. I will do better. I will get stronger and help you defeat this terrible enemy," says Maya, on the verge of tears.

"Maya, you have it backwards," says Vida. "You are the one chosen to defeat the Dark Menace and I am here to help you. I wish it were the other way around and that I could take the burden from you, but I can't. Time is running out, we have to accelerate your training. You have to become more physically fit and focused. We will only get one chance to destroy the Dark Menace."

Maya sees black spots dance across her vision and she thinks she might faint.

Chapter 26

Vida is all too aware that her granddaughter has her limits and that she can only push Maya so far. "I know you are scared, Sweetheart, there are many things to be scared of; but as you don't have to go to school today we are going to have some fun. I want you to experience something special. This won't be part of your initiation, but it will give you practice in going back in time."

Maya is excited at the thought of going back in time but is also nervous by what she sees as her failure with the lionesses. "I'm ready for anything, Grand-mother. I won't let you down, I promise."

"I've told your mother that we are taking a little trip. Let's visit your ancestors," says Vida.

"What do you mean, my ancestors?" asks Maya.

"I'll tell you when we get there," says Vida.

Excited, Maya grabs her grandmother's hand and, stepping into a parallel universe, they find themselves in a field with some large stones. Maya is shivering. It's cold and it's raining; it's not just raining it's pouring. The howling wind is blowing sheets of rain horizontally. Maya hears a loud clap of thunder above her and, before she can say "one Mississippi," lightning slashes its way across the sky, striking the ground less than a hundred yards away and hitting a small tree.

The tree bursts into flames despite the rain, and Maya can smell burning wood mixed with smoldering moss.

The storm is on top of them and the air crackles with electricity as the energy ricochets off the rocks. There's a second crash of thunder and the sky is illuminated again. This time the lightning hits one of the big stones, splitting it down the center. The spectacular light show continues as they huddle together. Maya, too enthralled to be frightened, looks in wonder at the amazing scene around her.

"Bloody English weather," says Vida.

Maya is starting to realize that when her grandmother takes her on one of her trips, she always seems to be appropriately dressed. At the moment she is wearing a heavy wool robe that's covered in mud. The stinging wind is driving the rain into her face and she can feel the water trickling down her neck. She cinches her corded belt more tightly and pulls the hood forward so that it's almost covering her face.

Maya no longer sees Vida but she can hear her voice, and the icy rain on her face is almost refreshing. That night, lying alone in the cold, hard, hole in the ground, has strengthened her and, in spite of the storm, Maya no longer fears the cold, in fact she's feeling warm and flushed with excitement.

"You said that I was going to visit my ancestors," says Maya. *"Are they here? Who are they?"*

"All in good time, Sweetheart," says Vida. *"Remember, you have to learn patience."*

Letting out an exasperated groan, Maya peers at her surroundings and realizes that she is at Stonehenge, a place that has long fascinated her. The stones are huge and she can understand why this was used for astronomy, the whole circle of stones is an observatory.

Am I really at Stonehenge? thinks Maya, a little overwhelmed; *is this the power that I am destined to have? Can I just think of a place and instantly go there?*

"Maya, don't let this go to your head, I am just showing you some possibilities; remember that with great power comes great responsibilities," says Vida.

Stung by her grandmother's admonition Maya remembers that she must feel humble and grateful, but her adrenaline is pumping and her excitement is getting the better of her.

Taking a deep breath and trying to calm herself she studies the huge stones. Apparently they have been positioned so that ancient astronomers could track the stars and planets as they progressed across the sky. Maya had read that, once a year, the rising sun strikes one of the stones; it lines up with the opening in another stone and illuminates an area that was the High Altar. For the Druids, the most holy place in their circle of stones.

"Maya, you are doing a wonderful job of warding off the elements, keep using the techniques that I've taught you. I want you to sit at the base of one of the stones, press your back against it and tell me what you see."

Maya did as her grandmother told her to do, and then said, *"I see men in heavy wool robes with hoods, just like mine. I hear a voice telling me that they are astronomers, philosophers, architects, magicians, and seers. What an amazing group of people. I am being told that they are also farmers who live in harmony with the land, these are not Celtic Druids; this group is Alexandrian."*

"What do you think that means?" asks Vida.

"That they have a strong connection to their Egyptian counterparts," replies Maya.

"Tell me about the voice you heard." says Vida. *"Do you know if it was a man's or a woman's voice?"*

"I'm certain that it was a woman's voice," says Maya.

"That was my grandmother, Dinara," says Vida.

"My Great, Great, Grandmother?" asks Maya, in awe. *"The woman in your photograph, I was actually listening to her voice? How amazing, will I hear her again?"*

"I don't know, Sweetheart, that's up to her," replies Vida.

"Can you shift your connection to Alexandria," asks Vida.

"I will try," replies Maya, and then she remembers that grandmother had said that she was going to meet her ancestors, plural. Was this a test? *I had heard Dinara's voice but did I miss something important?*

The landscape changes and Maya is sitting beside a beautiful river that leads to an estuary that feeds into the ocean. The air feels soft and is infused with multiple fragrances, from salt water to blossoming Lotus trees.

The landscape shifts again and she is in a city with cobblestone streets that all seem to be leading to one central point. *"Tell me what you see,"* says Vida.

"This is so exciting.   I see incredible marble temples and one magnificent building that radiates energy," replies Maya. *"It is surrounded by lush green gardens with ornamental pools; there is even a zoo with exotic animals, and a man is inside one of the cages, he might be feeding them. He doesn't seem to notice me.   Wait a minute the animals are getting agitated. Can they see me?"*

Maya looks over her shoulder as she hurries away from the zoo and, for a brief moment, it looks as if a dark mist is swirling around the animals.

Lulled by the beauty around her Maya continues her conversation with Vida and sends her images with her mind.

"This place is astonishing. I'm walking beside pools where the banks are covered with papyrus reeds; red and gold fish dart between lotus blossoms, and the colors flash as they reflect the sun.   White birds with long necks—they might be Cranes—are wading in the water and, when they catch a fish, you can see the fish as it slides down the birds' gullets. The colorful flowers and their pungent perfume are overwhelming. Peacocks are strolling amongst trees that are in full bloom, and the date palms are weighed down with fruit.

"Men are sitting on benches in the shade, deep in conversation, while others seem to be arguing, but are smiling as they wave their arms around. I see men carrying scrolls as they walk in and out of the building. Beautiful music floats through the air, it sounds as if it is coming from stringed instruments, but I can't see where it's coming from."

"Can you go inside?" asks Vida.

"Yes, I think I'd better. The animals are roaring and trumpeting and I hear men shouting. They sound afraid. I'm walking inside right now," replies Maya. *"Fortunately nobody seems able to see me."*

"That's good, Darling, because I'm not sure that women would be allowed inside those hallowed halls. Tell me what you are looking at."

"This place is huge. I'm walking through an exquisite room with carved Greek columns. There are heads carved into the tops of the columns that look theatrical, but more than just the masks of tragedy and comedy. The walls are covered with mosaics and they depict the gardens and trees that are outside, it's as if they are trying to bring the outside in, without the heat. Everything is very cool in here. The mosaics are stunning with the colors ranging from a light pink to a deep blood red. The many hues of green bring in the cool colors of the lush gardens and the gold is the color of the fish in the ponds. There are busts of what look like Roman emperors or Greek gods and some of the mosaics depict scholars carrying scrolls. This is starting to look like one of our Universities."

Maya walks into the next room. *"Grandmother this is a large hall that has mosaics showing men performing operations; or perhaps they are doing autopsies, they must be doctors, or men studying medicine. There are tables, and, oh! There's a table that looks as if there's a dead body lying on it and young men are entering the hall and sitting in seats like our bleachers. I'm getting out of here; I don't want to see anyone cut up."*

Maya hurries into the next room. *"Now I'm in a hall that has mosaics of the planets and stars and equipment that might be primitive telescopes, but it has so many doors. I'm getting confused, I don't know where to go next; it's as if reality, or at least the reality that I'm in at the moment, is shifting. The colors are fading and everything is starting to look grey and I can feel the walls closing in on me."*

Maya opens a door and is enveloped in a black mist. She slams the door and runs. She hears Vida's voice in her head. *"It's alright sweetheart, the Dark Menace is trying to distract you, just visualize a wall of white light around you and keep walking."*

Maya isn't walking she's running and then stops and leans against one of the columns to catch her breath. *"That was frightening, but I'm alright now and I'm moving into the next room.*

"This is where the music is coming from. It looks as if the students are having a lesson, what magnificent instruments, Mom would love this.

"There are several smaller rooms where men are writing on pieces of papyrus as they lean over scrolls that have been spread out over large tables. The walls are covered with shelves, and men are on ladders stacking scrolls into compartments. Now I'm

walking into another room and I see men sitting at smaller tables. They are scribes; they are copying documents onto the papyrus scrolls.

"Where am I? This is overwhelming."

"Darling, you are in the fabled Royal Library of Alexandria, considered one of the Seven Wonders of the World. A building that houses a collection of thousands of papyrus scrolls containing the works of brilliant scholars from around the globe."

"I'm in one of the Seven Wonders of the World?"

"Yes, Darling, you are," Vida says. *"Every document ever written was copied and housed in its beautiful halls. It was dedicated to the Muses, the nine goddesses of the arts; it's just one part of the Museum of Alexandria. The library was later burned by Julius Caesar, and some think that all its ancient scrolls were destroyed. Others think that some of the work had been housed in smaller libraries around the city and, much later, was acquired by the great colleges and learning institutes of Europe."*

"I have to get out of here. The shouts are getting louder and I can hear men running. I sense the Dark Menace is close and I'm feeling very vulnerable."

"Sweetheart, you can leave whenever you want, you are the one in charge. But before you come home, if you are up to it, I'd like you to go to the Great Pyramid of Cheops. You are close by and one of your initiations will be inside the pyramid; I'd like you to become familiar with it. You already know what it looks like, just visualize it and you will be there. And it

will put some distance between you and the Dark Menace."

"*I thought that the Dark Menace could move wherever and whenever it wants,*" says Maya.

Not wanting to frighten Maya further, Vida avoids answering. "*We'll get into that later, just leave, now.*"

Chapter 27

"Grandmother I'm at the pyramid.   It was astonishing; I got here instantly, but I just want to sit down and close my eyes for a moment. There was something very frightening in that last room at the museum."

When Maya opens her eyes it's nighttime, and a blood-red full moon seems to be balancing on top of the pyramid.   It's illuminating everything around it with a pink glow.

"Darling, describe what you see."

"From where I'm standing it looks as if there are also two smaller pyramids.   But I can't see the Sphinx. I know it's around here somewhere, I've seen pictures of it."

"Don't worry about the Sphinx right now.   I want you to find the entrance to the pyramid and go inside."

Walking slowly through the deep sands around the outside of this huge edifice, Maya draws her hands across the enormous stones. Just as she thinks that she might have missed it, Maya realizes that it is above her and she sees some stone steps leading to an opening. Walking up the steps she finds the entrance and, holding her breath, walks inside.

It takes her eyes awhile to adjust to the darkness. The moon outside was so bright that it almost felt like daylight; but as soon she stepped into the pyramid the darkness slapped her in the face; she feels as if she is wearing a blindfold. There is no light at all and she has no idea where she is going. Maya cautiously feels her way through dark chambers and tunnels, her knuckles scraping against the rock walls. She jumps as something scuttles by her, and then relaxes as she hears squeaks. Snakes don't squeak.

The air is stale and she realizes that her feet are kicking up clouds of dust. Her mouth is dry and the dust is getting into her throat and she's having difficulty breathing. Removing her headscarf she ties it around her face, covering her nose and mouth, but that seems to give her even less air.

Climbing a ramp she feels pressure in her chest and stops to catch her breath.

Hitting her head on the ceiling, she can feel the walls closing in as the tunnel gets narrower and lower. Almost doubled over now, she can feel the air becoming fresher and can see some light ahead of her.

The space opens up; she is able to stand and she can breathe again. Maya walks into a small room that has an airshaft with moonlight streaming down from an opening above her; it's highlighting a stone sarcophagus.

Maya hears her grandmother's voice. *"You are in the Queen's chamber, Darling, but I want you to go higher to the great chamber that was thought to be the resting place of Pharaoh Khufu, also known as King Cheops."*

Maya slowly makes her way to the King's chamber, but it's empty except for an intricately carved sarcophagus. If there were riches in the chamber to help the King on his journey to the next life, they were stolen by looters long ago. The chamber is cold and Maya shivers as she walks up to the granite coffin; Maya is surprised that it's not bigger. The Egyptians must have been a fairly small race of people; she touches the stone, tracing the hieroglyphs with her fingers.

"Maya, this sarcophagus is where you will be tested for the initiation."

Maya gasps at the thought, and her throat constricts until she thinks she might choke.

"You've been practicing moving objects with your mind, and it doesn't matter if it is a small statue or a heavy granite lid; the principle is the same. I want you to focus and push the lid of the sarcophagus to one side, giving you enough room to get in. This is just a test. You will only be in there for a few minutes, and I will be right with you, so you don't need to panic."

Oh, really, thinks Maya.

"Yes, Darling, really," responds Vida. *"When you are inside, I want you to use your mind to slide the lid back into place. It's very important that you control your fear because you will have to slow your breathing. In the final test you will be in the sarcophagus for some time, and there is only a finite amount of air."*

Maya's legs are shaking but she does as her grandmother asks, and climbs into the cramped space;

silently thanking her friends for the small grave that was dug for her. It was just about this size. Maya's entire body is trembling as she slides the lid back into place. Inside, it is pitch black, not a fragment of light to give her any hope of air, and she fights the panic that is creeping up on her.

"Darling, you are doing wonderfully, I'm very proud of you, but you still need to slow your breathing and raise your body temperature, your fear is making you feel even colder.

"Visualize stroking beautiful Mango, and feel Frederick lying beside you; he is completely relaxed, in fact he is snoring, and you know that I won't let any harm come to you."

As Maya relaxes she is able to slow her breathing. After a few minutes she realizes that she has become Sekhmet, the lion-headed Goddess of War, and a War Goddess can easily lie in a little box, for as long as it takes to get the job done.

"Maya, you are almost finished, I want you to slide the lid off the sarcophagus and step out. Now slide the lid back onto the box."

"Do you think some hot soup would hit the spot right now?" asks Vida, *"I do, it's time to come home."*

Stepping into the parallel world Maya feels herself hurtling through space until she plops onto a chair in her mother's kitchen.

"Just in time for dinner," says Eve, smiling. "I have the onion soup you like, and some treacle pudding," one of Maya's favorite desserts. "Your grandmother's staying; you two have a lot to talk about."

Maya can hardly keep her eyes open during dinner, so Vida leaves, saying that they'll talk tomorrow; she is anxious to know exactly what happened in the Great Library. The Dark Menace had managed to block her ability to see Maya and the fearful things that she was experiencing. This has never happened before and could become catastrophic.

Chapter 28

It's a beautiful sunny day in late November, the air is crisp and there are still a few piles of golden leaves on the ground, but Maya has been too busy to notice. Time is running out. She's been working with Vida and her mother on the art of healing, one of the crucial steps to initiation and she knows that she has to pass this test.

Vida's husband, Athos, Maya's grandfather, was very knowledgeable about herbs and he taught his daughter Eve everything he knew.

With Vida's knowledge of the chakras, and her mother's knowledge of herbs and plants, Maya is quickly becoming adept in the healing arts, but she is feeling a lot of pressure. Maya tries to push her fears aside but knows that if she fails just one of her initiations she fails everyone. Who then will fight the Dark Menace?

Learning about herbs and healing energy has taken up so much of her time that Maya hasn't been able to go into the forest with Rose and Amul. Maya is still a little nervous around Rose, but her grandmother doesn't appear to be concerned, so she pushes it to the back of her mind.

Maya knows that Amul and Rose are still working on various forms of martial arts and Maya realizes that she is a little jealous. She misses the physical activity and she misses Amul.

Maya has known him since she was five years old and thinks of him as a brother, but she has started having feelings that are not exactly sisterly.

Rose and Amul do come over for dinner two or three times a week and, once, when Amul was saying goodnight, he accidentally brushed the inside of her wrist. The electricity that shot through her was so intense that she had to run up to her room. Judging by the look in his eyes, Maya was sure that Amul had felt it too. She knew that he wouldn't push her; he was waiting until Maya was ready.

Vida is very pleased with Maya's progress; in fact, she is sure that her granddaughter will complete her initiations before her sixteenth birthday, but that's only four months away and the pressure is on. The dragons have done a wonderful job of keeping the Dark Menace at bay, but she senses that the enemy is getting stronger, in fact it is changing color; it is developing a pink tinge as it soaks up more blood.

There have been several events recently that have greatly alarmed Vida.

A large iceberg in Greenland, more like an ice field, had collapsed, indicating that global warming is accelerating more rapidly than she thought. And there have been even more atrocities around the globe, including the bombing of a children's hospital and a refugee camp. This has caused so much fear and bloodshed that it's almost beyond comprehension, and Vida has come up with an idea that she wants to talk to Magnus about. In fact she has several ideas that will increase the amount of light on the planet.

"There has to be a way to slow down the Dark Menace," thinks Vida. *"It is getting stronger every day. We just need to hold it back until Maya has completed her initiations, then she will have the protection of The Sisterhood."*

Chapter 29

"Pisces, I'd like to talk to you about Planet Earth," says the elderly unicorn.

"Yes, Magnus, how may I help you?"

"I assume that you've been watching what's happening on Earth, and how helpful the dragons have been."

"Yes, I have," replies Pisces. "Is there anything I may do to help?"

"The Earthling named 'Grandmother' has contacted me with an idea that I think is quite brilliant. She is suggesting that we ask the whales to help raise the vibration of Earth."

"How are they going to do that?" asks Pisces.

"I would like you to ask them to sing louder and more often."

"Sing?" replies Pisces.

"Yes, sing. You are familiar with the beautiful whales' songs; we can even hear them up here. Grandmother thinks that their songs can make Earth a happier place, so that the Dark Menace doesn't have such a vicious grip on certain areas of the planet. She thinks that the energy generated by their songs might pierce the force field of the enemy. If that happens, and the whales' frequency can fragment the darkness, it will be much easier for the dragons to incinerate the Dark Menace. Also, the whales' frequency is very different to that of humans, so Earthlings won't detect a difference, they'll just feel happier.

"The Dark Menace fears the light, and, when the people on Earth are happy, there will be more light."

"What an intriguing idea," says Pisces, "I will ask them immediately."

Pisces talks to the whales and they are excited at the thought of helping to heal the earth. They say that they will increase the volume of their music and sing more frequently.

But the Dark Menace has anticipated this move and is sending out the whine of mosquitos to block the transmission of the whales' song. Their beautiful song is now being transmitted as a jagged staccato that is discordant, and almost too painful to listen to; and the darkness gets darker.

Chapter 30

Maya is unlike most girls her age. She loves to go to bed because she has such wonderful dreams. Safe in the knowledge that the dragons are protecting her, she slips sideways into another realm.

Tonight she is walking in the forest on a path of white quartz that glows in the moonlight. Frederick is at her side, stopping every few minutes as he encounters another glorious smell. Maya is almost hypnotized by the shimmering leaves that dance as they reflect the moonlight bouncing off the path. Suddenly three Eagle feathers float down and land at her feet. As she stoops to pick them up, a black cloud blocks the moon.

Maya looks up nervously, afraid that the Dark Menace has penetrated her defenses. She freezes as she sees a big black shape hovering over her; but then breathes deeply as it doesn't appear to be threatening. Frederick isn't growling; in fact he appears to be very relaxed.

As Maya watches, the black shape takes the form of a huge dragon and it's holding something in its claws. Maya is excited that she is finally going to see one of the dragons that are protecting her, but this one seems different.

Maya asks the dragon his name and he says, "Raphael."

"But you are the Archangel who is the Guardian of Humanity," exclaims Maya.

"You are correct," replies the dragon, "but I'm also the Angel of health, healing, and abundance, and I'm here to guard humanity and help you heal Planet Earth."

"But why do you look like a dragon?" Maya asks, puzzled.

"I can take on any form that humans understand," replies Raphael. "As you wanted to see one of the dragons who are protecting you, I decided to manifest as a dragon, and I'm going to give you someone to help you."

As Raphael says this, he releases what he has been holding in his gigantic claws, and a baby Dragon floats down and lands at Maya's feet. Maya gazes in wonder at this infant and realizes that Raphael has given her his son, his most precious gift.

The infant is making mewing sounds, almost like a kitten, then it sneezes and fire comes out of its snout and Maya starts to laugh. This makes the baby giggle and it rolls around on the ground flapping its tiny pink wings.

Maya watches, fascinated by the spectacle in front of her, and reaches out to touch the baby as it stretches and starts to grow. As Maya strokes the infant, it looks adoringly at her with eyes that are deep black holes. As is grows, it continues to snort fire and Maya becomes concerned; but looking around she realizes that everything is green and lush and that there's nothing nearby that could ignite. Soon the infant bursts out of its pink baby skin and is taking on a blue green hue that is starting to shine in the moonlight.

Raphael is still above her, looking down at them both. He says that he has to leave, but his son will stay to protect her and the unicorns when they travel on their final journey around the globe.

Raphael bows to Maya and she understands that, if necessary, his son will give his life to protect her. This dragon will be her personal dragon, and she says that she will call him Raif.

Maya realizes that she is lucid dreaming. She knows that while dreaming she is able to see the dream from several different realities and analyze what is happening.

She is astonished and humbled by the incredible gift that she has received from Raphael, and, as her mind and body are trying to make sense of this experience, she is overwhelmed with gratitude to have been given such an exquisite gift and access to such an exciting parallel world.

Her grandmother had told her that gratitude has the highest vibration; that it's even more powerful than love, and now she believes it.

When Maya finished telling her grandmother about her dream, she sees that Vida has tears in her eyes.

"Maya, my sweet, I'm constantly in awe of the energy that wants to protect you, but also alarmed that the Angelic Kingdom feels that it needs to help; it means that the Dark Menace is even stronger than I thought," says Vida.

"Grandmother, I really need more information. Raphael seems to know more than I do. He told me that his son will protect me on my journey around the globe. What does this mean? I know that I'm going to take the tests that will enable me to be initiated and replace you as Priestess, and you say that Rose, Amul, and I are going to ride unicorns; but to do what? And you are going to ride Pegasus, why? I thought that the dragons were protecting me, keeping the Dark Menace at bay while I sleep; but you've also told me that I'm the one who is supposed to save the world, not you. I'm completely confused. I'm merely an ordinary girl with an extraordinary grandmother. How am I going to save the world?" Maya is looking agitated, and her cheeks are flushed.

Vida takes Maya's hands. "Darling, I wanted to wait until you were initiated before giving you the whole story because the tests alone are daunting; but I will tell you how you are going to save the world. On the eve of the summer solstice, you, Amul, and Rose will ride the unicorns and I will be riding Pegasus as we circle the globe. We will have the protection of the dragons and, as you can see, the angelic forces will also help. I have told you about some of the sacred sites in countries around the world and, on this one day, Gustav, with our help, is going to inscribe these sites with information. The Dark Menace is going to try to stop us. It thrives on the misery that it creates and has to be eliminated. To put it simply, we are going to go to war with the Dark Menace; we will destroy it and inscribe a Manifesto into these sacred sites; and it will be released simultaneously so that the world can live in peace."

The joy that Vida had seen in her granddaughter when she had laughingly told her about the baby dragon has drained out of her body. She looks like an empty shell, blank, expressionless. Realizing that Maya is in a state of shock, Vida releases her cold but clammy hands and reaches for an afghan to wrap around her. Rubbing some lavender oil between her palms, Vida sweeps her hands around Maya's aura, filling in the gaps where her energy has leaked out.

"This is why I didn't want to tell you the entire story, but getting information in pieces was just going to frustrate you. I'm going to give you some hot soup and then take you home. You need to lie down and I will sit with you until you feel better, and then you can ask me anything and I promise you that I will answer all your questions."

It's Saturday and Vida knows that Eve is in Finchfield at the farmer's market, which is fortunate, because her daughter Maya is pale and walking like a robot when they arrive at the house.

After putting Maya to bed, Vida stacks crystals around her granddaughter, running energy back and forth to remove any negativity from her energy field. Upon hearing Eve's return, Vida goes downstairs to tell Eve that Maya is in bed resting, that she has a slight fever, but that she will stay with her all night. Concerned, Eve goes upstairs to check on her daughter;

but seeing that Maya is sleeping soundly she returns to the kitchen, secure in the knowledge that Vida is the best nurse in the county.

Vida knows that this is going to be a critical night and blames herself for not giving her grand-daughter the information more gently, but what's done is done and she will protect her granddaughter at all cost. *"If Maya is not strong enough to fight the Dark Menace, so be it; I will find another way,"* thinks Vida.

Beads of perspiration cover Maya's forehead and Vida holds a cool wet cloth to her brow, but Maya is kicking her legs and fighting the covers. It almost looks as if the snakes are back. Vida can see that Maya's temperature is rising as a battle rages within the child; she is fighting with herself, deciding if she is strong enough for the task. This is not something that will be forced on her. She has free will and can choose whether or not she wants to fight the Dark Menace. Maya's face is white and her body soaked when, exhausted, she suddenly goes limp and falls into a deep sleep.

Vida, her face grey with concern, holds vigil beside the child. Waking from what seems to be an eternity, Maya smiles at her grandmother.

"I am ready! I can take whatever the Dark Menace throws at me. But first, let me get though the initiations, and I'm really hungry. Do you have any treacle pudding?"

Relief floods Vida as she strokes her granddaughter's arm, "I'm sure your mother has some. I'll go and check."

As Vida leaves the room Maya is not feeling so brave. *Am I really ready to take on the Dark Menace? Once I'm initiated will The Sisterhood be able to protect me? What if something terrible happens to Grandmother?*

Chapter 31

"I think it's time to talk more about energy fields and how you can use them to your advantage," says Vida.

She sees the change in her granddaughter. Maya is more mature and has more understanding and resolve. Vida wishes that she had given her the information she needed earlier, but it's been a balancing act, trying to decide what information she could handle and what to withhold. Vida doesn't know everything, this is a new experience for her too, and she just wants to protect Maya.

Vida takes both of Maya's hands and holds them firmly. She looks into Maya's eyes until she's sure that she has her full attention. "Darling, I've taught you how to see energy, how you can shift your vision slightly to the side to see what others are unable to see, but there's a lot more to it. You can project this energy to form a protective wall around you, and you can use this energy to repel, or return the negative energy that is directed towards you. You can literally bounce it back from whence it came.

"Something that has manifested into form is a lot easier to defeat than a concept. I've shown you how to use the energy in your hands to create a bubble of protection around you, but there is far more power at your disposal when you learn how to use it.

"Let's try it now; I want you to connect with the universal energy field. Focus on your root chakra at the base of your spine, then bring the energy up your body, and then shoot it out through your fingertips."

"My hands are really tingling," says Maya. And then her mind drifts to Raif, the baby dragon.

"Damn it, Maya, focus! This could save your life," snaps Vida.

Shocked by her grandmother's words Maya slams back into the moment.

Vida takes a deep breath. "Now continue the energy up your spine, past your heart chakra to your crown chakra and out through the top of your head."

"Wow, it's as if fireworks are going off and light is falling in a waterfall all around me."

"Now you've got it, Darling," says Vida, "and I want you to practice this daily."

Vida gets up and stretches; the tension in her back surprises her. This hasn't happened before. She sits down and concentrates on Maya, her violet eyes almost boring into her.

Maya shifts in her chair, uncomfortable under such scrutiny.

"I also want you to practice manifesting this energy so that you are able to build a wall of white light six feet thick around your property, and surround your house with rainbows of light, not just on the sides and top, but underneath.

"The Dark Menace is relentless, and you have to be constantly vigilant; be aware at all times that it is increasing its efforts to defeat you. But I also know that you have extremely powerful protection—the Constellations, the Animal Kingdom, and the Angelic Kingdom; they all want you to succeed, and once you have completed your initiations you will have the protection of The Sisterhood.

"Darling, I know that you are struggling but you have to defeat the Dark Menace, and lift this thick, sticky morass of misery that is trying to envelop the globe; but be assured that I will be with you every step of the way."

Maya's mind wanders and she wishes that Amul were with her right now. *He is so strong and I feel so safe when he's with me. I know that he will protect me and he's keeping an eye on Rose.*

It's the weekend and Vida wants to prepare Maya for another initiatory test.

"Sweetheart, you know who Sobek is, you have a papyrus of him on your bedroom wall," says Vida.

"Sobek, is the Guardian of the Nile, the Crocodile God of Strength and Power and protector of armies," says Maya.

"That's right, Darling, and your papyrus shows the Egyptian God Osiris, God of the underworld and the afterlife, overseeing the weighing of the heart. There are many depictions of this important Egyptian ritual.

"In your picture the scales of judgment are being held by Anubis, the Jackal-headed God of mummification. He is also the protector of the dead and is the guardian of the necropolis. The Crocodile

God, Sobek, is witnessing this ancient ritual."

"The heart of the deceased is weighed against a feather," says Maya, "and if the feather is heavier than the heart, the departed isn't able to cross the river and continue on to the next life."

"Exactly," says her grandmother. "My Sweet, you are going to swim with the crocodiles."

Maya's hands start to shake and her legs feel so wobbly that she has to sit down.

When she was very small, every night before she would go to sleep, her mother had to look under the bed to make sure that there weren't any crocodiles hiding in the darkness. When she outgrew her fear of crocodiles and became interested in Egyptology, her grandmother gave her this special picture.

She loved looking at Osiris but always felt a twinge when she looked at the Crocodile God. "I'm going to swim with Sobek?" asks Maya, her voice quivering.

"Yes, Sweetheart. In your final initiation you will have to, so I'm going to start preparing you now."

"Will I really have to swim in the Nile?"

"Yes you will, Darling, but you know that you are protected, and that I'll do all that I can to keep you safe."

Vida hadn't told the child of her concerns that the Dark Menace was gaining strength, there was no point in alarming her; but Maya will need extra protection when she makes herself vulnerable for this particular test. Vida has already talked to Magnus about getting help from Hydra, the Snake Constellation. Draco has offered more help, although he has his hands full organizing the dragons. Draco has also offered to send a meteor shower, or Draconid, which will confuse the enemy and fragment its thickest layers.

"Darling, we are going to slip sideways into the adjoining world and when we arrive you will find yourself standing on the bank of the Nile. You've already been to Alexandria and the Great Pyramid, so this should be easy for you."

"But, Grandmother! Crocodiles! What if I panic?"

"If you panic, Hydra will be there to help you."

"Hydra? I'm already panicking. Crocodiles and snakes, can it get any worse? I don't think I can do it."

"Darling, we've worked on your fear of snakes, and when you bit off the head of the serpent, you absorbed its kundalini energy and claimed your power as Priestess.

"What is Hydra going to do?" asks Maya, shivers running down her back.

"She is going to guide you through the tunnel," replies Vida.

"What tunnel?" asks Maya, in a shrill voice. "I thought I was going to be swimming in the Nile,"

"You will be swimming in the Nile, Sweetheart, but you will have to find the underwater tunnel that leads from the Nile to the center of the temple dedicated to Sobek and Horus. You will have to hold your breath for a long time and you will be in almost total darkness. The river is full of silt, and any movement stirs it up, so you will have to feel your way along the bank to find the opening."

"What if I can't find the tunnel?" asks Maya.

"That's where Hydra will help, she will be swimming alongside you and, if you can't find the opening, grab onto her tail and she will guide you through the tunnel. Hydra is on your side, she's been watching your progress along with the other constellations, and she wants you to succeed."

Maya thinks that she's about to throw up. Just the thought of grasping a snake's tail makes her feel faint.

"Remember, Darling, you have to quiet your mind so that you can activate your reptilian brain in order to communicate with Sobek. You need to show him that you are not a threat.

"We've practiced slowing your breathing which will help you when you are holding your breath under water. Getting into your reptilian brain will also help you acclimate to the cold water. You will hear my voice in your head guiding you and, if you have a question, you just have to think it.

"I know that this is a lot for you to handle, but each time we do one of these exercises it makes you stronger. The work we are doing isn't just to help you pass the initiations and take my place as Priestess, these exercises are giving you the confidence and strength you will need when we have the final battle with the Dark Menace."

Maya is standing in some reeds on the bank of the Nile. The sun is blisteringly hot and the cool water looks inviting. In the distance she can see the tall sails of two Feluccas and, as she watches them skim across water, Maya wonders if they are transporting goods across the Nile or if tourists are taking a cruise.

She hears Vida's voice in her head. *"Don't get distracted Maya, you're not there to sightsee. Are you ready?"*

Maya nods her head and dives into the water. As Maya swims she is trying to remember everything that Vida has told her. *Slow my breathing; get into my reptilian brain; I'm not a threat to Sobek, communicate with him, Hydra is here to help me.*

As Maya swims she is almost blind. She has stirred up the silt and has lost all sense of direction. Unsure where to go she feels something beside her, it is Hydra. Maya is both relieved and repulsed by Hydra's presence. She hears her grandmother's voice in her head. *"Darling, take hold of Hydra's tail, she will guide you."*

Suddenly the water gets very still. Sobek is here, gliding silently as crocodiles do when they are about to attack. If he is able to grab onto Maya with his powerful jaws he will roll and thrash until she is incapacitated.

Maya is on the verge of a panic attack, but stills her fear as she hears Vida's voice in her head. *"Darling, tell Sobek that you are here to help; if your world is destroyed, his will be destroyed too. Tell him that you need his protection to find the tunnel and enter the temple. Explain that you are being tested and, if he allows you to proceed, you will be back to complete your initiation and defeat his enemies. Ask Sobek to protect you when you return and request that he not impede your progress."*

Sobek has almost reached Maya when suddenly she becomes very calm. She looks directly into his prehistoric eyes and communicates with him using images and a form of language that she isn't able to understand, but he does.

Sobek turns away, the water clears and Maya can see the opening to the tunnel.

Silently thanking Sobek and Hydra, Maya surfaces for a moment, then, taking a deep breath, swims into the tunnel. Just as she thinks she is about to explode and can't hold her breath any longer, she sees some light. Frantically, Maya swims towards the light and surfaces, popping up out of the water into the center of the temple.

"*Wonderful, Darling, you have managed to navigate your way into the most holy temple dedicated to Sobek. He understands that when you return for the final initiation, you will not be a threat. In fact, Sobek will help you now that he realizes how important your task is, and how important your success is to his survival.*

"*Darling,*" says Vida, "*it's time to go home, and some hot tea with honey will be waiting for you. You can't see me, but you can feel me, so reach out and take my hand.*" Instantly they are back in Vida's kitchen.

Vida smiles as she hands her granddaughter some tea.

Wrapping her hands around the hot mug Maya wonders what her next test will be. *If they get more difficult, I'm not sure I can handle it.*

Chapter 32

Despite Maya's positive experience with Sobek and Hydra, Vida is worried. Maya is not as strong and focused as she needs to be. She realizes that her grandchild is juggling school and her initiations, but she needs something to challenge her physical body, and so Vida decides to teach her archery. The English longbow, when used correctly, is a very powerful weapon.

"Grandmother, I haven't talked to Rose and Amul for a couple of days," says Maya. "How are they getting along with their lessons?"

"Rose is blossoming, and Amul is a wonderful teacher," replies Vida.

Again, Maya feels a pang of jealousy, and again is feeling heat in areas of her body that she doesn't want to think about.

"Sweetheart, they are in the forest right now, why don't we join them and see what's happening. But before we join them," says Vida, "I have something that I think that you will enjoy."

Maya sees that her grandmother is holding a bow and a quiver of arrows.

I didn't see the bow when we started walking into the forest, thinks Maya, and then she smiles. *Of course, Grandmother can manifest anything she wants whenever she wants. I wish I could.*

"Once you have completed your training you will be able to do many things that might seem impossible now," says Vida.

When will I remember that grandmother can read my mind?

"Yes, Sweetheart, when will you?" asks Vida.

Maya grins.

"Using the longbow will strengthen your arms and, when you are focused on your target that's all you can think about," says Vida. "It's not like a shotgun where you just point it in a general direction and you are bound to hit something, this takes great concentration and discipline."

Maya takes the longbow and as she strokes the wood it feels like an old friend. She plucks the linen string and she can hear it singing to her.

This is mine, she thinks, *this is definitely mine.*

Vida watches Maya's reaction and knows that she has made the right choice. Maya was born to handle a longbow, and Vida wonders why she hadn't thought of it before, particularly as her second in command, Artemis, has traditionally used a bow.

"Are the others going to have a bow too?" Maya asks.

"No," says Vida. "They will have their Kali sticks but I have a feeling that this is the weapon for you."

And when Grandmother has a feeling, it might as well be written in stone, thinks Maya.

"You are right," says Vida.

Maya looks at her grandmother, laughs, and says, "You're always tuned into me."

"Right again, Darling."

Maya caresses her bow and says, "This is absolutely the weapon for me, and I think I might have used it in a previous life."

"You could be correct, Sweetheart," says Vida. "When it presented itself to me I knew that you and the bow had a history.

Rose and Amul are in a clearing that is dappled with sunlight, and the shadows play on their bodies as they circle each other.

Maya and Vida arrive silently and watch them from a distance. It's almost ethereal as Rose and Amul fight each other with the Kali sticks. Rose's coordination is unbelievable; she is so strong and light on her feet that Maya feels irritated just watching her.

Rose gets to play with Amul while I'm supposed to save the world, thinks Maya, *I hope he hurts her.*

Amul isn't pulling any punches, he is making Rose step into her power to defend herself. His strength and perfect timing takes Maya's breath away.

As soon as Maya and Vida step into the clearing, Rose and Amul stop fighting and, all smiles, run towards them, giving them both big hugs.

"Sorry," says Amul as he pulls back, realizing that he is wet and sticky, and has sweat trickling down his face, "we've been having quite a workout."

As he wipes his face on his sleeve, he says, "What do you think of our student?"

"Yes," asks Rose excitedly, "what do you think? I'm having such a great time, and I've lost four pounds in the last month," she says triumphantly.

"Don't lose any more," replies Maya. "You're looking too good."

Rose gives her a hard look.

Vida walks over to a soft spot under one of the trees, sits down and calls to everyone to join her. "Amul, Rose, I've explained to Maya what I am planning and I need to give you the details of our mission," says Vida. "I asked you to trust me when I told you that Maya needed help strengthening her body so that she can pass her initiations, but it's a lot bigger than that. You've ridden the unicorns and are learning how to fight, but these activities don't have anything to do with her initiations." Vida is studying their faces and sees curiosity and a little fear.

"Grandmother, I'm grateful that you've taught me new skills and I'm much stronger than I realized. But if this has nothing to do with her initiations, why have we been working out?" asks Amul.

"You've heard about the terrorists and the bloodshed that is happening all over the world, and you know that the planet is dealing with global warming," says Vida. Rose and Amul nod their heads. "This is being caused by an enemy that I call the 'Dark Menace' and it is Maya's destiny to stop this monster from destroying the world, and I would like you to help her."

Their curiosity has been replaced by astonishment and disbelief.

Maya had already given Amul some information and he doesn't want Vida to know that Maya spilled the beans; but, of course, she does. Vida continues as if she is completely unaware of the collusion between Maya and Amul. "It will be dangerous and it is purely voluntary, nobody will think less of you if you decide not to join us," says Vida. "I'd like you to think about it before we go any further with your training."

Amul gets up and paces back and forth. "I knew there was more to it," he says, "but I had no idea that it was this big."

Rose is sitting with a strange expression on her face; it's almost as if she is trying to hide a grin.

"I don't need to think about it," says Amul, "I want to help any way I can. If Maya is risking her life, I want to be with her. In fact I would like to take her place. I know that I could defeat the Dark Menace, I don't want Maya risking her life."

Maya gets up and throws her arms around him and, looking up into his beautiful face, says, "I'm very grateful for your offer, but I don't think that Grand-mother would allow it." She looks at Vida. "It seems that I have been chosen to lead this battle. No one else can do it, not even Grandmother."

Vida looks at Amul and says, "If there was any way that I could take Maya's place I would. The thought of her risking her life breaks my heart, but this is her destiny, it's not mine or yours."

"Rose," says Vida, "take all the time you need to think about it. The only condition is that you can't tell your family or friends about this. Even Maya's mother doesn't know the details."

"I want to join you," says Rose. "I want to help you destroy the Dark Menace."

But Maya is worried, she still sees Rose's open mouth and all those teeth and thinks, *Can I really trust her*?

"In that case," says Vida, "let's continue with your training, and you can still drop out at any time."

"Look what I've got," says Maya as she shows them her bow.

A target on a stand appears out of nowhere.

She's done it again, thinks Maya.

Vida smiles.

"Rose and Amul, continue your workout," says Vida, "but, Maya, I want you to practice hitting the target, I'll show you how it's done."

Vida takes the bow and fits the arrow into the string, pulls the arrow back while focusing on the yellow spot in the center of the target. She lets go and the arrow hits the bullseye.

"Let me try," says Maya.

Taking the bow from Grandmother, Maya copies Vida's stance and, fitting the arrow into the string, inhales, holds her breath and lets the arrow fly. She hits the target dead center.

"Well done, Darling, you have done this before," says Vida. "You can practice this at home. I'll set up a target in the garden and, whenever you have ten or fifteen minutes, I want you to shoot some arrows. You will have to do this on the fly, quite literally. You won't have the luxury of warming up; much of what you do will be spontaneous; it has to be an automatic response.

"Once you get used to the longbow, I'll let you try a smaller one. You will be using the bow while you are riding Gustav, and a smaller bow might be easier to handle," says Vida. "But you will know which is the right one for you; even though the longbow is bigger, you two have a history and it is tuned to your energy."

They all practice for another hour and then Vida says, "It's getting late and Eve still needs some help in the garden."

Vida doesn't need to look at her watch, in fact she doesn't wear one; she has her own internal clock.

"All hold hands and we'll take the shortcut home."

As Amul takes Maya's hand she feels a tingle of electricity, just as if she had activated a chakra.

"Okay, everyone, hold on tight," says Vida, as they step into the adjoining realm.

Instantly they are back at Maya's house. Eve has been expecting them and has iced tea, berries, and homemade cookies on the table.

When they have had their fill, Amul excuses himself and Eve asks Rose to join her in the garden.

"Mother, I'll help too," says Maya.

"You still have a lot of work to do with your grandmother," says Eve. "Rose and I can manage."

Maya is surprised by her disappointment.

Maya is getting stronger and more powerful every day. Now she has her daily archery practice, and her five-mile run is getting so easy that she wants to increase it.

The problem is time, she has so much else to do. The solution is to manipulate time, to slip into a parallel world where anything is possible. She still excels in school, has accepted her classmates' jealousy and nightly puts her homework under her pillow; but Maya is also able to get the exercise she needs to strengthen her body.

The healing work that she has been doing with her grandmother has shown that she is a natural born healer, with great skills and compassion for the patient.

She is maturing into an accomplished young woman who is determined not to let the Dark Menace take hold of Earth. She understands that there are areas of Earth that are darker than others, where people have been fighting each other for thousands of years and their hatred of each other is all they know; it's so deep, it's almost bottomless.

She hears the news and knows that the number of extremists is growing. Grandmother has told her that the Dark Menace stimulates the fanatic's hatred by slipping its poison into their minds and preying on their ignorance. The zealot's methods are so terrible and so cruel that their opponents have lost all hope.

The Dark Menace feeds on blood; and there has been so much blood spilt, it's almost as if some parts of the land are running red with it.

Vida was just informed that a Norwegian fiord has collapsed from the temperature increase, and has another idea that she wants to talk to Magnus about. Solutions keep coming to her, the stronger the Dark Menace gets. Danger stimulates her imagination, but she sometimes wonders if the adrenalin rush is healthy, considering the consequences of failure. Her goal is to protect her granddaughter and she has to make sure that her concern for the environment doesn't take precedence over Maya's safety.

Vida was disappointed when the Dark Menace found a way to block the whale's songs, but she thinks that this idea is even better than the last.

Magnus knows that before the Elders left Atlantis for their own planet, they gave the unicorns amazing gifts; now Vida thinks that it is time to put these abilities to the test and use the Ley Lines.

Ley Lines look like a power grid that encircles Earth; and Vida suggests that the unicorns use their gifts and turn up the voltage. The average person can't see this power, and the wildlife and environment will not be affected. It is only the extra-sensitive people who will feel the increase.

With the power turned up and more light covering Earth, even though people can't see it, they will feel happier. However, the Dark Menace will be able to see the additional light and the fear of it will reduce its ability to manipulate people and throw the world into further chaos.

Vida's other suggestion is that the unicorns increase the occurrences of the light shows, also known as the Northern Lights, or Aurora Borealis, and have them light up the dark lands.

The brainwashed and superstitious terrorists will be fearful if they think that an unknown force is attacking them. And they are right to be fearful; the force for good is going to destroy them.

Magnus agrees to both suggestions and is excited about the idea. He is sure that more light will slow the Dark Menace, it might even paralyze it.

Chapter 33

It's evening, and the family has finished their dinner. "Darling, I want to do some more work on the chakras," says Vida.

Maya has had a long, exhausting day at school, but, as usual, she aced her exams and is feeling elated at the thought of learning something new. She knows the pressure is on and she has to complete her studies quickly so that she can become initiated. There are only three months until her birthday.

"Let's go upstairs and look at some energy," says Vida.

It's starting to get dark but Vida doesn't turn on the lights.

"Darling, I want you to look at me and tell me what you see; chakras are a lot easier to see in reduced light," says Vida. "Remember to shift your vision."

"I'm not seeing anything, everything looks grey," says Maya. "I know that chakras have color, I've seen them in your hands. Why can't I see them?"

"I don't know, Darling. Let me tune into you so that I can see through your eyes."

Vida is starting to feel alarmed; everything does look grey through Maya's eyes. Has the enemy penetrated Maya's vision? And is it preventing her from seeing color? She calls in The Sisterhood and, together, they focus on driving the Dark Menace from the house, but it's becoming more difficult; the enemy is getting stronger and, each time Vida challenges it, her energy reserves become depleted. She doesn't tell Maya that the enemy had penetrated her mind; her granddaughter has enough to deal with.

"I've loosened things up for you, Sweetheart, try again," says Vida.

"Now I see color," Maya says. "There are wheels of colored light spinning at the primary chakra points; but I also see many smaller wheels spinning at different levels of your body and I see a cord of silver light from the top of your head that extends upwards beyond my line of sight."

"Wonderful, Darling; now I want you to look down at your body and tell me what you see."

"I've lost focus, my vision is blurring. Everything is grey again."

"Hold on, Sweetheart, I'm not sure why you are having problems. Sit down while I figure it out." Vida is angry. She rains fire down on the dark mist and hears a high-pitched scream as the Dark Menace disintegrates. "Alright, Sweetheart, I think I've taken care of the problem, try again."

Maya looks down at her body. "This is exciting. I see my own chakras spinning."

"Walk to the mirror and tell me what you see," says Vida.

"I see a silver cord of light that extends up from my crown chakra, just as I saw yours, and I have the feeling that it goes up to the heavens. How is this possible?" Maya asks.

"Remember that I told you that everything is an illusion, that we are living in a world where we have agreed that this is a house and we are in a room seeing things that others have difficulty seeing. We can use this 'second sight' to our advantage.

"The Dark Menace exists in a depressed world where things are exactly as they seem. The enemy keeps the land under its control so that it's dark and desolate. It's afraid of the light because it knows that, when people are able to see beyond the darkness, they will no longer be fearful. But we are going to show them the light.

"Now I want you to go into the next room and close the door," says Vida, "Shift your vision and try and see what I'm doing."

"You want me to see through the wall?" questions Maya.

"Yes, Darling, it's quite easy, when you get the hang of it."

Maya walks into her small bathroom.

"What am I doing?" asks her grandmother, raising her voice.

"You're reading a book."

"Was I reading a book when you left the room?"

"No, you weren't," replies Maya.

"Sweetheart, I want you to do these exercises every day," says Vida. "Now come back into your bedroom."

Maya throws open the door to her bedroom, she's breathless with excitement.

"I'm going to go downstairs and I want you to tell me what your mother is doing," Vida says. "I want you to send me pictures of what you see; I don't want you to verbally tell me, I just want you to send me the answer with a picture."

"I'll do my best," replies Maya.

While Maya is focusing on her new challenge, Vida calls an emergency meeting with The Sisterhood. This communication is done instantly in the adjoining realm. She explains that the Dark Menace is back and that they have to find a permanent way of keeping it out of the house.

"*Sorry, Darling, I was distracted for a moment.*" Maya is hearing her grandmother's voice in her head. "*I'm in the kitchen with your mother; let me know what you see.*"

Maya sends Vida a picture showing her mother putting the dinner dishes into the kitchen cupboard.

"*You are absolutely right!*" says her grandmother's voice in her head. "*You're spot on. Remember to practice daily.*"

Vida walks upstairs to Maya's bedroom and sits in the rocking chair. "Looking through walls and seeing the colors of the chakras is fun but this next piece of information can save your life," she tells Maya.

Maya looks startled, and it finally sinks in, this is not a game.

Vida explains, "I'm going to teach you how to open your third eye to its fullest extent so that you can use it as a searchlight. This is your personal flashlight and it will be very important on your final ride.

"Start by focusing on your third eye while you are meditating. Then visualize your eye opening.

When I first did this the shock of electricity that went through me was amazing, so don't be concerned if that happens to you."

Vida continues, "When your eye is open I want you to visualize light coming from it. The light will look like a laser or the beam from a lighthouse. After you have tried it a few times while meditating, try it in your dark bedroom; you will be amazed at how it can illuminate everything around you."

Maya is bouncing up and down on the bed she is so excited.

"Also, as you look at people through your third eye you can see how they are feeling by the colors around them. Whether they are excited or depressed, the colors will be quite different. This can give you information as to whether this person is a friend or enemy.

"Sweetheart, you have a big responsibility," says Vida. "What you are learning now can not only save your life, but also save the lives of your friends."

Maya's joy and excitement flows away from her like water poured from a jug. *I'm going to be responsible for the lives of everyone,* she thinks, and she shudders at the thought.

As Vida walks into the kitchen, Eve says, "I'll walk out with you," and they walk into the garden. "Mother, I know we have talked about this before but I'm very concerned about the way you are pushing Maya." Eve tries to keep her voice under control, but her anger is getting the better of her. "I think you need to slow down; you seem bound and determined to catapult Maya into adulthood, and I feel as if you've taken my daughter away from me."

Now Eve is on the verge of tears. "What has happened to the little girl who wouldn't go to sleep until I searched the bedroom for crocodiles? The child who would play with the bees without getting stung? And who would love to slurp honey from the comb? The tenderhearted child who would bury every dead creature she found and who would cry for hours over a baby chick that didn't survive?

"You want to turn her into a warrior, a killing machine, someone who's supposed to save the world. How do I know that she will survive; and is the world worth saving?"

Tears are streaming down Eve's face as Vida takes her daughter's hand. "Eve, what you are describing is called 'growing up.' You can't hold onto your baby forever, she's a young woman now. For your sake, and Maya's, you have to let your daughter go, and we can't slow down, we have to speed up.

"If Maya is unable to pass her initiations she won't have the support of all the entities who want to help her. If that happens, then heaven help us, literally. I don't know who can take her place. I wish I could, or you could, but we can't. I believe that the world is worth saving, and Maya is the one who has been chosen to lead the fight; but I can't guarantee that she will survive. I can't guarantee that any of us will survive."

Eve sits down on an old wooden bench surrounded by her beautiful flowers. She covers her face with her hands and starts to sob.

Chapter 34

"Did you just hear what Grandmother said," asks Cancer. "She thinks that Maya might die in the battle with the Dark Menace."

"She hasn't even taken her tests yet. What happens if she doesn't pass her initiations?" asks Ursa Major.

"We have no control over what happens on Earth," repeats Taurus, trying to get his point across.

"You're no help," Leo comments. "The girl was wonderful with the lions."

"Leo, you're prejudiced because she likes cats," says Ursa Major. "We have to be realistic; Earthlings are destroying their planet and we can't do anything to stop it."

"I disagree," says Draco. "I wouldn't be sending in my brothers to help if I thought the cause was hopeless. It's my dragons who are keeping her safe so that she can pass her tests."

"And I wouldn't be sending my beautiful Sarita if I didn't think that it would help," says the Swan Constellation."

"And I'm going to help Maya," says Sagittarius, projecting his deep strong voice.

Surprised, they all stop to listen.

"Of course," says Leo, as he turns towards the Centaur, half-man, half-horse. Maya is going to use a bow as her weapon; you must be very excited."

"Magnus," interrupts Virgo, "I have a problem. I had asked if I could help the girl called Rose and I have been watching her closely. I think she is working with the Dark Menace, and I now believe that she is Maya's enemy."

"How do you know this," asks Draco.

"Draco, I realize that you've been very busy with the dragons, but I know this because I've been watching her," replies Virgo, with a touch of sarcasm.

The constellations all start talking at once.

"How can we stop Rose?"

"She was Maya's friend."

"If Rose helps the Dark Menace, they all might lose."

"If they lose, we lose, how can we help?"

"What happens if Maya dies?

"Alright," says Magnus, "everyone settle down. We are here to help the Earthlings but it is simply because we don't want to be destroyed by their stupidity; although I have to admit that I have become attached to Maya and I don't like to think of her friend betraying her."

Hydra jumps in, "I know that we are invested in saving ourselves; but when you look at the larger picture wouldn't you prefer to have an Earth that is stable and harmonious? I don't want to be dragged down because of the Dark Menace."

"What is the Dark Menace?" asks Scorpius. "On the surface and in our time frame it seems to be an insignificant blip; but to the Earthlings it's a huge monster."

"But what happens if Maya is killed?" repeats Leo, looking miserable.

"Well," says Magnus, "we are going to work with Grandmother to help Maya through her initiations; and it seems that the Dark Menace is a monster that we are destined to defeat, and we will do our best to keep Maya alive."

"I hope our best is good enough," says Leo.

Chapter 35

It's Saturday, and Maya has a quiet breakfast with her parents. Vida arrives and tells Maya that they have finished all the practice runs and that this next test is for real. This will be the first of five initiations that Maya will have to complete in order to become a Priestess and join The Sisterhood.

"Darling, I am very proud of you. You have worked extremely hard and become a strong and capable young woman. I know that this is the right time, and I have absolute faith that you will complete all the tests with ease."

Maya has also had a growth spurt. She is now five feet and six inches tall, quite lean but muscular and, to her delight, she has developed breasts, they are not as big as she would have liked, but at least it's something.

Rose and Amul walk up the porch steps and Maya looks questioningly at her grandmother.

"I asked Rose and Amul to join us; this is a very big day and they wanted to see you off on your journey," says Vida.

Practicing what Vida has just taught her, Maya opens her third eye and scans Rose. There seems to be a grey mist around her. *Maybe it's my imagination,* thinks Maya. *Rose keeps complaining of headaches, perhaps there is something else going on.*

"Rose, I can see that you are not feeling well, maybe you should go home and lie down," says Maya.

"There's nothing wrong with me, I'm feeling fine and who are you to tell me what to do?" says Rose.

Maya is about to tell Rose that she is becoming defensive, but she bites her tongue and softens her tone. "It's just that I can see by your aura that you aren't completely in your body, and that can endanger all of us," says Maya.

"What nonsense, I'm fitter and stronger than you are and more focused. I've watched you mooning over Amul; you're the one likely to endanger us all," replies Rose angrily.

Amul flushes but steps in. "Rose, I'm concerned about you. You've changed."

"You bet I've changed, I'm no longer the little girl who has to walk in the shadow of the great Maya, and I know that you like me more than her."

Amul starts to protest and glances at Maya. He has a pleading look in his eyes as he says, "Rose, I'm sorry if you think I've been leading you on but," he hesitates not wanting to hurt Rose's feelings, "but I just think of you as a friend."

Rose is furious with Amul for what she sees as his betrayal. She was trying to drive a wedge between Maya and Amul, but it doesn't seem to be working.

Vida has been watching this scene, and had hoped that Maya would see Rose's deception, and the fact that she is trying to distract her; but although Maya is confused she is still loyal to her friend. Vida has to let Rose expose herself; Maya must be able to distinguish between a friend and an enemy.

"Rose, are you sure that you want to continue working with us? No one will think less of you if you decide to drop out. This is my fight, not yours," says Maya.

"I made a commitment to you and your grandmother, and I intend to keep it," says Rose, "and I don't appreciate being attacked by you."

Maya sighs and holds up her hands, as if saying, "I surrender."

This is not a good way to start to my initiations, thinks Maya. *I have to push Rose out of my mind; I can't allow her to distract me.* And then she thinks, *I wonder if that was her intention?*

"Maya, you understand that you will be on your own during the tests, and I can't help you," says Vida; all eyes are on her now. "But I have taught you everything you need to know to accomplish your tasks. I will be giving you instructions and you will hear my voice in your head when it's time to move on to the next test."

Maya is both intoxicated and a little anxious at the thought. She knows how important it is to become a Priestess and how many entities are relying on her to succeed, but it's also a lot of pressure. Knowing that once she has completed the tests she will be able to move forward in time excites Maya. At the moment she can only go backwards, which is great fun; but Maya realizes that she's not here to have fun. *Grandmother had even said that being able to travel forward in time might save my life.* She shivers at the thought and the wedge of fear gets larger.

"Grandmother, I am ready, and I won't let you down," says Maya, smiling nervously.

"I want you to move into a parallel dimension and make your way to the Egyptian temple of health and healing adjacent to the city of Thebes, what we now call Luxor. There will be people waiting for you near the Karnak complex."

Maya is standing on the Nile's bank, but facing away from the water with her back to the pink cliffs of the Theban desert. Maya has read many books about Egypt and has seen the stunning photographs, but nothing could have prepared her for this vast complex of temples, the city of 100 gates. Over thousands of years, thirty Pharaohs contributed to its construction, praising a variety of gods and goddesses. The temple of Amun-Re covers approximately 50,000 square feet with 134 massive columns. The small temple that Maya is seeking is one of the most ancient and is built beside a crescent lake. It is next to the temple dedicated to Mut, the Mother Goddess, or Earth Goddess.

Maya is wearing a simple white gown, and she notices that everything around her is lush and green as she trails her hand through the reeds. There are swaying date palms providing a little shade, but the sun is strong. She can feel the heat penetrating her skin as she moves towards the small temple that is glowing in the shimmering light.

This temple's design is simple and classic. It is

not an edifice dedicated to a god, or a ruler, it is understated and actually more important; it is dedicated to healing.

As Maya reaches the entrance, two young women, no older than Maya, also dressed in white, greet her. They lead Maya into a room where there are three small pools. Standing in the cool fragrant room, relief floods her body as her temperature decreases. The women move, almost in slow motion, until one is standing on each side of her.

They gently remove the cord from around her waist and then release the tie at her throat. Her gown slips to the floor and someone behind her gathers up the garment.

One of the women picks up a small stone jar and pours liquid over Maya's head and massages her scalp. The other woman takes a soft cloth and gently washes her entire body in circular motions.

With one young woman on each side of her, they take Maya's hands and lead her to the first pool, slipping off their gowns before leading Maya down the steps and into the water. Once in the pool they continue their massaging and cleansing ritual.

Maya has a feeling of absolute bliss. The water is cool and the fragrance of the liquid is intoxicating. The stroking of her body is stimulating and soothing at the same time.

The young women take her hands and lead her to the next pool. This is a more invigorating experience. The water feels completely different with a more pungent aroma.

Again the young women cleanse her body, and

the water in the pool seems to be drawing out all pain and stress; it's as if she is going through a major detoxification and she feels as if she could fall into a deep sleep.

The two women take her hands and lead her to the third pool. It is so astringent that Maya's not sure if she can handle it. She feels as if her skin is being stripped away from her body, as if she is being flayed alive.

The pain is so intense that she is afraid that she might faint. The women push down on her shoulders until she is submerged. Gagging as she surfaces Maya tries to spit out the terrible tasting water, but she has already swallowed a good amount and she can feel it burning her throat and, as it travels to her intestines. Her stomach cramps, and she feels as if she is going to vomit.

The women take her hands again and almost carry her across the pool to the steps on the other side. Maya stumbles up the steps as the women lead her to a small waterfall. They prop her up and, as she stands under the waterfall, mercifully, all the pain washes away and Maya feels completely renewed. When she looks down at her body she is amazed that her skin is still there, red and angry looking, but still in place. She had expected that it would be hanging in strips.

The women have dressed themselves, and gently slip another white gown over Maya's head. After fastening the tie at her throat and fastening her belt, the women take her to a bench where they gesture to her to lie down, and she immediately falls into a deep blissful sleep.

After she awakens, the women lead her into a room where several people are lying on stone tables. The two women guide her to the first table and then leave.

Maya looks down at a young girl on the table who is obviously in pain, and Maya passes her hands over the girl's body in an effort to find the break in her energy field.

Feeling her hands drawn into an area by the kidneys, Maya knows what she has to do.

Connecting to Universal Light, Maya draws energy through her crown chakra, down her arms and into her hands, and she fills the area around the woman's kidneys with healing light.

Seeing the energy swirl in little spirals of pink light that corkscrew throughout the young girl, she watches as the pain leaves the girl's body.

As the girl relaxes, Maya passes her hand in a downward direction across the front of her own body, cutting the energy cord. This is a vital part of the healing process. She has to cut the thread that has been connecting her to the girl so that the patient doesn't continue to draw energy from her. Then Maya steps towards her next patient.

Maya can see, even before she reaches him, that this man requires a very specific herb to remove the poison from his system.

As she thinks of the herb, she sees a glass bottle on the small table in front of her. Maya puts a little on her fingertip and tastes it to make sure that she has chosen the correct remedy.

Gently, she gets her patient to drink the liquid,

but he needs more. Maya knows that, to save his life, this man needs a rare unguent, a special ointment.

Thinking of it, the unguent appears in her hand. She rubs the ointment all over his body and sees his life force retuning as she fills him with Universal love.

Maya performs her ritual of cutting the energy cord to break the connection.

Now, she moves towards the next patient.

But before she can reach him Maya stumbles. She feels a little dizzy and confused as if something is trying to take control of her. She pauses for a moment as she tries to regain her balance. The energy surrounding her feels completely wrong. The palms of her hands are bright red and she is filled with pain. Trying to stabilize her body she walks up to the man on the table.

Maya passes her hands over the patient and can see that there is a break in his heart. The man is filled with a very deep sorrow that borders on despair.

Knowing that repairing the tear in his heart will only temporarily alleviate his distress, she passes her scarlet hands over his body looking for something more, something that has caused the tear. This is not just an emotional issue, there has to be something physical causing his pain, but she seems to be making him worse.

As Maya looks at him in horror, his heart breaks in half and small black fissures are appearing all over his body; he is on the verge of fragmenting.

Maya's own pain almost overwhelms her, but she manages to cool her system as she fights to regain control of herself. As the red fades from her hands she literally puts the pieces of the patient back together. Then filling his brain with joy and stimulating all the pleasure receptors, Maya surrounds the man with love and watches as his broken heart closes. He is whole again.

Shaken by her experience and, with her body burning again, Maya can see that she almost killed the man. What were the black fissures? And why was her patient on the verge of fragmenting? Had the Dark Menace penetrated the healing temple?

Exhausted and shaking, Maya moves slowly to a stone bench. Easing herself down like an old woman, she presses her burning back and fevered head against the cool stone wall.

Suddenly ice replaces the heat in Maya's body. *This first test was supposed to be easy, what if I can't handle the next one? I can't allow the Dark Menace to take control of me. I have come too far to lose now.*

Chapter 36

Maya is filled with doubt as she hears her grandmother's voice in her head. *"Darling, I want you to make your way to the Great Pyramid. There will be someone waiting to escort you to the King's Chamber and King Cheops' sarcophagus."*

"But I almost just killed a man," says Maya.

"You didn't, the Dark Menace did," says Vida, *"and you put him back together again. You're doing fine, just focus on your next test."*

Dressed in the thin white gown and sandals of the initiate, Maya shivers in the cold desert night as she walks along the wide imposing path of crushed stone. She can feel the gritty sand between her toes and the straps of her sandals are starting to irritate her sensitive skin. She sees a woman, also dressed in white, standing next to the pyramid. The moonlight is bouncing off the side of the glistening imposing edifice and the small woman's body casts a long shadow onto the pathway. Fascinated by the daunting sight, Maya doesn't notice the dark shadow following her. When Maya reaches the lady in white, the woman motions for her to follow.

It's even colder inside the pyramid and, as they make their way through tunnels, at times having to crawl on their hands and knees to navigate through small spaces, Maya fights her claustrophobia. The woman is leading Maya into areas of the pyramid that are foreign to her, and, suddenly, they have to lie flat and drag themselves on their bellies across the rough stone. Maya's knees are scraped and bruised and she's already exhausted, but they have now reached an area where they can almost stand. Bending over so they don't hit their heads, they climb some stone steps. Scented oil lamps light their way, but the perfume of the lamps catches in her throat and doesn't cover the musty smell of the ancient stone dust.

Entering the Queen's Chamber there is a welcomed draft of fresh air that Maya remembers from her previous visit. It's coming from a shaft in the ceiling of the chamber, and the perfectly angled stone shaft was constructed in such a way as to catch the moonlight. Maya inhales deeply as she stands in a beam of light that illuminates the small room and the Queen's sarcophagus.

She would like to stay longer to breathe in the fresh air, but the woman leads her into more tunnels as they continue their climb. When they reach the King's Chamber, the woman gestures towards the sarcophagus and leaves.

Maya knows what to do. She has practiced this with her grandmother and, on one level, feels unafraid; but her teeth are chattering from the cold and, although she is reluctant to admit it, fear. Walking towards the granite casket she is gripped by a feeling of sheer terror and her body starts to shake. Running her quivering hands over the hieroglyphs she forces herself to get control of her emotions. She knows that if she can't curb her fear she will die.

Vida had told Maya about people who fall into icy water, and how the cold had saved their lives when their brains slowed everything down. Maya is already very cold but she focuses on lowering her body temperature even more and, as she slows her breathing, she visualizes the lid of the sarcophagus sliding to one side.

She knows that the sarcophagus is empty. Looters had removed the king's body and the surrounding treasures long ago, but it's still very creepy.

Vida is watching Maya, but there are some things that she hasn't told her.

As High Priestess Vida was able to choose the tests for her student but The Sisterhood chooses the severity of the tests for the initiate and doesn't allow the teacher to be part of that process.

If Maya passes all her tests she will replace her grandmother as Priestess of the Egyptian order of The Sisterhood, and Vida will step down.

The Sisterhood wants Maya to succeed. They watched as Vida trained her pupil to become a capable warrior, a strong young woman who will be able to defeat the Dark Menace; and once she has become a Priestess, and wears the jeweled breastplate, The Sisterhood will be able to protect her.

Maya will become a Priestess but not High Priestess. That position is chosen from the group of seasoned Priestesses who have gone through years of rigorous testing and The Sisterhood has already chosen the next High Priestess.

As Maya climbs into the sarcophagus, she tries to block the myriad thoughts that are trying to penetrate her frozen brain. She smiles at the one image that gets through. It's going to be a really tight fit; she has grown since she was last here.

Using her mind to slide the lid back into place Maya pulls her knees up to her chest and wiggles her body until she is in the most comfortable position possible, then closes her eyes.

Imagining herself immersed in icy water she falls asleep.

Maya's eyes pop open. She has been dreaming about an unseen enemy chasing her. In a dream, or under hypnosis, the body responds as if it is experiencing the actual event so that her breathing has accelerated, using more oxygen. Maya has a pain in her chest and knows that she needs more air.

What she doesn't know is that the black mist had slipped into the sarcophagus with her; the Dark Menace is lying beside her.

Maya feels her mind and body slipping away. She is floating in the darkness, not fearful, but sorry that her family and friends will be heartbroken by her death.

Aroused by the scraping sound as the lid slides off to the side, Maya gasps and spontaneously inhales, gulping large quantities of air. Not yet understanding where she is, Maya lies as if in a coma. Slowly, as oxygen fills her body and brain, she realizes where she is and that she has survived and completed her task.

She lies in the sarcophagus for several minutes as she warms her body and slowly increases her intake of oxygen. She doesn't want to get the bends like a diver surfacing too rapidly. When she feels that she has stabilized, and has regulated her breathing, she wiggles her fingers and toes and feels the blood flowing back into her limbs, but she has a deep pain in her joints, probably from being deprived of oxygen. As the warmth invades her being, she reaches one arm out of the stone box and stretches her cramped muscles. She manages to turn onto her back and stretches out the other arm. Willing herself to sit up, Maya feels her life force seeping back into her body. But her body rebels and starts to go into spasms. Her muscles are cramping so badly that she can see her body contort. Waiting for her body to relax, Maya takes slow deep breaths until she feels that she is able to stand. Silently, she thanks her grandmother for the years of yoga instruction and the importance of focusing on the breath. She had taught her that, when you breathe correctly, and you are completely centered, anything is possible.

Carefully stepping out of the sarcophagus she almost falls and sits down hard on the cold floor, bruising her tailbone. Regaining her equilibrium, Maya commands herself to stand and she visualizes the lid sliding back into place.

Most of the oil lamps have burned out, just a few are sputtering in the darkness, and the smell of the oil is nauseating. Realizing that she is going to be walking down steps and ramps virtually blind, she moves slowly, carefully putting one foot in front of the other. At first she feels as if her body is rubber; but then she feels her limbs tingle as energy starts to flood her body as she navigates her way downward. Some areas of the descent are quite steep and, at times, she has to use her hands to find the entrance to the tunnels.

Blood is running down her face from repeatedly hitting her head when the ceiling height changed. As she wipes the blood away with her hand she can feel a large gash on her scalp. Her body is still very stiff, and crouching is painful. The perfume from the extinguished oil lamps is giving her a headache and making her feeling light-headed. Maya tries to contain a coughing fit and almost chokes when she inhales a large gulp of the ancient dust. It's almost a relief when she reaches the passage where she has to lie on her belly. This time it is a little easier as she is going downhill. Fortunately, some of the tunnels are so narrow that Maya can reach out and touch the walls on either side, keeping her steady, and she pauses when she needs to regain her balance.

Reaching the Queen's Chamber, she blesses the light penetrating the shaft. Maya rests for a while, marveling at the skill of the architects and builders who were able to construct a monument that was positioned so perfectly as to attune to the stars and constellations. Measurements that, even today, archeologists don't entirely understand.

Having regained her strength, Maya continues her downward journey. Feeling her way along the walls she realizes that there are tunnels that go off to each side, but as long as she keeps going downhill she should be able to find the entrance. She knows that there are chambers below ground level and prays that she doesn't take a wrong turn and end up in the bowels of the pyramid.

Her descent seems to take forever, but, bleeding and bruised, she finally finds the entrance and staggers out of the pyramid.

As Maya steps outside, the light momentarily blinds her, and she shields her eyes with a hand until her vision adjusts. Squinting, she sees that the sun is overhead. It must be about noon, and she wonders how long she was in the sarcophagus.

She stumbles and falls to the ground and feels the sand grinding into her skin. Closing her eyes for a few minutes she waits until she has regained her equilibrium, then looks down and sees her torn fingernails and bleeding hands.

Looking around, she sees a group of old men squatting in the shade next to several stone jars. They are dressed in traditional galabeyas and are deep in conversation.

They study her as she walks unsteadily towards them. A mangy dog appears from nowhere and barks at her. One of the men calls to the dog but, growling, it continues its menacing advance towards Maya. The man calls again and, turning, the dog slinks, head low in submission, back to its master.

She must look a sight; she can feel blood trickling down her face. Her white gown is covered with dirt, sweat, and blood, and the hem is torn and frayed.

Maya, not sure if she can walk a straight line, cautiously approaches the men. They barely acknowledge her; after all, she is a woman and not worth their time, but, bound by their tradition of hospitality, they indicate that she can help herself to some water. Gratefully she ladles water into a cup and sips, she wants to gulp it down, but knows that she has to drink slowly. The men gesture towards a shallow basin. She takes the ladle and pours the cool water into the basin and washes her hands and feet; then, holding the ladle over her head, lets the water trickle over her bloody face. Tearing a strip from her dirty gown she dips it in the water and binds it around the gash in her head.

Thanking the men, she retreats to a place that's as far away from them as possible, but still in the shade. As Maya examines her bleeding arms she grumbles at her grandmother for not fully preparing her for the initiation, and then she hears Vida's voice in her head. *"Sweetheart, I can't prepare you for everything, but you were wonderful, I'm very proud of you, but you do realize that with your healing ability you can heal yourself. I haven't suggested it because you are under a lot of stress and I want you to use all of your energy for your tests. I will clean you up before each new initiation but it's something to remember if things get too bad and I'm not able to get to you in time."*

Not able to get to me in time, thinks Maya, *what on earth does that mean? Will there be times when grandmother abandons me?* In spite of all she has accomplished, all the tests she has endured, the thought of having to go it alone brings a level of panic that almost paralyzes her.

Chapter 37

"*Maya, I want you to make your way to the Temple of Edfu; it is dedicated to Horus. This is not part of your initiation, but as Horus has taken an interest in you, I think you should visit his temple and thank him.*" There it is, that voice she trusts more than her own, the support she needs to become a true warrior.

But wait, I can't visit the Sun God looking like this, thinks Maya and then remembers what her grandmother has just told her.

Maya had been seeing more of the falcon as she walked in the woods. Each time he would come a little closer, but he's obviously very cautious as he checks her out. The thought of going to a temple dedicated to Horus is very exciting.

Finding herself standing in front of the temple of Edfu, Maya looks at her hands and sees that her scrapes are healed and her white gown is pristine. Touching her scalp she can feel that the gash has healed and her hair is clean; it's no longer matted with blood, and she feels a surge of energy flow through her body.

Thank you, Grandmother, she says silently.

The temple is on the west bank of the Nile and has an enormous black granite statue of Horus guarding the entrance.

The regal falcon, son of Isis and Osiris, is wearing a crown, the symbol of his divinity. Seth murdered his brother Osiris and Horus was later revenged for his father's murder when he defeated Seth in battle, receiving the title "Ruler of the World." Horus is reborn every day, and the temple is dedicated to birth and renewal.

Maya bows to Horus before she walks past the beautiful columns covered with hieroglyphs that frame the entrance to the courtyard. Maya moves through the courtyard towards massive doors that protect the inner courtyard.

As she stands in front of the doors, they swing open. Glad to be out of the blistering sun, Maya walks through the doors into a fragrant, cool oasis. Fountains and small waterfalls cool the air. Granite benches line the sandstone walls and people gather to recount the heroic deeds of Horus.

Women who are ready to give birth ask him for a safe delivery and a healthy child. Women who are childless ask him for help in conceiving a child.

She moves to one of the benches and, closing her eyes, asks to speak to Horus.

Almost immediately she hears a voice saying. *"How may I help you?"*

Maya says that she is here to thank Horus for his interest in her, and to ask for his protection.

"Of course, you have my protection, otherwise

you wouldn't be here. I will be with you, and protect you during the battle. The falcon that you have seen in the woods will ride on your shoulder, as my emissary."

Joy and relief flood Maya and she says how grateful she is. She tells Horus that if she can be of service to him in the future, to please call on her. As Maya sits absorbing this exciting information, a dark feeling envelops her. It's almost like a premonition. What if the falcon is killed in the battle? Could she handle the guilt?

The wedge of fear is getting bigger and a wave of nausea rolls over her. *It's not the falcon who is going to die*, she thinks; *someone else is going to die*.

Chapter 38

Exhilarated by her experience with Horus, but frightened by her premonition, Maya is anxious to get this part of her training over with.

When she hears her grandmother's voice she asks, *"What's next?"*

"Darling, you had a grueling experience in the pyramid, are you really ready to proceed?"

"Bring it on," replies Maya, grimly.

"Sweetheart, you are going back to talk to the lions and the Goddess Sekhmet. The lions might give you some trouble; you are going to be severely tested."

Unlike the last time! Maya thinks.

"I'm ready," she says.

Almost immediately Maya is in the same arena as before. And, although she knows that it is day, the sky is black with sand that swirls like a reverse tornado, it is a Khamsin, a massive sandstorm. As she tries to stand upright in the howling wind, she can just make out a sound in front of her, and assumes that it is the door to the arena opening. She spins as she hears a similar sound behind her. Two doors? Perhaps twice as many lions? Feeling the sand tearing at her skin and filling her nose and mouth so that she can hardly breathe, Maya starts to panic.

She hears a snarl and is pushed from behind. She can't see anything through the swirling sand and is completely blind, but she's aware that the lions know where she is, they can smell her and she can feel them. She is pushed again and her heart starts thumping. She feels a paw as its claws rip her dress. She's pushed again and falls. Knowing that she can be killed with one bite to the back of her neck, she struggles to her feet. The sound of the growls overpowers the howling wind.

Still unable to see them she is aware that she is surrounded. Her brain is on overload. She senses that these are male lions, but she is confused. Usually there is a maximum of two males in a pride, but this is an artificial grouping. There must be female lionesses with them. She is pushed again and stumbles into another lion and it screams as its strong tail lashes her. Maya jumps as a lion roars, and then she hears a sound that appears to be a cross between a grunt and a scream, as if the animal is forcefully expelling air.

Now the ground beneath her feet is rolling and, as the wind dies down, she can hear stones crashing around her. It must be an earthquake. When the wind-whipped sand subsides she can just make out the lions. There are nine of them. They are being thrown around by the shaking ground and are fighting with one another. Maya can see that some of the columns surrounding the arena have fallen and she can't see Sekhmet's throne. As the lions fight and bare their fangs she can see their foaming saliva spray the air as they shake their heads.

Maya is so disoriented that she longs to sit on the ground but fears that the animals will pounce if she does.

"Remember, they are just bigger versions of Mango." she hears her grandmother say. *"You must get control of them."*

Knowing that her fear can kill her, she tries to calm herself and imagines that she is Sekhmet, the lion-headed Goddess.

Despite her attempt at serenity, Maya feels sweat trickling down her neck, between her breasts, and down to her belly. Her thin gown is torn from the lions' claws and stained from her perspiration. The swirling dust is turning the gown a light coffee color and she can see marks that probably came from the lions' tails and saliva. In other words, she's a mess. Maya fights even harder to control her emotions.

The shaking has stopped and the lions are moving towards her on both sides, snarling, with their ears flat against their heads, as if they are looking for their next meal.

Maya projects tranquility and complete dominance. She is the one in charge, and they are simply her subjects.

But Maya's attempt at dominance isn't working. The lions are biting one another as each one seems to be trying to assume its own dominance within the pride, and she wonders who will be the first to attack.

As they move towards her, Maya feels as if she is in a Roman arena about to be sacrificed. Afraid that she is about to leave her body, she talks herself back. She knows that the only way she can pass the test is to gain control.

The ground starts to shake again, it must be an aftershock, and the lions get very agitated.

She doesn't understand why they are so aggressive, but assumes it's all part of the test, and then she sees a black mist swirling around the animals. The lions are on the verge of attacking, she can almost feel one clawing her back and biting her neck, when Maya floods them with love.

Holding her breath and wondering what to do next, Maya sees the black mist start to dissipate. Almost hypnotized by the massive power of these animals she watches their rippling muscles and swishing tails as they begin to circle her. Maya turns as one of the animals lashes her with its tail knocking her on her back.

Thinking that this is the end, and that she is about to die, Maya closes her eyes and stops breathing. Feeling hot breath on her face, and then a burning sensation, her eyes fly open but she remains motionless. It feels as if her skin is being rubbed with sandpaper as a lion licks her face. Maya lies on her back for about five minutes while two of the other lions nuzzle her. Then very slowly, not wanting to annoy the animals, she moves her body so that she can stand.

Wanting to gulp the air, but forcing herself to breathe slowly, she waits to see what will happen. The lions surround her and lie down. Ahead of her, Maya sees the familiar throne of Sekhmet, and, holding her breath, she steps over and around the lions and walks toward it.

The lions are watching her intently but are no

longer aggressive. One of them rolls onto its back, and a couple begin to groom themselves. As Maya mounts the platform she sees that she is wearing the long gown of Sekhmet. The lions continue to watch her fixedly, and, as she sits on the throne, they get up and saunter towards her. Maya talks to the lions, apparently in their language, and as they lie at her feet she puts her hands to her face. Maya can feel the fur and knows that she has become Sekhmet the lion-headed Goddess, and knows that she has passed another test.

Maya is energized. The more tests she completes, the stronger she feels. She has become the warrior, Sekhmet, the Goddess of War. She can see herself riding Gustav, with Rose and Amul beside her. This is her destiny and she is finally claiming her power.

Chapter 39

"Darling, do you want to continue your journey, or rest for a while?"

Maya's adrenaline is pumping as she tells her grandmother that she wants to continue. She knows that she has to speed up the process.

Before she had started her initiations her grandmother had told her that an oil pipeline had burst in Alaska, spewing it's black crude over the frozen tundra and permafrost, making its way to the pristine waters where the salmon spawn. The ocean is now covered by black oil that is spreading for miles across the water, just as the Dark Menace is laying down a black blanket across the land, smothering everything in its path.

"Alright, Sweetheart, you are going back to the Nile but a little farther south, to the temple of Kom Ombo, to visit Sobek. Hydra will be waiting for you, but there will be other obstacles. Be careful, and look at everything around you; I know that there will be some surprises."

The adrenaline is dissipating and, as Maya wonders, with some trepidation, what additional challenges await her, she finds herself by the river.

It's early morning at the end of the flood season

and the thirsty fields are soaking up the life-giving waters of the Nile; but it also means that there are many more creatures moving through the muddy water. Even with the progress Maya has made, one of her biggest fears is, still, snakes.

Maya is assailed by a confusion of smells—death from the rotting vegetation and life from the new shoots that are struggling up out of the mud.

Maya knows that Sobek, the Crocodile God, is expecting her and has told her that he won't be a threat.

Trying to reach the river's edge, Maya has to wade through the mud and, as her feet make sucking noises, she wonders what else is out there and who or what might hear her.

She is about to dive in, when the water looks as if it is boiling. It churns and roils as three gigantic hippos surface. Maya gasps in surprise, tries to stop her forward momentum, but slips in the silt and slides into the muddy river.

Maya knows how dangerous hippos can be. They are extremely fast and can bite a person in half.

When they hear the commotion the animals turn towards her and start swimming in her direction. The bank is too slippery to climb and she can't drag herself out because there's nothing to hold onto.

Even if she were able to climb out she couldn't outrun them. Taking a deep breath she dives deep into the water hoping that the hippos won't follow her. As she swims she can see them above her, their huge legs are moving as if they are running on land. Hoping that she can put some distance between herself and the hippos before she needs to take a breath, Maya tries to fight the panic that is almost paralyzing her.

Sensing Hydra next to her, Maya grasps her tail. Feeling herself being propelled through the water at high speed, she goes limp and, as she releases the snake's tail, Maya knows that she's drowning.

As she sinks, only half conscious, Maya is vaguely aware of something beneath her. It feels hard with a rough texture, and it's lifting her to the surface.

It is the Crocodile God Sobek. With her lungs filled with water, some part of her brain wants to grasp the air with her fists, but she knows that she is dying.

With Maya on his back, Sobek swims to the edge of the river and climbs out, digging his huge claws into the mud. As Maya slowly regains consciousness she realizes what has happened and, rolling off Sobek's back, she lies on her side and empties her lungs of water. Blacking out again, she falls into a deep sleep.

When she opens her bloodshot eyes, the sun is high and she can feel her burnt skin pressing against the leathery hide of the giant crocodile. Sobek, this twenty-foot reptile, is lying silently beside her, guarding her from the circling vultures.

Silently thanking Sobek for saving her life, Maya looks around at her surroundings. She has to find some water and shade before she can find the tunnel that leads to the temple.

Feeling lightheaded, and struggling to stand on shaky legs, she sees some palm trees in the distance and, through her haze, thinks it might be an oasis where she can find fresh water.

Willing her legs to move towards the palms, the fog in her brain starts to lift and she remembers that the Nile is a freshwater river. She has all the water she needs right in front of her. It might be a little muddy, and goodness knows what bacteria might be in it, but as she has already swallowed a large amount, a little more won't hurt.

Looking deeply into Sobek's heavily lidded eyes, and using his language, Maya expresses her utmost gratitude to this beautiful creature.

Knowing that she still has to complete her task by reaching the sanctuary in the center of the temple, Maya slogs through the mud to the river's edge and dives in. Surfacing she takes small gulps of water and starts to feel more balanced, more centered.

The flood has changed the topography and, as Maya feels her way along the bank, she wonders whether silt might have filled up the tunnel. She has an idea of where the tunnel is, but is still disoriented after the frightening experience with the Hippos.

The experience has depleted her energy, and she talks sternly to herself to get it together. Maya knows that she has many resources available to her; she just has to ask for guidance. But when you are under stress and need help the most, that's when you forget the basics.

As if light suddenly penetrates her scull, Maya understands what the tests are all about. You simply have to remember what you have been taught, trust those teachings and use the tools you have been given.

Why have I been looking down, when I should be looking up? The Kom Ombo temple is a large structure and if I can see it from the river, I will have a better idea of where the entrance to the tunnel is.

As Maya is feeling pleased with herself at this revelation, she feels a snake slither by. It's not Hydra, and Maya's blood turns to ice. The snake turns and comes back towards her.

It seems aggressive and Maya tries to swim out of its way, but she hears a voice in her head. *"Listen to me, I am Renenute, the Snake Goddess, protector of the harvest and consort of Sobek. I will not hurt you. He has sent me to guide you through the tunnel."*

Maya asks Renenute if she should touch her, but the snake replies that it's not necessary, to just follow her.

Maya surfaces, takes a deep breath then dives down, back to the snake.

Peering through the silt, Maya sees an opening and, following Renenute, she swims through the tunnel and pops up in the middle of the temple of Kom Ombo. Climbing out of the water, Maya sees something that she hadn't noticed the first time.

This is a temple with two sanctuaries; it is a temple of dualities. One temple is dedicated to Sobek, the creator of the Nile, leader of armies, and the destroyer of enemies. The other temple is dedicated to the falcon Horus, the God of birth and new beginnings, the divine child of Isis and Osirus.

It's a temple dedicated to both the higher and baser aspects of your being. It gives you the opportunity to become whole, by accepting and integrating the light and the dark within yourself.

Looking around, Maya sees a young woman walking towards her. The woman takes her hand and leads her to a bench. When she is seated, the acolyte gives her something to drink. Sipping the delicious liquid, Maya immediately feels the life force flowing back into her body.

The woman smiles as she leads her into a dimly lit, fragrant room. Another woman enters and the two acolytes remove Maya's gown. They bathe her and then indicate that she should lie on a table, face down. They pour oil over her body and place warm rocks on the main chakras in a line up her back.

With a woman standing on each side of her, they start to massage the soles of her feet pressing the power points and pulling each of her toes. They work in circles as they massage the muscles in the backs of her legs. Moving up to her thighs, they alternate between gentle strokes and deep pressure. Reaching her buttocks they remove the stones and apply even more pressure to her torso, pressing deeply into the muscles of her back and shoulders with their elbows.

One of the women kneels on her back applying pressure to areas that Maya didn't even know she had.

They gesture for her to turn over, and then massage the tops of her feet, and stroke between each toe. Just as Maya relaxes into a feeling of bliss they work the meridians on the front of her legs. The pain catches her by surprise and she gasps.

Ignoring Maya's groans of pain the women move up the chakra points to her belly, paying particular attention to her digestive tract and removing all toxins. After massaging her breasts they each take a hand and, pulling and flexing her fingers, they put pressure on the joints. Working their way up her arms the women press her shoulders with their elbows then move to her neck. Then they stretch her with one acolyte pulling on her feet and the other with a hand under each armpit.

After massaging her face, and paying great attention to her ears, they scrub her scalp and pull her hair.

Covering her face with fine cloth, a fragrant liquid is sprinkled over the fabric and Maya falls into a deep sleep.

When Maya awakens she has no idea how long she's been sleeping, but has completely regained her strength and feels totally refreshed. As she starts to stand, she hears Vida's voice. *"That was a wonderful nap, Darling; there is only one more test for you to take. Are you ready to continue?"*

"Yes," replies Maya, *"I'm more than ready, I feel wonderful."*

"Alright, Sweetheart, I want you to make your way to Queen Hatshepsut's Temple, in the Valley of the Queens; you'll know what to do when you get there."

Chapter 40

Maya has seen pictures of this temple; it was a revolutionary design by the architect Senmut. Deir El-Bahari is almost contemporary, consisting of vast terraces with wide ramps that connect multiple levels, and Maya is awed by the imposing building in front of her.

As she walks towards the temple along a path of crushed rose quartz, Maya has never felt so hot, and feels embarrassed to be entering Queen Hatshepsut's temple wearing a stained garment drenched in perspiration.

Queen Hatshepsut is the only woman to rule ancient Egypt, and she is one of Maya's heroines.

With the relentless sun beating down on her, Maya's breathing becomes labored as she starts to climb a ramp. Seeing a black swarm in the sky ahead she grabs onto one of the beautifully carved Sphinxes lining her path. Thinking that it might be locusts, and wondering what other Egyptian plagues she will have to endure, the ball breaks up and heads straight for her.

To her horror she sees that these are not locusts but bright red mosquitos the size of locusts, and she has nowhere to hide when they attack. Waving her arms as she tries to protect her face she is bitten repeatedly all over her body by these enormous insects.

She knows that Egyptian mosquitos can carry deadly diseases, but these seem like something from another world. Maya recoils as she watches an insect uncurl its long proboscis, injecting its venom through her punctured skin. The poison is making great welts all over her body and she can feel her face swelling. Their high-pitched whine is so loud that Maya feels as if something is drilling into her skull, and a river of pain washes over her. Dragging herself up the ramp from Sphinx to Sphinx she makes her way to the first terrace. As Maya collapses, the insects continue to feed on her body, sucking out blood and injecting poison.

Dazed, she thinks of Rose and her strange encounter with a mosquito. It had been too early in the season for Rose to be bitten, and Maya had dismissed her friend's complaints. Perhaps these are not ordinary mosquitos. Is it possible that the Dark Menace has changed from a mist and manifested into this form? She knows that the enemy took control of the serpents at night while she slept; perhaps it can take on any form it wishes.

Almost unconscious from dehydration and the poison that is flowing through her body, Maya knows that she needs water to survive and, in her stupor, wonders if she will live to complete the test.

The mosquitos depart as quickly as they arrived and, gasping, Maya crawls up the second ramp. Even in her confused state Maya is able to admire the beautiful obelisks that line her path.

Using every ounce of her willpower Maya pulls herself to her feet and sways as she stands in front of two massive, intricately carved doors. The doors swing open and Maya feels herself glide or float through the entrance. In almost total darkness she has the sensation of walking through a rain forest with the gentle moisture washing away all her pain, penetrating her skin as if her entire body is drinking this life-giving liquid.

Moving forward, unsure whether she is walking or floating, she moves into a dark room that appears to be a narrow hall, and she feels a gentle breeze. It's so delicate and soft, it almost feels as if the wings of a hundred hummingbirds are fanning her. Free of pain and delighting in the sensual experience, Maya pauses as her body temperature cools and the poison recedes. As she relaxes she inhales a perfume that is so sumptuous that it awakens her taste buds.

Walking in the dim light, her eyes slowly adjust to the darkness and she can see that the walls and columns surrounding her are covered with paintings and hieroglyphs. The space appears to open up and, as she walks, she sees two rows of small lights, about waist high, one on each side of her. It's difficult to see in the low light, but when she looks at her arms all the welts from the mosquito bites have disappeared, and as she strokes her skin it feels soft and smooth.

Moving further into the room, and as her vision improves; Maya realizes that the small lights are the eyes of animals. Shifting her vision, she is able to make out the shapes, and sees that they are big cats, black panthers, and feels a thrill as she realizes that these are live animals, not statues. The gleaming golden eyes of these magnificent animals glow in the dark and follow

Maya as she walks between them.

There is a burning smell now, rather like incense, but it's creating smoke that makes it even harder to see. Peering through the haze, Maya sees some light in the distance. Moving forward through the fog, the hall opens into a chamber that has a shaft of light illuminating a large granite block covered by magnificent jeweled cloth.

Walking towards the stone block, Maya realizes that it is an altar and bows her head in reverence and submission.

On top of the altar are three stone caskets that glow from within. The one in the center is taller than the other two. The caskets have lids and Maya wonders if they are sealed. Running her hands over the cool stone of the altar, Maya can feel that it is covered with hieroglyphs and symbols.

Standing in front of the altar, she is drawn to the casket on her left. Maya tentatively reaches out and touches the casket.

Emboldened, she tries to shift the lid. It lifts easily and the chamber becomes a kaleidoscope of light. The casket is filled with precious jewels, rubies, emeralds, sapphires, and amethysts, a rainbow of color and power. The crystals glow from within, and the radiating colors bounce off the walls and ceiling in a riot of color that is almost disorienting.

Moving to the casket on her right, Maya lifts the lid and the light almost blinds her. There is every shade of gold, from the brightest yellow of the sun, to the deepest rose gold that looks almost copper.

The casket is filled with goblets, breastplates,

necklaces, bracelets, earrings, and all manner of gold and jeweled articles. She hears a voice in her head telling her that priests and priestesses have used these treasures since the beginning of time. They are priceless historical artifacts, which even include the goblet used by Jesus at the last supper.

Maya is astounded by the information and, although awed by the beauty of these irreplaceable treasures, she is drawn to the casket in the center. She removes the lid but, as it is taller than the others, she can't see inside it.

Maya hears a voice telling her that she has to choose one of the caskets. She must make a decision, but she hasn't seen what's inside the third casket. Maya clears her throat and, glad that she still has a voice, says aloud that she chooses the casket in the center. Then holding her breath she slowly reaches into the casket.

Her heart races as she feels movement, and momently freezes as she becomes aware of what she is touching. Keeping very still she allows the snakes to wind their way up her arms. She holds her breath as their tongues flick in and out as they slither across her shoulders and wind themselves around her neck.

She hears the snakes whispering to her. They are telling her that she is one of them, that she has absorbed the energy of the Goddess and that they will protect her. Slowly withdrawing her arms from the casket she stretches her arms out to the side. Stepping back from the altar Maya bows her head in reverence and gratitude.

There is a pink glow around Maya as she glides,

almost motionless, towards a chamber on her right. Part of her brain is focused on the snakes, not wanting to anger them, but also knowing that they are her friends. She seems to be floating as she enters the anti-chamber. The room's walls appear to be covered with rose quartz, which casts a pink glow. As Maya looks up, high above her the light is sparkling white as if the ceiling is covered with diamonds, and it is. She floats towards an altar that has a large book in the center.

The book's cover is encrusted with jewels and as she stands in front of it, the sacred text opens. The pages fan at great speed creating a small whirlwind, a vortex of energy, and Maya, wrapped with the snakes, is drawn into the Akashic Records, the history of all that ever was and all that ever will be.

Maya hears Vida's voice in her head. *"Sweetheart, in spite of your fear, you were able to completely open your heart chakra. Only someone who has the purest of intentions and who has been stripped of all defenses can be pulled into the Akashic Records. This will give you power beyond your wildest imaginings.*

"Maya, you have passed with flying colors, I'm so proud of you. Would you like to come home?"

"Yes, please, Grandmother, I have so much to ask you."

"And I'll answer all your questions; I'm at your house," she hears her grandmother say.

Instantly Maya is at home, sitting at her kitchen table.

Eve is all smiles and gives her daughter a big hug and kiss on the cheek.

Vida is beaming. She is thrilled that Maya has completed her initiations in spite of the fact that the Dark Menace was able to penetrate the layers of protection that were wrapped around her grandchild. Vida is now able to give Maya the gift that will ensure her protection, but she will do it later.

Maya is now a member of The Sisterhood, a Priestess in her own right, and she has the skills and tools that will ensure her victory.

Now Vida has to prepare everyone else for the coming battle.

Chapter 41

"Hydra," calls Leo, "did you see how Maya handled the snakes? Wasn't she brave, and they were so beautiful." Leo is still afraid of Hydra and thinks that praising the snakes might soften her attitude. "You've changed your tune," says the Snake Constellation. "Yes the snakes were beautiful and I think that I should have some credit for helping Maya when she was swimming in the Nile."

"But you almost drowned her," snaps Sirius, the Dog Star.

"Technicalities," says Hydra. "The stupid girl should have held her breath longer."

"She's not stupid, she's going to save the Milky Way, and it was the snake Renenute who led her into the temple," says Sirius. "You might be bigger than me but I'm the brightest star in the night sky and I'm not afraid of you."

Leo wishes that he hadn't said anything. He likes the Dog Star and knows that Sirius feels a connection to Frederick the way he does to Mango, but he thinks that this argument is only making Hydra more aggressive and Leo's sure that Sirius isn't going to back down.

"Are you still at it?" interrupts Magnus. "I'm

trying to help Maya save our Universe and you are still bickering like children.   If you don't have anything good to say about Maya, don't say anything.   Hydra, you try to intimidate the other constellations because of your size; I'm beginning to think that you have an inferiority complex.   It seems that the majority of Earthlings don't like snakes."

    Leo smiles.

Chapter 42

Maya is glowing with delight; her father has arranged his schedule so that he can join the family for a celebratory dinner. Rose and Amul are on their way, and everyone is very excited by her success. Frederick and Mango get some special treats and are allowed in the dining room to sit with the family.

Eve's wonderful dinner is enjoyed by all and everyone wants to hear about Maya's adventures. Maya is thrilled to be home with the people and animals she loves best but is only able to give them generalities about her adventures. The family realizes that they can't be privy to the details of her initiations, and recognize that these are sacred rites that are shared only with other initiates. Everyone completely understands and is content with the fact that Maya is back with them, safe and sound.

After Maya's favorite dessert of treacle pudding, Rose and Amul help Eve clear the meal and wash the dishes. Rose is looking flushed. Maya attributes it to the hot dishwater and the excitement of her return, but when Rose takes off her sweater Maya can see three large welts on her neck. Maya turns to her grandmother but can't get her attention; she doesn't seem to want to look at her.

Maya's father goes to his office for what is likely to be a long night of work. Frederick and Mango follow Maya as she goes to her bedroom; but Maya is still thinking about Rose and what appears to be mosquito bites on her neck and wonders if there is something that her grandmother doesn't want her to know.

Vida is the most relaxed she has been in months. Her beautiful strong and powerful granddaughter has completed a remarkable task and now she is more than qualified to become a Priestess of the Egyptian Order. Vida enters Maya's bedroom and finds her sitting on the floor so that she can be closer to her pets.

After stretching his long shaggy body across the bedroom floor and putting his head on Maya's feet, Frederick is soon sleeping but whimpers and twitches as he dreams. Maya smiles and wonders what animal he is chasing. Meanwhile, Mango's purr is almost deafening as he sits in Maya's lap, gazing at her through his beautiful golden eyes.

Sitting in the rocking chair Vida asks, "How are you feeling, Darling?"

"I feel absolutely wonderful, Grandmother. What an extraordinary experience!"

Vida already knows how Maya is feeling, she has been in her granddaughter's mind and body every moment, but she wants Maya to express herself in her own way.

"Is there anything that concerns you or that you are curious about?"

"Yes, there are many things, but first I want to

confirm that, while I was in Egypt, I was also still here in this house. It's a little overwhelming. All the challenges were so real, so terrifying in fact, that it seems amazing that I could be in two places at once. I know we've gone over this and you've explained it many times, but it still seems that I experienced what most people would think was impossible. It's difficult for me to believe, and I've just done it."

"Sweetheart, I can assure you that you were in this kitchen while at the same time you were in Egypt. In fact you were sitting at the kitchen table and your mom was holding your hand. Eve knew that you were going through the initiations to replace me, but she had no idea what the initiations were and, when you heard my voice in your head, even though I was at the table with Eve, she couldn't hear what I was saying. I was projecting the thought to you, just as we did when we practiced seeing through walls and sending pictures of what we were saying.

"Your mother wanted to be with you every step of the way. She knew that you were in danger but she also trusted me to take care of you. You should be very proud of her, I know that the two of you have had your differences, but she only wants what is best for you and she realizes that you have a destiny to fulfill. And, yes, you are right; many other people do think that it is impossible to be in two places at once, that's why you can never tell anyone," says Vida.

"We've still got a lot to talk about so I think we should have some tea. Will you go and get it from your mom? I've already sent her a message, so it's waiting for us."

Maya has a surprised expression on her face.

"Yes, Sweetheart, your mom can hear my thoughts, when I want her to; and it speeds things up."

Putting Mango on the floor and lifting Frederick's head from her feet Maya goes downstairs to fetch the tea.

Handing her grandmother a mug, Maya sits back on the floor and Mango jumps into her lap.

"I want to learn more about the Akashic Records, but, before I get to that I want to ask about the giant mosquitos; they were the size of locusts and quite deadly. I felt that the Dark Menace was able to manifest itself into these insects.

"Remember when you set fire to the tree stump and the Dark Menace knocked me down and I told you that I had seen Rose's open mouth with all those teeth coming at me. Well, I had a similar feeling when the locusts attacked me at Queen Hatshepsut's temple; I didn't see Rose's face but I think the Dark Menace has infected her. She's been complaining about a mosquito for some time and said that she felt that it was boring into her ear. And when you showed me how to open my third eye I scanned Rose and could see a grey mist or cloud around her. I know that she wouldn't willingly do anything to hurt me, but could the Dark Menace, in the form of a mosquito, inject its poison into her, making her an enemy instead of a friend?"

Vida gets up from the chair and walks around the room. As she thinks about Rose she can feel the tension flowing back into her body. "This is something that I have also been concerned about," she replies. "And, although I know she loves you, this might be something that is beyond her power to overcome. I'm sure she has no idea what is happening to her but we have to watch her, while assuming that she will continue to protect you."

"I tried to get your attention when we were in the kitchen. Did you see the bites on Rose's neck? I have the feeling that you know more than you're telling me," says Maya.

"Yes, Sweetheart, there are things that I can't share with you at the moment, but I will give you more information as soon as I can."

Frederick gets up to stretch and Mango jumps off Maya's lap, so she takes this opportunity to move to the bed and pulls her favorite comforter over her crossed legs.

"Now," says Vida, changing the subject, "what is your question about the Akashic Record?"

"What is the Akashic Record, the big book that I was pulled into?"

"That's a good question, with a complicated answer. The Akashic Record is a history of everything that has happened, and everything that ever will happen."

"You mean that everything we do or experience is predetermined?"

"In a way, Sweetheart. But because humans have free will we can still determine our own fate, we can change our history, and, consequently, the history of the world."

"What do you mean, 'the history of the world'?" questions Maya.

Vida sets her mug down on the table next to

her.

"I have explained to you that we are all connected, and what we do affects everyone else; well, this is a prime example of that law."

"It's a law?"

"Yes, Sweetheart, we are all governed by certain laws, or ways of doing things. These are 'truths' that humans have lived by for thousands of years. Adhering to these truths is what we do when we live in the light; when we break these laws, and we hurt others, we descend into darkness. Some people call it 'Karma,' or, to simplify, what goes around, comes around. Of course, not everyone can be good, kind, or understanding all the time. We are, after all, human, and we are still in the learning stage. Good people do thoughtless, unkind, and hurtful things every day, and we all make mistakes. The object is to recognize our mistake and apologize to a higher power for our misdeeds and ask for forgiveness. This is the way we learn."

"Okay, I understand what you are saying, but I had the feeling that I could manipulate time."

Mango jumps onto the bed, nearly knocking the mug from Maya's hand. She laughs and strokes him tenderly.

"Manipulate might not be the right word. You know from our travels that we have been able to go back in time. We visited the Druids, for example. Now, because of all your hard work, you will be able to go forward in time."

"I'm not so sure that I want to see into the future," says Maya.

"Seeing into the future can be helpful, because it can tell us the strength of the Dark Menace. We need to see the future so that we can plan our strategy, and it's important to use every tool at our disposal. We are dealing with a very powerful and determined foe; the Dark Menace is literally fighting for its life.

"Sweetheart, I'm going to anoint you as Priestess in a very simple ceremony. These days, nothing elaborate is necessary. There used to be a weeklong celebration when a novice was sworn into the Order. We could perform the ceremony in the adjoining dimension so that your fellow Priestesses could witness the event, but even that will take time that we don't have. This doesn't mean that you are any less than those who have gone before; in fact, I would estimate that you are one of the most skilled and accomplished women ever to be accepted.

"And as I am still High Priestess, and my second in command, Artemis, hasn't assumed my position yet, I'm going to break a rule. I am going to allow your mother to witness the transfer of power. Officially she is not supposed to see the ceremony, but she has gone through so much, knowing that you were in danger but trusting me to keep you safe, that I want her to be with you."

Vida walks to the top of the stairs and calls to her daughter.

Maya gets off the bed as her mother enters the room. Eve is smiling as she gives Maya a big hug, and Maya thinks that she hasn't seen her mother look this happy in months.

Taking Maya's hands, Vida gives her a kiss on

each cheek and then takes a vial of oil from her pocket. She kisses the bottle then rubs the oil onto her hands and sweeps the air around the outside of Maya's energy field. She has to stand some distance from Maya, because the young woman's energy field has grown exponentially during her tests. Taking her hands again, Vida kisses Maya's fingers, then, with her back to Eve so that she can't see, Vida traces a symbol on Maya's forehead and says something in a strange language.

While she is speaking, Maya looks at her grandmother and sees something that she hasn't seen before. Across her chest, Vida is wearing a gold breast-plate that is covered with jewels. Maya knows what it is, because she had seen a similar breastplate in the casket during her initiatory test in Queen Hatshepsut's Temple. Eve sees it too and gasps.

When Vida finishes speaking she touches the breastplate, says some more words, lifts it off her body and places it on her granddaughter.

"What just happened, am I dreaming?"

"No, you are not dreaming, Sweetheart. I just transferred the power of the Priestess to you."

"Just like that? It's that simple?" says Maya.

"Just like that, Sweetheart. This part is simple, but what you had to endure to reach this point was not simple; you should feel very proud of yourself, and you now have the protection of The Sisterhood."

"But, Grandmother, won't this leave you unprotected?"

"I shall be fine, Darling, I have many layers of protection, and now that you have achieved your goal and have become a Priestess, the Dark Menace will try even harder to reach you, and I'm not going to let that happen. You and I can see the breastplate but your mom no longer can."

She glances at Eve and her daughter nods, confirming that she can't see the breastplate.

"I will let Rose and Amul know that you are wearing it, but they won't be able to see it until we begin our ride," says Vida.

"Shall I always wear it? What about when I'm in the shower?"

"Darling, it is now a part of you, you won't feel it and it will stay in place whatever you do.   The jewels are very powerful; they will not only protect you but deflect any negative energy.   Remember your dream about the Ruby in your back?   Well that Ruby will always be in you, this is the same kind of thing but with the energy increased a thousand fold.

"And there's one more thing," says Vida handing Maya a small package.   "Happy birthday, Darling."

Maya's eyes widen. "It is, isn't it, I'd completely forgotten."

"We didn't, but we didn't want to distract you from your tests. Open the package."

Maya unwraps the silver combs and tears come to her eyes as she remembers that her grandmother had told her that she could have them on her sixteenth birthday. She wraps her arms around Vida and kisses her on the cheek, overwhelmed with love for this remarkable woman.

"Your mother has something for you, too," says Vida.

Maya unwraps her mother's gift. It is a bright yellow, silky-soft scarf and Maya gives a squeal of delight. Eve winds it around her daughter's neck then, giving her a big hug, says, "Your grandmother chose the color, she says that yellow is your power color, and that you should wear it on your ride. Happy birthday, Sweetheart."

"We'll have a bigger celebration once we have defeated the Dark Menace, but now I think you should go to bed," says Vida. "You've had a lot of exciting adventures, and tomorrow we have to get back to work. If you've lost track of time, tomorrow is Saturday. Rose and Amul are joining us in the forest and I've got a surprise for you."

Chapter 43

The birds wake Maya at 5:30. Their songs are so elaborate it's as if they too are celebrating her return. As she lies in bed inhaling the wonderful aromas in the garden, and with the gentle breeze from the open window sliding across her body, she truly believes that anything is possible.

This is a new day and I'm no longer a child. I'm a strong and accomplished woman and I'm a Priestess with a Sisterhood who will protect me. Maya feels a surge of power, and confidence floods her entire being; energy is running through her body in a way that she has never experienced before. Getting out of bed, Maya gives Mango and Frederick hugs and kisses, but they leave her alone while she performs her morning ritual of meditation and yoga.

Vida, Rose, and Amul arrive after breakfast and they all walk into the forest together in silence.

The birds are singing their joyful songs so loudly that it is almost deafening. Animals watch the group as they pass, some from behind the trees, others boldly walking out of their hiding places.

The group continues to walk, enjoying the beauty around them, and Maya sees the falcon watching her intently. Each time she sees him he is a little closer.

A beautiful fawn, who still has its spots, peers at them from between the foliage, and then, its mother, an older doe, steps out into the open.

As they trek deeper into the forest, it becomes apparent that the forest animals are aware that a big change has occurred and they are here to show their support.

Sitting on the soft pine needles, the group takes water and snacks from their bags.

While he's munching on nuts, Amul gets the fighting sticks out of his backpack and hands two of them to Rose; Maya already has her bow.

They are just about to get up when Maya signals for them to wait. She sees that the falcon has followed her and is perched in a tree at the edge of the clearing. She was hoping that he would seek her out; in fact, before she left the house, she had picked up a long leather gauntlet that a friend had lent her. Putting on the gauntlet, she moves away from the group and walks a little closer to the magnificent bird. The falcon hasn't taken his beautiful eyes off her.

Standing in the middle of the clearing she puts her left arm out to her side and starts calling to the bird, making a low whistling sound.

Maya is perfectly still with her arm outstretched when the falcon leaves the tree and circles around her. Vida, Rose, and Amul are watching, expectantly. The bird circles her three times and then lands on her arm.

Maya is thrilled but stays perfectly still. She talks to him and, after a few minutes, takes her right hand and strokes his back. He looks directly at her with his incredible eyes and then gently pecks at the glove.

Still talking, she slowly moves her left hand to her shoulder and the falcon hops on. As he grips her shoulder, and his talons penetrate her skin, Maya reminds herself that she has to wear protective shoulder padding from now on.

Maya remains perfectly still while he sits looking at everything and everyone around him. She holds out her arm and he hops back onto the glove, then flapping his wings he takes off. He circles three times and then flies away.

The group continues sitting quietly on the ground until Rose can't take it anymore. She jumps up and Maya stiffens as her friend runs towards her. Rose flings her arms around Maya almost knocking the breath out of her, which was good. Maya hadn't realized that she had stopped breathing and she shoots a quick look at Vida. Everyone is so excited that they all start to talk at the same time.

"That was amazing, what a beautiful bird."

Vida is smiling, confident that the hawk, as Horus's emissary, is going to give Maya another layer of protection.

"That was an extraordinary experience," says Vida, "and I'm most grateful to Horus for his protection; but you all need more practice fighting. I'm going to create a dome of light that will protect you as you use the Kali sticks in new ways.

"And one more thing," says Vida, "while you fight, you are all going to be flying."

"Flying?" The word came out with such force

that Maya, embarrassed, covers her mouth with her hand.

"Flying might not be the right word, but, yes, Sweetheart, I'm going to teach you all how to manipulate gravity; and you'll also find out how powerful the fighting sticks are and the damage they can do. You won't be able to fly for long distances but you have to learn how to get back to your unicorn in case you get knocked off."

"But if we get knocked off, surely the unicorns will wait for us to get back on," says Maya.

"They won't be able to stop because they will be flying too," says Vida. "The unicorns have wings."

"No they don't," says Rose, "I didn't see any wings."

Maya and Amul agree with her.

"I assure you that they do," says Vida. "You'll see when we work with them tomorrow."

The kids look at Vida in astonishment.

Vida flicks her wrist and white clouds envelop the tops of the trees that have bent inward, creating a ceiling, or dome, that covers the clearing. This will ensure their privacy; Vida doesn't want anyone else to see the fire or lasers that she's planning on using.

"You've all been with me when I've transported you back to the house. We did that by slipping into the next dimension and you became invisible; but this is a little different. You're only going to be able to fly short distances. We will be manipulating gravity, a little like a yogi who is able to levitate. But those holy men have meditated for years to achieve a higher level of consciousness and we only have a few weeks to practice."

Now that the shock has worn off, Vida is looking at three excited faces.

"Forget about the unicorns for the moment. I want you to focus on what we are going to do next," Vida says.

"Rose and Amul, you've already worked with the sticks; and Maya, I'm very impressed with your skill with the longbow, so the next step is to learn how to lift off the ground and fly. Of course, to begin with, I'll be giving you a little help, but after you practice you'll be able to do this all by yourselves.

"Put your weapons at the side of the clearing. Now stand up straight and think of yourselves as being very light, almost weightless. Then visualize yourselves lifting off the ground. You might feel a little tingle as you do this; after all, gravity is just an illusion. You can do anything when you get beyond the concept that we have limitations.

"I don't want you to look at your feet. Fix your gaze on something above you and visualize yourself gliding towards it," says Vida.

Rose is already looking up and almost shoots into the air. She is so astonished that she looks down and then spectacularly plummets to the ground.

Maya and Amul have only been able to lift up about two or three feet and, as soon as Rose falls, they glide back to the ground. Concerned, they both run over to her. She is sitting up and rubbing her injured shoulder.

"I thought that we weren't supposed to get hurt," says Rose, angrily.

"I was talking about using the sticks," replies Vida. "I didn't expect you to shoot up like a rocket."

"Well, I did, and my shoulder is killing me," says Rose.

Vida goes over to her and holds her hands over Rose's shoulder.

"There, that should take care of the pain, but you should sit out the rest of the session," says Vida. "Maya and Amul, I want you to keep practicing."

Maya and Amul are having fun. They have lifted about twenty feet off the ground and are competing with each other, trying to knock the other down, laughing all the time.

"Amul, come back down, pick up your sticks and hand Rose hers," says Vida. "Maya, collect your bow.

"I know you are having fun but you'll soon see that this is no laughing matter, you are going to be working with powerful weapons and you have to learn how to control them," says Vida.

"Rose I don't want you to do anything with the sticks except hold them. Do either of you notice anything different about the sticks?" asks Vida.

"Yes," says Amul. "They are slightly heavier and there's something that I hadn't noticed before. At the end of each stick there is a slight indentation where the bones in my wrist rest."

"That's correct. Let's start with one stick at a time. Rose, I don't want you to do anything, just watch," Vida repeats. "Amul, point your weapon at the tree that's on the far side of the clearing. Now push down on the indentation with your wrist and you'll feel a small section that you can turn to the right," says Vida. "Make sure you are pointing at the tree as you turn it."

An almost transparent blue-white beam shoots out of the stick and cuts the tree down the center; his weapon is no longer a rattan stick, called a "Kali"; it has become a laser, a fearsome weapon.

"Wow," say Amul, Rose, and Maya, almost simultaneously.

"It's all right, I'll put the tree back together," says Vida with a smile.

Maya looks over at Rose and is frightened by the expression on her flushed face. Rose looks excited; it's almost as if she is hungry for the power in the stick; a shudder runs through Maya's body.

Maya looks over at her grandmother, but she doesn't seem to have noticed.

"The sticks can also shoot fire," says Vida. "Amul, point the stick at the same tree and turn the control to the left."

Amul does what he's told and flame shoots out of the stick, setting what remains of the tree on fire. Vida smiles at the looks on the kids' faces.

"I said that you are going to be using powerful weapons," says Vida. "These are not toys, they kill and you have to respect them.

"Now, Amul, lift off the ground and point at another tree and fire at it. Keep firing at the trees and experiment with both the laser and fire. See what you feel most comfortable with; you now have a choice, depending on your target."

Vida has Maya practice hitting the target with

her bow. She corrects Maya's stance and then tells her to keep firing the arrows.

"Rose, if your shoulder is feeling better, bring one of your Kali sticks and come and stand beside me," says Vida. "Now point your weapon at that tree and fire." The tree explodes in a ball of flame, Rose looks triumphant, and her face is flushed.

"Rose, I'd like you to partner with Amul. Stay focused on him so that you don't shoot up again," says Vida. "Eventually you will be using two Kali sticks, one in each hand, but while you practice I just want you to use one stick each. So leave the other at the side of the clearing. Now lift off the ground and point your sticks at each other and turn them on. You will feel the heat but you won't get burned. I want you to feel the energy of your weapons; but be prepared, the force might knock you backwards."

"Is there a way to control how much fire comes out?" asks Amul.

"Yes," says Vida. "You can control the intensity by how far you turn the control. It's very subtle so you should keep practicing until you feel comfortable. It needs to be automatic, as if it's an extension of your arm."

They start slowly, each afraid of hurting the other; but Rose gets knocked flat on her back by Amul's weapon. She glares at him. They adjust the power and soon realize that they can feel the heat but are not getting burned. They become bolder, both in their aerial maneuvers and in attacking each other, and Rose becomes quite aggressive.

Amul is holding back, but when Rose is

successful during a particularly tricky maneuver and knocks him to the ground, he hits her hard, sending her spinning. Amul is laughing but Rose is not, she looks angry.

"Maya, join in and lift off the ground," says Vida.

Maya becomes airborne and starts shooting her arrows that burst into a flaming mist. Amul joins her, firing his laser; she can't feel any heat but she can imagine the destruction it would cause. Maya is thrilled. Not only can she fly, she can do flips and rolls while, at the same time, firing arrows from her longbow.

"Sweetheart," says Vida, "there's one more thing I want you to try," and she holds up a Kali stick, but this one is a little longer.

"I've been working with the sticks for months, but now I thought that I was going to use the longbow," says Maya.

"This is just another possibility," says Vida. "I've been watching how the Dark Menace moves and you will probably be fighting in close quarters. This might be a better weapon than the bow. Just give it a try; you'll instinctively know what is right for you. You'll only be using one stick; you might even want to take both the stick and the bow." Vida hands Maya the stick. "I've made this one a little different."

Maya can feel a difference in the weight and notices the little indentation.

"Point it at that tree and turn the end to the right."

A flame explodes from the stick. Maya looks

astonished and thinks, *How can something so small have such force*? "What is it?" she asks.

"Your Kali stick is now a flamethrower," says Vida, "and I added some white phosphorous, which makes the flame burn even hotter and longer."

Vida doesn't tell Maya that the bombs that are raining down on Syria contain white phosphorous, causing terrible destruction and catastrophic burns for the citizens living in what is left of their cities; she doesn't want to upset her.

Lifting into the air, Maya practices with her new weapon, realizing that this might be a better choice, depending on how the battle proceeds.

They all practice for another hour or so and then Vida says, "It's a good start and I'm glad you are having fun, but you all might be dead by now if this was a real battle."

They all look shocked at the thought.

Vida flicks her wrist and the dome disappears.

"We'll come back tomorrow and keep working. You have to learn how to attack, as well as defend yourselves. It's time for dinner let's go home," says Vida.

Under the protection of the dome, they spend Sunday morning fighting, Rose and Amul with the laser/flame sticks and Maya alternating between her flamethrower and the longbow.

After a lunch break, Vida calls the unicorns. As the magnificent animals walk into the clearing there's a collective inhale as the group gazes in wonder at the beautiful beasts that are going to carry them on their perilous journey.

"I still don't see the wings," says Maya. "I'm sure when we rode them in the forest they didn't have wings."

"They did, Sweetheart, you just didn't see them. We have a lot of territory to cover in one night, so it is essential that we fly," Vida says. "That's why you need to be able to get back to your unicorn if you get knocked off.

"Leave your weapons on the ground. At first, while you fly, you'll want to hold onto your unicorn's manes until you get the hang of it, but once you are comfortable, let go; you'll need your hands free so that you can hold your weapons."

Gustav walks up to Maya and kneels before her so that she can mount him. Blanca and Simone do the same. They have practiced riding the unicorns in the forest but this is something new and they all look a little anxious.

"Everyone, hold on tight and grip with your knees," says Vida, as she gestures to Gustav.

The unicorns unfurl their beautiful wings and they all take flight.

Soon everyone is smiling. The unicorn's flight is so smooth that they can hardly believe they are flying; it's fun and exhilarating at the same time.

After about twenty minutes, Vida calls them back to the ground so that they can retrieve their weapons before taking flight again. Once they are in the air, Vida starts to shout directions as she orchestrates the battle.

"Rose, I want you to fall off Blanca and then fly back to her. But, Blanca, make it difficult for her.

Remember, everyone, this is going to be a chaotic situation. The Dark Menace is going to be attacking and we're not sure what form it will take. The dragons are going to be flying in and out. You will recognize them by the circles of light on their foreheads, but they are very fast and you don't want to incinerate one of them with your weapon. Amul, I want you to guide Simone towards Maya and bump her, throwing her off Gustav, but remember that if you hit her with your laser, she is dead."

Falling, Maya momentarily forgets that she can fly but pulls up short before she hits the ground and, smiling, makes her way back to Gustav. Soon she is sweating, they all are. They all practice falling off their unicorns and then successfully navigate the obstacles as they fly back to their beautiful animals.

"We are going to do this every afternoon after school," says Vida.

Maya is feeling encouraged by her performance and her confidence is building. She kisses Gustav on the nose and, as Vida releases the dome, the unicorns fly away.

The Dark Menace has been slowly changing.

It started when the dark energy began to get a pink tinge around the edges. As more blood was shed and greater atrocities occurred, the pink took on a darker hue and spread throughout its own energy field. The dark energy is absorbing the blood and its energy field is becoming as red as the blood it feeds on.

The plan has to be in place by next month so that they can ride on the eve of the Summer Solstice, and Vida needs to spend some more time with the unicorns, dragons, and Magnus. The battle is being prepared like a precise military maneuver; but when magic and the Dark Menace are involved, anything can happen.

For many years, Vida has been working with people from around the globe who are appalled by the way some people treat the earth and are desperate to save it from destruction. Now that the Dark Menace has emerged, and because of the terror caused by this bloodsucker, the timetable and goals have changed.

Everyone realizes that this will be a battle not just to save the planet but also to save the Cosmos.

Chapter 44

"Darling, we are going to move forward in time, so that you can see what we will be fighting for. Only you and I can go forward, we can't take Rose, Amul, or the animals. What you see might shock you because we will be looking at the future; but be assured that I, and many others, are working hard to make certain that what you are about to see doesn't happen."

They step forward to a place that is blisteringly hot. So hot that Maya is afraid that she might not be able to breathe. The area is desolate and the smell is overwhelming. The ground is covered with small rocks, or pieces of what might have been buildings; but they look as if they have been pulverized. Maya pulls her scarf over her mouth and nose, trying to keep the dust from choking her. The ground is flat and in every direction, all they can see is black sulfur-smelling smoke rising from cracks in the parched earth. There are no people, vegetation, or animals of any kind. It is a desolate wasteland.

Maya looks at her grandmother in horror. "Is this what we will become?" asks Maya.

"Not quite, Sweetheart. We are going to move forward again."

Maya is shivering uncontrollably and she can

hardly see. They are standing in a dark ice field, and black smoke swirls around them. There is no light from the sun; it has been completely obliterated by smoke and ash. Maya realizes the only reason that she can see is because Vida has opened her third eye and is using it to illuminate the terrible landscape.

"Maya, use your training and get control of your body temperature, you will freeze very quickly if you don't warm the core of your body."

"Will we be able to recover from this?" whispers Maya.

"No, Sweetheart, we won't. The people have squandered all their resources, and countries used nuclear weapons against one another, which poisoned the ground and blocked the sun. They caused tsunamis that flooded the earth and the water turned to ice. Humankind was able to recover from the last ice age, but this time they won't. They have killed everything, even the smallest microbe, and nothing will come back. The planet will become a block of ice that will spin off into space. This is why the constellations are so worried, because our destruction will affect them."

"You said that you have been working with others to save the planet, who are they?" asks Maya.

"There are many native peoples around the world who have been working for generations to keep Earth in balance, but their abilities are limited. They don't have the advantages that we have. It is the 'White Man' who has lost his way and has created a planet that is about to self-destruct."

"Let's get out of this terrible place," says Maya.

Chapter 45

The unicorns have already received all the information they need.

It's an ambitious plan that involves covering the globe in one night. The group will visit many of the sacred sites and monuments around the world. Using his golden laser horn, Gustav will inscribe the monuments with a manifesto that will contain all the information necessary for the world to thrive, not just to survive.

If the sacred site is a lake, he will write in the water. The document will be invisible until it is released to everyone, simultaneously. Because they will not be visiting every country, when the information is released it will be projected onto the sky in the language of that country. Everyone, whether in Senegal, Iceland, or Chile, will receive the same information.

If there is a tribe or group of people who don't have a written language, for instance, the Dogon Tribe of Mali, who believe that they are descendants of aliens from Sirius, they will see the Manifesto projected in images that they understand. This information will also be imprinted into their brains so that there is no confusion about the meaning of the Manifesto. They are free to use the information or not. Their history will be honored and there won't be any pressure for them to change.

Politicians, dictators, corrupt groups, or religions will not be able to change the information. This knowledge will ensure that poverty, famine, and aggression will be erased.

The information will include how to grow crops so that every country can be self-sustaining, and how to find water and build reservoirs to hold it. Everyone will be given the tools and the knowledge to construct homes, build cities and infrastructure. The document will show how people can control their population, and keep a balance between what they have and what they need. There will be complete religious freedom so that everyone can worship in their own way, providing it doesn't cause harm to others. All countries will be given details of practical ways they can use wind and laser power that will eliminate the need for fuels that are causing pollution and global warming. Each human and every creature in the animal kingdom will be respected for the role each plays in keeping the planet in balance.

As they fly over countries where there is darkness, the unicorns will be shining light onto the land and raise up temples and antiquities that have been destroyed by religious zealots. Stones that have been sleeping in the ground for thousands of years will be pulled upright, and monuments that have been buried and long forgotten will reappear.

The people will embrace the light and see how powerful it is. The only people who will be frightened by these events are the evil ones who are causing the bloodshed. These oppressors will see that there is a power much greater than them, and they will have to choose between living in darkness or the light.

Vida realizes that these are lofty goals and that the fearmongers and tyrants, who have lived in hate for hundreds, if not thousands, of years, might refuse to change. That is their right. Humans have free will and may evolve as they wish; but they will not be allowed to harm others.

The Dark Menace is going to do all that it can to continue causing strife and bloodshed; but without blood to feed on, the enemy will shrivel up and die, and Vida is determined that the Dark Menace will be eliminated.

Vida tells the kids to meet her at her house so that she can prepare them for what else lies ahead. Sitting around the kitchen table, as they munch on their favorite cookies, Vida explains the plan. They already know that Maya is going to ride Gustav, Rose will ride Blanca, and Amul will ride Simone. What Vida hasn't told them is how the other animals will be involved. She tells the group that a white swan, named Sarita, who is the daughter of Cygnus the Swan Constellation, will be in first position as vanguard, and that other swans will take her place as needed. Vida pauses, so they can absorb what she has just said. Maya is looking grave, and her eyes are glistening as she holds back tears.

"When you say that others will take her place, you are telling us that Sarita is likely to be killed?"

"Yes, Darling, many will die, but they are all willing, human and animal, to give their lives to prevent this global catastrophe.

"Now what I'm going to say next might sound as if we are children, playing dress up, but I assure you that it is necessary. You will be wearing special garments not only so that others can identify you but because your garments will help you step into your power. The old adage, 'clothes maketh the man' is true.

"Maya will the wearing the headdress of Sekhmet, the lion-headed goddess of war; and her personal dragon, Raif, the son of Archangel Raphael, will be flying above her. She will have Horus on her shoulder and, as you know, her weapons will be the longbow and a flamethrower. Maya will be in the lead position behind Sarita and will be dressed in white. Her third eye will act as a beacon, sweeping from side to side, adding to the light from the unicorn's horns. Rose and Amul will be riding behind Maya. Rose will be riding Blanca and will be on Maya's left. She will be wearing a crown of red roses and her gold garment will have a red rose embroidered on her chest. Amul will be on Maya's right. His garment will be purple and his headdress will be a coiled cobra. Both Rose and Amul will have their modified Kali sticks. As good as our defenses are, there will be times when the Dark Menace is able to slip through, and we have to be ready."

Vida tells them that she will bring up the rear riding Pegasus. Her totem is the wolf and she will be wearing wolf's pelts and a wolf helmet.

"Draco's dragons will be flying beside us, above below, and behind us so that we will have protection on all sides. The Dark Menace is going to try to infiltrate our defenses, it is very powerful and might take on a form that looks like one of us."

Rose and Amul look shocked at the thought.

"How are we going to know who to fight?" exclaims Maya.

"Darling, you know that the Dark Menace is afraid of the light; well, everyone, including the dragons, will have a circle of light on their foreheads. Everyone, that is, except you and I. My Sweet, your third eye will be wide open acting as a beacon, and there will be no mistaking that searchlight."

"I will be riding Pegasus backwards?"

"Backwards?" exclaim Rose and Amul, simultaneously.

"Yes," replies Vida, "I will be bringing up the rear and my third eye will be acting as a beacon to search the darkness to see who might be following us."

Chapter 46

The Dark Menace has a level of intelligence that has surprised Vida. She sees it adjusting its tactics as the situation changes, and is grudgingly impressed. This gives her an even bigger challenge, and Vida is at her best when challenged.

She is sure that the reason the terror and chaos have accelerated is so that the Dark Menace can accumulate blood. This means that it will be heavier and less maneuverable, which gives them an advantage.

Vida decides that they can start their journey at a lower altitude and, as the battle progresses and the enemy uses up its fuel, becoming lighter, they will have to fly higher. The problem will be when they encounter the heavier, denser foe guarding the sacred sites.

Tomorrow is the eve of the Summer Solstice, but there is no music or joy in the house tonight. Vida, Maya, and her parents, Eve and Philip, have just finished dinner and are sitting around the table talking. Maya can see her late Grandfather Athos standing behind Vida with his hands resting on her shoulders. Behind them she can see Dinara and Fedor. As she strokes the beautiful cherry wood and oak table, Maya looks up to see Grandpa Joe with his arm around Grandma Fergie Ferguson. They are both smiling at her as they stand behind her father. Mango is sitting on Maya's lap, looking directly at the Fergusons and Frederick is lying at her feet. The animals are aware of the spirits in the room; they sense that something serious is about to happen and are quietly alert.

Eve has known for some time that there is going to be a battle to bring back the light. She has seen the Dark Menace creeping into the house and knows how hard her mother has worked to protect Maya, but she still feels left out. Eve held her tongue as she pushed her fears aside and proudly watched her beautiful young daughter mature into a strong resourceful woman.

Vida explains the plan to everyone and Philip, hoping that nobody notices, is trying to control his shaking, sweaty hands by grasping his thighs under the table. He asks how he and Eve can help. Vida says that the best way to help is to visualize a positive outcome, and see the family returning home, triumphant.

The unicorns are going to use their lasers to create a force field around the group, ensuring their invisibility from everyone on Earth. Because of the many time zones they'll be flying through, and the fact that they will be invisible, Vida has decided that they will fly tomorrow morning, not wait for nighttime. At least when they start their journey they will be flying in daylight, it will give them an advantage over the enemy. The Dark Menace still avoids the light, whenever possible.

Rose and Amul are in their own homes having dinner with their parents. Amul and Rose's parents are completely unaware of their children's plans for tomorrow. There is no point in telling them, they would only be frightened and wouldn't understand the enormity of the situation. The best thing is to have a normal evening together and get a good night's sleep. They need to be well rested for the battle tomorrow.

The full moon is streaming through the window, and Maya has slept fitfully, at one point getting so wound up in the sheets that she thought the snakes were back. She usually loves sleeping in the moonlight, and knows that the light will be to their advantage on the ride today; but she has a feeling of foreboding and keeps seeing Rose's face. There's a damp muggy heat that saps one's energy. The air is still, and there's not even the slightest breeze slipping through the window. She almost feels as if she is suffocating and, at one point, rushes to the window. Holding onto the windowsill and not wanting to admit her fear, she desperately inhales what little air there is.

There are no sounds coming from the garden. It's as if everything has been put on hold. There are no chirping crickets or scuffling small animals, no hooting owls or barking foxes, just silence. She remembers a dream that was confusing. It was good and bad at the same time. Her grandmother was very prominent in the dream and Maya tried to hold onto the images, but they slipped from her grasp and she can't shake an ominous feeling. Tired and frustrated, even more fear creeps in when she realizes that, although it's a full moon, the mocking birds haven't sung a note all night. Not a good omen to start this crucial day and she resists the urge to jump out of bed and look at her Tarot cards. Maya closes her eyes and drifts into a light restless sleep.

Waking with a start she glances at her clock and jumps out of bed. Looking out of her window she inhales sharply. The cloud formation is one she has never seen before; it's as if she's looking at something from another world. It's sinister and optimistic, beautiful and frightening, at the same time, a little like her dream. Layers of clouds with fuzzy stripes of a moody dark grey, that blend into a lighter grey, tinted with shades of lavender that turn to purple, then merge into a pink orange and bleed into a pale white. It's as if she is looking at a cross section of Earth that shows the striations, layers of silt, sediment and rock that have built up over billions of years. The clouds change as she looks at them and she realizes that she is a part of this planet, a minuscule part, a fragment, but still an important part of the planet and she will do anything and everything to keep her home, this Earth, alive. It's foreboding but exhilarating at the same time.

She'll remember these colors in her head forever, but reaches for her camera and takes a shot, just in case. Before running downstairs Maya reaches for her Minoan bee necklace. Placing it around her neck she tugs on the chain making sure the clasp is secured.

Smiling at her mother as she walks into the kitchen, Maya gives Eve a kiss on the cheek, but Eve can see that her daughter hasn't slept well. Getting an icy feeling in the pit of her stomach, Eve pulls her daughter to her. Laughing, Maya thinks that the aroma of lavender that surrounds her mother is the most comforting smell imaginable; it even beats treacle pudding.

Trying to cover her fear, Eve puts Maya's favorite breakfast in front of her daughter, telling her that she'll need fuel for the long ride ahead. Thanking her mother, Maya forces the food down her dry throat with gulps of herb tea. Philip comes into the kitchen and gives his daughter a big hug while trying to hide the concern in his eyes. Almost simultaneously, Vida arrives and wraps her arms around Eve holding her for a long time, and whispering into her ear that she won't let any harm come to Maya. Mango and Frederick are staying close to Maya, but even they are silent, no purrs or nudges, they are just watchful.

Vida takes Maya's hand and gazes into her granddaughter's green eyes with such love that Maya gasps. "Darling, I have taught you everything that I know. You are the one chosen to defeat the Dark Menace and now I hand you the reins, you are in charge. We have discussed the route that I would use, but now it's up to you; you can make your own choices. This is an enormous responsibility, but your instincts are always correct, follow them and we shall win."

Rose is looking pale and complains about a ringing in her ears as she and Amul walk up the porch steps together, each holding their sticks. Maya is concerned by Rose's vacant stare. She almost doesn't recognize her friend; it seems as if the life has been pulled out of her eyes, and Vida can see that neither

Rose nor Amul has slept well.   Before they left their homes, Rose and Amul had told their parents that they were going to be spending the day with Maya and not to worry if they were a little late getting home.

Maya is about to pull Amul aside to express her concerns about Rose when the rest of the family walks onto the porch to greet the kids, and they all sit in the white wicker chairs.   They don't even notice Eve's beautiful roses climbing the porch posts, or their powerful fragrance that's permeating the air.   It's humid, already hot, and Maya is sweating.   Everyone is aware of the silence; it's as if every creature is waiting for something to happen and holding its collective breath.   The bees have stayed in their hives, and Eve had to prop open the gate to the coop because the chickens were huddled in the back and didn't want to come out.   Eve had told Liam that she wouldn't need him until 9:00, so that everyone would be gone before he arrives.

Philip tries to make light conversation, saying that it's going to be a real scorcher today.   Everyone smiles and agrees but nobody is interested in small talk.   Even the colors and fragrance of the beautiful flowers in the garden do nothing to lift their spirits.

Maya picks up Mango for one last cuddle. Putting him on the floor she rubs Frederick's ears and drags her fingers through his long coat.   She stops and, parting the fur, finds a foxtail.   "I'll get it out when I get home," she tells him, as he pounds his tail on the wooden deck.   She longs to take her animals with her, but knows that they need to stay here with her parents.

There's movement in the trees as the

magnificent black unicorn emerges from the woods. Gustav, followed by the two white unicorns and Pegasus, walks silently into the garden. The unicorns' gold horns have white light spiraling around them and Eve inhales sharply as she reaches for Philip's hand. This is the first time that either of them has seen the unicorns or any of the animals.

Walking up to Gustav, Maya looks deeply into his amazing eyes, then rubs him between the ears and kisses him on the nose. Snorting, he throws back his head and paws the ground as she mounts him. There's a familiar cry from the woods and Horus swoops in and lands on Maya's padded shoulder. While Rose and Amul hop onto Blanca and Simone, Vida jumps onto Pegasus. When everyone is seated, Maya gives a slight flick of her hand and instantly they are all dressed for battle.

Maya, dressed in her white gown, has her new yellow scarf wrapped around her neck and is wearing the breastplate on the outside of her garment. The spectacular colors of the jewels flash in the light and illuminate the face of Sekhmet, the lion-headed goddess of war. Beneath her mask Maya is wearing her special garnet earrings. The large rectangular ruby that is embedded in her back is now visible and there are lines of energy wrapping around her upper torso, connecting the breastplate to the ruby, ensuring that she is protected on all sides. She will use her third eye as a searchlight but she can also use it as a laser, if needed. She has her longbow slung over one shoulder along with a quiver of arrows and is holding her flamethrower.

Rose, in gold, and wearing a crown of red roses, is holding her sticks. Amul is wearing his purple robe with the coiled cobra on his head, and he too is holding his sticks. Maya thinks he looks stunning.

Vida wears the helmet of a wolf, her totem animal. She is dressed in wolf pelts, completely unaware that Dinara had been devoured by wolves and that she has wrapped herself in her grandmother's energy. She holds a sword that can both slice through the enemy and shoot fire from its tip. Seeing that everyone is in position, Vida flips around so that she is facing backwards.

Sarita flies into the garden and the white swan positions herself in front of the group. Raif, Maya's personal dragon, the son of Archangel Raphael, is hovering above her. They can all see the circles of light on the dragon's foreheads and know that they are protected on all sides. Draco will send in more dragons, as needed.

Deciding that she wants to use only one weapon, Maya takes the bow and quiver from her shoulder and calls to her mother. Handing Eve the bow, she gives her mother a quick kiss on the cheek, then she lifts her hand and they all take flight, and, as if to say good-by, hover briefly over the house. It is a spectacular sight with beautiful Sarita leading the way. Eve and Philip are mesmerized. They watch their powerful daughter, Sekhmet the Goddess of War, as she sits astride Gustav with Horus on her shoulder. Rose and Amul flank Maya, and Vida follows on Pegasus. The wingspan of the unicorns and Pegasus is amazing and their coordination is exquisite; it's as if they are performing an aerial ballet.

Maya nods to the unicorns and they shoot sparks into the sky as they surround the group with the force field making them invisible. Eve, with Mango on her lap, holds Philip's hand while Frederick gazes into the distance as if he can still see the group. The four of them sit on the porch immobile, Eve and Philip unable to speak; there is nothing to say. Now they just have to wait.

Chapter 47

"Let's go to Sedona," says Maya. Flying in tight formation, invisible to all but each other, they speed over the countryside. They skim over lakes, rivers, and the magnificent Sierra Nevada Mountains where the cool wind stings their faces.

The temperature rises as they fly over Death Valley and they are buffeted as the Dark Menace slams into the dragons, but they manage to escape without injury.

They'll be reaching Las Vegas soon, and Maya wonders if the Dark Menace will take advantage of the negative energy surrounding the city, and she decides to take the group to a higher altitude. Before reaching the city they hit a wall of icy rain. It's more than freezing rain; they are flying through a blinding hailstorm.

Shivering and surprised by the unexpected weather, Maya takes Gustav into a dive and, as they race across the city, Maya thinks about the tourists who had hoped to be baking by the turquoise pools and gambling in the glitzy hotels. Hail in Las Vegas at the Summer Solstice! What is the world coming to? *What, indeed,* Maya thinks grimly, as she and Gustav rejoin the group. She would have liked the unicorns to shine some positive energy onto the city, but Maya is anxious to reach Sedona, so they speed across the Colorado River.

Sarita looks splendid as she flaps her magnificent wings, but as they reach the Grand Canyon the enemy engulfs one of the dragons and then another is torn from the group. The carnage has begun. The screams of the dragons crack open the pale blue sky, and fluffy clouds appear from nowhere and envelope the magnificent beasts, gently lowering them to the ground. Draco's dragons are the first line of defense, and these two beautiful creatures are the first to sacrifice themselves.

Aware of the powerful energy that is generated by the vortex in Sedona, the Dark Menace wants to stop this journey before it begins; it wants to prevent them from reaching the red rocks.

Rose and Amul look over at Maya to make sure that she's all right just as the enemy slams them again, taking out two more dragons. Again their screams echo through the clouds.

More dragons take their place. Maya isn't sure how many there are, but she can see six. Even though she has all this protection, the wedge of fear is now creeping into Maya's soul and she's feeling cold, wet, and not quite so confident. Vida has put her in charge and she had bravely said that she was up to the task; but is she? Trying to reassure Rose and Amul she smiles as if to say, "We've only just started," and then flashes them fire from her fingertips.

Maya can feel the energy of Sedona long before she sees the spectacular red rocks. They are glowing in the morning light, shimmering with power. The stunning outcroppings have deep canyons filled with lush vegetation, but there must have been a recent thunderstorm, because the creek is now a swollen river. The constantly changing light forms strange shapes on the desert floor and Maya doesn't notice that, hidden in the shadows, one of those shapes is the Dark Menace.

Maya and Gustav lead the way as they dive towards the canyon floor and Maya feels a wave of hot moist air. She has already selected the rock that will be the first to receive the Manifesto. As they descend, the Dark Menace assaults them on all sides trying to envelop them with a sticky black mist, similar to what she had seen surrounding Rose, but a thousand times bigger.

The dragons attack and the smell of burning blood is nauseating. Maya can taste it as it sticks in the back of her throat and she has difficulty swallowing. The screams from the Dark Menace are deafening when the fire-breathing dragons incinerate pools of the enemy's blood. The closer the group is to the ground the more vulnerable they become. More waves of sticky black mist envelop them and Maya is knocked sideways, almost losing her balance. Gripping with her knees and holding tightly to Gustav's mane she quickly recovers and fires her flamethrower at what looks like black tar. Whatever the black stuff is, it's flammable and when the white phosphorus hits it, the explosion of fire is so intense that it knocks Gustav and Maya backwards. Horus briefly takes flight, but lands back on Maya's shoulder and gently nibbles her ear. She can hear him telling her that she is protected, and that no harm will come to her, but her cheeks are already scorched by the flames.

Wow! thinks Maya, *I must reduce the velocity when I'm that close.*

Vida swings her sword as she turns around to make sure that Maya is safe. Glancing up, Maya silently thanks Raif, knowing that he will defend her to the death. It's also reassuring to see the circles of light all around her, and she knows that the dragons are close by, but they have lost so many already, and this is just the first stop.

Using their Kali sticks, Amul and Rose send a shower of sparks as they shoot fire at the enemy. They all know that the Dark Menace is afraid of Maya and that she is the prime target. The enemy is fighting for its life and it is stronger than anyone anticipated.

After Gustav encrypts the rock with the Manifesto, Maya urges the black unicorn to a higher altitude. The Manifesto will be invisible until it is released to the world with everyone receiving the information simultaneously. The information will be written in each country's own language, with no chance of misinterpretation. Nations will be shown how to stop global warming, grow disease-resistant crops, and capture fresh, clean water.

Thinking that the Dark Menace is heavy with blood and momentarily unable to reach them, Maya has the group hover over the vortex, absorbing its positive energy; but Maya is wrong and they nearly lose two more dragons. The Dark Menace must have found a way to store blood; it no longer seems so bloated, and Maya tells the group that they will have to fly even higher to stay beyond its reach.

Maya is surprised by the anger in the rocks. She receives a message saying that the rocks are not being honored and that people are desecrating the land. As they race away, and the red rocks become specs in the distance, Maya is still wondering about their anger.

Chapter 48

Before they make their way to Machu Picchu, the next sacred site, Maya wants to fly to New York City and Washington D.C., so they head east and slightly north, shining their light on the entire country, preparing the populace for the information that they will receive from the Manifesto. It's not an obvious light; it's not something that will frighten people or preach to them, thereby eliciting a negative response; it is a gentle optimistic light. Upon receiving this energy the people will become more hopeful and understand that their lives will be better if they decide to make some positive changes.

But the enemy is following them. It's trying to hide, but everyone knows that it is there. It has already spread its black tentacles, like a vast net, across the country. Maya can see the intersecting black rivulets that almost look like the reverse of the Ley Lines. It looks like a giant black fishing net that has captured the earth, and the Dark Menace is waiting to tighten the net, haul it in, and devour the unsuspecting fish.

Maya pushes her fears aside and has the unicorns shine their positive light on prisons, ghettos, and areas where people are in conflict and in need of help, and the energy lifts their spirits.

The group flies to the United Nations building in New York City, shining their light on the politicians and statesmen, who seem impotent against the genocide that is occurring in Syria. Vida prays that the unicorns can break the impasse, giving the statesmen new insights and inspiration so that they decide to find solutions instead of battling one another.

Turning south they fly unimpeded over the casinos of Atlantic City, and the unicorns imprint the patrons with information about the Atlanteans, showing how this ancient race with an indolent lifestyle and great wealth vanished after spiraling into misery through alcohol and drugs.

Having not seen the enemy for some time, Maya assumes that the Dark Menace is holding back until they reach the next sacred site. But again, she is wrong. The Dark Menace is hiding, determined to prevent them from reaching Washington D.C.

The enemy tears more dragons from the sky, turning it from an azure blue to blood red, and the shrieks and screams are deafening as Maya and Amul strike at the enemy with their weapons.

Maya realizes that she hasn't seen Rose for some time. Has she become separated from the group? She should have been fighting shoulder to shoulder with them? But then Maya sees something that makes her feel as if she's been punched in the belly.

The black tentacles of the Dark Menace are covering the House and the Senate, and the sight nauseates Maya. Their adversary has spread a blanket of suffocating darkness across the imposing buildings. Its heavy, sticky tentacles slide down the walls and it is creeping into the chambers and slipping through doors. The enemy wants to keep its hold on the lawmakers and continue to cause strife and gridlock. It has taken advantage of the petty, egotistical, power-hungry politicians who refuse to change a system that is hopelessly out of date; and the Dark Menace is poisoning everything it touches, stoking their fears.

The Sisterhood tells Vida that the same thing has happened at the Kremlin and that the Russian President is completely in the grip of the Dark Menace. Unfortunately, The Sisterhood is limited and, without the help of the constellations, they can do little to help. Maya is their only hope. She is the one chosen to defeat the Dark Menace and, when she does, the enemy will no longer have a hold on Russia. The populace will then be able to decide their own future, a future without fear and oppression.

Draco sends in more dragons, and Maya is relieved to see the circles of light surrounding them, and she feels triumphant and elated as the dragons burn up the choking mist, releasing the lawmakers from its grip, enabling them to see the advantages of working together and compromise.

But this gain is not without a huge cost. The enemy retaliates and Draco has to bring in more dragons to attack the Dark Menace; and these beautiful winged, fire-breathing creatures do so with renewed ferocity.

As they skim across the country they light up nursing homes that have become warehouses for the elderly, and the unicorns' positive energy facilitates a major shift in the way people receive care.

Plants wither and die when they fly over areas where cannabis and other drugs are grown. Flying over the beautiful countryside of West Virginia the unicorns target the shacks where Crystal Meth is made. The explosions of these homegrown labs are spectacular, and the group has to race to a higher altitude to escape the noxious fumes. Maya smiles with grim satisfaction as she hears the thunderous screams of the Dark Menace and knows that it has suffered a severe setback. Through the chaos and noise the unicorns wrap the populace with compassion so that the addicts are able to find help instead of being vilified. The Dark Menace has been severely wounded; it appears to have backed off and is allowing them to project light onto areas in need. Maybe it doesn't consider drugs a priority or perhaps it's waiting for a bigger target.

Flying over the Appalachians the Dark Menace is still holding back as the unicorns shine light on poverty and hunger, giving people hope that their children will have a better life.

Maya wonders what the Dark Menace is waiting for. The enemy that is manifesting itself as a formless mist is intelligent and resourceful. It obviously has a plan, and she wonders what it is and where it will strike next.

Chapter 49

"Draco, I want to commend you on the dragons' performance; they are doing a wonderful job.

"As they incinerate the enemy we can hear the screams from the Dark Menace up here. I do appreciate their tremendous sacrifice; you have lost so many, and the journey has only just begun."

"Thank you, Magnus, the dragons have all gone willingly, knowing that they are the first line of defense and that many will be lost."

"Cygnus, Sarita is doing a wonderful job of leading the group, I'm very proud of her."

"Thank you, Magnus, it means a lot to hear you say that," replies the Swan Constellation. "I have been worried about Sarita, because, as 'point woman,' she is so very vulnerable."

"Unfortunately, the Dark Menace is a lot stronger than we thought," says Magnus.

"But we are winning, aren't we?" asks Leo anxiously.

"Regrettably, the enemy seems to be able to slip into hiding places without being seen and is changing in ways that are difficult to predict. It is relentless as it attacks the vulnerable Earthlings; and, because its fuel is blood, it's getting stronger. I can only hope that we can defeat this evil energy," says Magnus.

"No disrespect," says Draco, "but hope isn't enough. I can't accept the possibility that we might lose the battle; I'll send in more dragons. But if the worst happens, and we do lose, what will become of us? Will the Milky Way survive?"

"I'm not sure," says Magnus.

Chapter 50

They have a lot of territory to cover before they reach the mountains of Machu Picchu. They will be flying over countries that are at war with the drug cartels, and knowing that a lot of blood is being spilt in Central America, Maya wants to prevent the enemy from having a fresh source of energy. She contacts Draco and asks him for additional dragons to precede the group, so that they can incinerate the blood that covers the land.

On their journey across Central America, the unicorns and dragons burn up the darkness, and there is a lot of darkness to burn. The ancient people had practiced human sacrifice for years, and the blood has soaked deep into the earth.

The unicorns lift up stunning pyramids and cities that have been buried for hundreds of years, and the people are awed by the changes around them; but they aren't frightened. It's as if this is something that they have been expecting. The group is still invisible, but they are preparing people for the Manifesto and showing them the power of the light.

These ancient peoples had extensive knowledge of superior building techniques and they had constructed their cities with aqueducts to deliver water to terraces so that they could farm on the most fertile soil. With the cities resurrected, those techniques can be used again in areas where modern machinery would be impractical.

Nearing Machu Picchu, the clouds part and Maya is able to see the Sacred Valley below them. The home of the Incas is considered to be one of the Seven Wonders of the World. It is also one of the major energy vortexes, and Maya can feel the powerful energy as they fly over it. The air thins as they ascend towards the sharp peaks of Machu Picchu's towering mountains that are penetrating thick clouds. Surprised that the Dark Menace isn't waiting for them they linger so that they can absorb the sublime energy. Each time they hover over a vortex they are invigorated and energized. The dragons become stronger and the unicorns more powerful.

The clouds part and Gustav inscribes the Manifesto into the brilliant azure sky. The writing looks like a white contrail; it fades almost immediately and will stay hidden until Maya returns home and reveals to the world how to heal the earth.

She experiences a different form of energy, a much softer energy, as they fly over the Lemurian Sun Temple of Ollantaytambo in Cusco.

Their adversary is waiting for them as they ascend to Lake Titicaca, thought to be the highest and largest lake in South America, and considered by the Incas to be the "womb of humanity." The attack comes in waves. This time the Dark Menace has singled out Vida and drops a black blanket of sticky mist over her, briefly blinding her. The Dark Menace is ferocious. It manages to smother three dragons and slips between the others. More dragons fill the space, but the enemy is already inside their defenses. Maya's body is starting to shake, she is exhausted, and the adrenalin has worn off. The black mist now feels like ice. *It must be the altitude*, thinks Maya, and she can see that Vida's wolf pelts are frozen, restricting her movements. The attack on Vida has shaken Maya, *What happens if Grandmother is killed and isn't here to help me?*

Raif rains fire on the Dark Menace, freeing Vida from its icy grip, and she is able to strike the enemy with her flaming sword. Maya, Amul, and Rose come to Vida's defense and the enemy screams as large portions of it are incinerated, and Maya wonders if she will ever be able to erase the screams and the smell of burning blood from her memory.

As they get closer to the water, Maya can see the floating islands made of reeds, home to the pre-Incan Uros. The Uros have lived on the sacred lake for thousands of years, even before recorded history. The group protects Maya and Gustav with a wall of flame as the black unicorn inscribes the Manifesto into the water.

They ascend quickly as Maya hears Vida shouting at them to fly higher, and that now is not the time for sightseeing. Irritated, Maya thinks to herself, *Who is in charge here*? Then she pauses as it finally sinks in that she is the one in charge. The reality blurs her vision, she literally feels as if she has been hit between the eyes. She looks over at Vida and feels a tremendous weight pulling her down. *Stop it*, she thinks, *pull yourself together, I can do this.*

Grandmother wouldn't have given me this responsibility if she didn't think that I was up to the task. But it's not just Grandmother who is expecting me to win, Magnus and The Sisterhood are expecting me to defeat the Dark Menace, and her thoughts trail off as if they are spoken words. *And I am supposed to save the world.*

Maya is subdued by the reminder but also excited because their next stop is Easter Island, but they still have a long way to go. Amul pulls alongside Maya and she feels comforted to have him with her as they continue their journey across Peru before reaching the Pacific Ocean. The dragons have burned up the blood in the earth so that the group can linger. Rose seems to have dropped to the back and Maya assumes that Vida is watching her. She looks in wonder at the Nazca Lines with the drawings of birds and animals that can only be seen from the air, and what appears to be lines carved into the rock indicating a landing strip; and she wonders who, or what, landed there.

Guessing that the Dark Menace is going to concentrate its energy on the sites where Gustav is going to inscribe the Manifesto, gives them some breathing room, and they are able to enjoy the flight between the chosen sites; but feeling guilty because she's allowed the group to sightsee, Maya urges the unicorns to pick up the pace. As much as she loves looking at Amul's beautiful face she pulls ahead. She can't allow herself to become distracted; they are not even halfway through the journey.

They can feel the temperature change and the increased force of the wind as they approach the Pacific

Ocean.

Skimming over angry waves, rising to approximately twenty feet and with plumes of salt spray in their faces, this part of the journey is not so enjoyable.

Buffeted by strong head winds, Maya recognizes that Sarita is tiring and gestures to the swan to move to the back of the group. Maya tells Raif to protect Sarita, as her grandmother and Pegasus move into first position, and she watches as Vida flips around so that she is facing forward as Pegasus picks up speed. The powerful wings of Pegasus hardly seem to be moving, but now that he has accelerated they are all flying very rapidly. Pegasus doesn't need any guidance; he knows exactly what to do.

When she became a hawk and flew up to the Milky Way, Maya had seen the earth from space, and she has seen the pictures taken by the NASA astronauts on their flights to the moon, but this is breathtaking. It's almost as if Maya has detached from herself and is looking down at Earth from a great distance. She is able to see the planet in a whole new light and is able to hear the sound that Earth makes as it pulsates, breathing in and out, a living vibrant planet. She recognizes it as the same sound that NASA was able to record. Each planet has its own distinct sound and vibration. Maya hears the hum of the earth as it reaches into her bones and captures her soul. It makes her more determined than ever to save the planet.

Feeing stronger and more determined as they get close to Easter Island, the sacred isle of the Birdmen, Maya can feel the vortex of energy long before she sees the magnificent heads. These incredible carvings made by the Moai people are positioned on the slopes of the sacred Rano Raraku Volcano. But she can also see the forms of the monoliths that are beneath the earth, hidden for thousands of years. Amazed by the spectacle below them, Maya momently drops her guard and loses track of Rose. With Vida in the lead, Maya feels anxious and realizes that Rose must be at the back with Sarita. At that moment the Dark Menace attacks. Waves of energy assault them on all sides. The dragons retaliate but Sarita is enveloped by the evil bloodsucker and is torn screaming from the group. Maya is devastated. *This is my fault,* she thinks, *if I had been in the lead, Grandmother would have protected Sarita.*

Maya is choking, she's unable to breathe and her eyes are burning as the enemy tries to smother her with a thick morass, a heavy blanket of bloody mist; but through the blood she sees that Rose has a triumphant expression on her face.

Amul pulls alongside Maya and as he burns the sticky blood off her body with his laser, she shouts at him to watch Rose, but he's unable to hear her.

Horus leaves Maya's shoulder and, trying to open a pathway for Gustav, the fearless bird flies directly into the bloody black fog, but has great difficulty as his wings are coated with what appears to be tar. The dragons join Horus, swooping in and raining fire on the enemy as they open a channel for Maya and Gustav to descend. Horus, his wings singed, lands back on Maya's shoulder. Maya is sickened by the loss of the beautiful and fearless swan and, knowing that somehow Rose was involved in her death, she blames herself for being distracted and allowing it to happen. Vida pulls alongside Maya and assures her that she isn't to blame, but it doesn't help.

Seeing the circles of light on the dragon's foreheads comforts Maya but also reminds her how many have been lost. The group raises some of the buried monoliths as Maya and Gustav spiral into a sharp vertical dive, enabling them to inscribe the Manifesto into a magnificent head before climbing swiftly to escape the enemy.

Maya decides that she needs the dragons to head the group, not the swans. Beautiful Sarita had done a wonderful job but she didn't have any defenses of her own, and Maya doesn't want to lose any more magnificent swans. Draco sends in additional dragons and two move into point position while Vida and Pegasus return to the rear. Maya wants Vida to watch Rose, but her grandmother is riding with her back to her.

Chapter 51

"What's next?" asks Amul.

"Uluru," shouts Maya.

"What?" Amul shouts back.

"Ayers Rock," she replies, and he nods.

"Where is Rose?" Maya shouts.

"In the rear with Vida," yells Amul.

Uluru is in the Northwest Territory of Australia, about 300 miles from Alice Springs. It is the sacred home of the Anangu people, a gift they believe they were given at the beginning of time. The monolith is approximately 500 million years old and, depending on the time of day, changes color from pink to purple to dark red. At sunrise and sunset the glowing rock transforms the surrounding landscape and sky into a scarlet ball of light. The Anangu people have a rich history of stories of the Dreamtime that originate from their magical monolith, and Maya is looking forward to seeing this extraordinary holy outcropping that the Aborigines have worshiped for thousands of years.

Skimming over the turbulent waters towards Australia, Maya's excitement grows as they leave the ocean behind and fly over the vast continent. In the distance, as they soar across the land, they can see a red flat-topped mountain rising about 1,000 feet from the desert floor; but, before they reach it, Maya feels a form of energy that seems familiar, but she can't place it. Before she can discern what it is the group is slammed from all sides by the Dark Menace. But something has changed. It's as if there has been a transformation, and, with an icy feeling in her stomach, Maya recognizes the energy.

Swarms of giant red mosquitos burst from the belly of the bloodsucker and slip between their defenses. It is the same mosquitos, the size of locusts, that had attacked Maya at Queen Hatshepsut's temple, but this time there are thousands of them.

Maya uses her flamethrower and, together with the dragons, they incinerate many of the mosquitos. Vida slams them with the fire from her sword but swarms are attacking them from all directions. Maya looks over at Rose, and her friend seems to be immobilized with a frozen look of terror on her face, she seems unable to use her weapons. Amul is almost knocked off Simone by the mosquitos and fights to keep his balance while cutting a swath with his flaming Kali sticks. This unexpected attack leaves the group gasping. The dragons cut a path through the mosquitos, giving the group room to escape and they fly to a higher altitude. Blanca takes control and flies Rose to safety.

Maya's left temple is throbbing as she flies Gustav towards Rose. She can see that Amul has regained his balance but has a grim look on his face. Nearing Rose, Maya can smell the pungent aroma of burned rose petals and sees that her crown of roses is missing. Rose is shaking and she still has the frightened blank stare.   Maya knows that they still have to reach Ayers Rock to inscribe the Manifesto, and she commands Amul to watch over Rose.

Amul looks at Maya with admiration as she takes Gustav into a deep dive leading the group as they try to penetrate a thick black fog.   But even though Gustav is using the light from his laser horn and Maya's third eye is wide open, acting as a searchlight, they are flying almost blind.   A wave of mosquitos targets Amul and Simone, separating them from the group.   The Dark Menace drops a blanket of black mist over them, temporarily blinding Amul and preventing him from using his Kali sticks.   Although the dragons swoop in to help, he loses track of Rose in the melee.

Seeing the group disappear into the fog, Rose breaks away and approaches Vida from behind.   Rose's face is distorted as she attacks Vida with a ferocity that can only have come from the Dark Menace and, using her Kali sticks, sets fire to Vida's garments.   Just as Maya turns, the fog lifts and a bolt of lightning sears the sky, illuminating Rose as Vida fights for her life, flashing fire from her sword. Maya, her heart pounding, hurtles towards her grandmother, firing her flamethrower. Thunder crashes around them, drowning out the screams. Amul has broken free of the mosquitos and races back to help Vida.   Raif wraps his wings around Vida to extinguish the flames but the Dark Menace smothers him.   The dragons attack, burning up the black sticky mist that has enveloped Raif, and the smell of burning flesh adds to the stench of burning blood.

The air crackles with electricity as the powerful

storm explodes and lightning hits one of the dragons. Maya wonders if the heavens have turned against them.

Rose seems to have the strength of ten men and her attack is so fierce that she is able to tear Vida from Pegasus, who has also been seared by the flames. Amul throws himself from Simone in an attempt to catch Vida, who is spiraling from the group when another wave of mosquitos attack. They swarm over Vida's body as they pull her towards the Dark Menace. Not realizing that he is on fire, and desperate to reach Vida, Amul lashes out at Simone as she wraps her white wings around him, extinguishing the flames.

Vida's radiant smile lights up her face and her deep violet eyes seem to send Maya a message of love as she hurls her sword towards her granddaughter before being dragged, spinning out of control, into the black heart of the Dark Menace. Rose is sitting on Blanca, immobilized; this young girl who is upset by the cries of cut flowers has just killed Vida.

Catching the sword with her free hand, Maya pushes her flamethrower into her belt and grabs Rose's Kali sticks. Unable to stop herself, even though Rose is staring at her with blank eyes, Maya takes Vida's sword and attacks her friend with a savagery that she didn't know she was capable of, slicing and incinerating her.

Maya feels a moment of triumph before taking a frantic dive into the swarm of mosquitos in a frenzied effort to rescue her grandmother. Maya fires her flamethrower and Gustav uses his laser horn, destroying hundreds of insects, but they are too late. Amul tries to reach Maya, fighting off the mosquitos with his flaming sticks, but he is too far away. Just as

Maya is about to be engulfed by the enemy, Raif swoops in. He spreads his giant burned wings over Maya and Gustav and lifts them beyond the reach of the Dark Menace.

Maya is shaking so hard that she almost falls from Gustav. Incapable of registering what has just happened, Maya knows from some deep place in her brain that she still has to inscribe this powerful rock with the Manifesto. The bolts of lightning keep striking and the explosions of thunder are deafening, but the dragons open a path for Maya and Gustav and they inscribe this magnificent monument. Then racing after Maya and Gustav, the group holds back the mosquitos as they ascend safely to a higher altitude.

Rubbing her eyes as if trying to erase the image, Maya is in shock, unable to comprehend that her grandmother is dead and that she has killed Rose. Then she thinks in horror, *Is Amul my enemy too? I had asked him to watch Rose and he left her alone.* She seems to be hallucinating, moving in and out of reality. *My beautiful grandmother, my protector, my touchstone, my teacher is dead, and I have killed my best friend. My grandmother is dead.* It's like a loop that keeps circling through her head and Maya keeps repeating it, *My grandmother is dead, and I have killed my best friend.* Maya's heart is pounding in her chest and she feels as if she will explode from the anguish.

I have difficulty killing my rabbits for our own dinner table, Maya thinks, *and now I've taken a human life. I've killed Rose,* and she realizes with a shock that she enjoyed her revenge.

They have to be at least two miles above sea level and the air is thin and cold, but Maya is sweating and her lungs are filled with so much air that she feels as if she will burst. Tormented by her actions, Maya starts to lose consciousness now feeling as if her lungs are filling with water and that she is drowning. Without her grandmother she no longer has anything to hold onto. She has lost her anchor. An overwhelming feeling of defeat engulfs her, all the tragedies, and all the deaths for nothing.

"On the contrary, Sweetheart," says the wind that caresses her face.

Hearing Vida whispering in her ear, Maya regains consciousness. Vida is telling her that she is with her husband, Athos, and is happy and without pain.

She says how proud she is of her warrior granddaughter, but that she has a job to finish. Maya has to defeat the Dark Menace, and she can grieve for her grandmother later. Vida also tells her that The Sisterhood has moved her deputy, Artemis, who is the new High Priestess, into the group.

Maya looks over her shoulder and sees a beautiful woman with long glossy black hair sitting astride Pegasus. The beautiful white winged creature now has a burned rump and is missing much of his tail. Artemis has strong features with a prominent Grecian nose and wide-set hazel eyes flecked with gold. This woman exudes power and is covered in bearskins, but her mask is on backwards so that she can look both forward and backwards at the same time. She has a small bow and a quiver of arrows slung over her shoulder and she is carrying a silver net.

The Sister who has taken Rose's place has an exotic air about her and is sitting proud and tall astride Blanca. Maya hears her grandmother say that this member of The Sisterhood is from Mali, and the name of this African Priestess is Olokun. This dark-skinned beauty is dressed in colorful robes of red, yellow, and turquoise and is wearing a towering headdress. And she has brought a formidable weapon with her. Unlike the honeybees that have been revered for centuries by many cultures, Olokun's bees have only one purpose. They are fighters and their purpose has been to defend planet Sirius B.

Olokun's ancestors, the Dogon Tribe, believe that they are from the white dwarf star Sirius B, and Olokun had asked the Elders for permission to bring the bees with her. These giant bumblebees, the size of Gustav's hoofs, are unable to live in Earth's atmosphere so they are floating in transparent Spheres in the atmosphere of their home planet.

Every bee volunteered to defend the group and, knowing that it will have a short lifespan, they plan to project themselves into the heart of the Dark Menace, poisoning the blood that the mosquitos feed on and killing the insects. Olokun has warned the group that the Spheres are deadly but that they need to familiarize themselves with everyone to avoid touching them accidentally. Very carefully the Spheres float around the group so they can understand the energy of each person, knowing that an accident would mean instant death for the Sphere and the person they touched.

Chapter 52

Even though the constellations are light years from Earth, their bond with Maya and the family is deep and they have been shaken by the ferocity of the battle.

Magnus calls to the Wolf Constellation. "Lupus, the Earthling called Grandmother fought bravely. You should feel very proud that she had you as her totem. It's very difficult for all of us. Cygnus has lost beautiful Sarita, and it is kind of the girl not to ask for more swans to take her place. Sarita was very vulnerable to attack. Draco mourns the dragons and I'm very grateful to the Elders of Sirius B and Olokun for bringing hundreds of their beautiful bumblebees into the battle. They all left knowing that very few would return, but we knew from the start that this was going to be a fight for the very existence of the Milky Way."

"Magnus, we do understand," says Ursa Major, "and I am very proud that the new Priestess, Artemis, is wearing the bear pelts. Earthlings have a myth that Artemis is the daughter of Zeus. Apparently Zeus was a very powerful God, they called him the 'Sky God' and it looks as if the Dark Menace is losing its strength, maybe Zeus has something to do with it."

"It is the sacrifice of my brothers that is winning the battle," grumbles Draco, and the other constellations murmur their agreement.

Chapter 53

Trying to push her grief and guilt aside, Maya feels as if she is an alternate reality, but her mind keeps going back to Amul. He nearly died trying to save Vida, but was this a ruse to mislead her? Is he really on her side?

As they speed towards Cambodia, Artemis falls behind so she can practice with her silver net without hitting anyone. Curious, Maya looks back and watches in amazement as Artemis whirls it around her head. She releases it and this small net fans out, covering a large area; it hovers for a while and then reduces in size and returns to the High Priestess. With pride, Maya thinks of her wonderful Grandfather Athos and the little statue of Artemis that he had showed her.

Maya talks to herself as she urges Gustav forward. *Focus,* she thinks, *the only thing that I can concentrate on is defeating the Dark Menace, don't get distracted.*

Flying over Cambodia the group hovers high above Angkor Wat, waiting for the mosquitos. As soon as they come into sight the Spheres swarm the vast temple and Artemis casts her silver net, capturing and incinerating vast numbers of the deadly insects. Surprised by the unexpected reinforcements, the Dark

Menace pulls back, giving the group time to swoop in and inscribe the Manifesto.

Racing back to a safe height Maya leads the group to Varanasi where Artemis casts her net, and the Spheres strike at the mosquitos, clearing a path and giving Gustav time to inscribe the Manifesto into the very heart of India, the Ganges.

The Dark Menace seems to be shrinking; there appear to be fewer mosquitos and Maya wonders if it is changing its strategy. She assumes that it must be gathering its resources for a final onslaught. Racing unhindered across the stunning sacred mountains of Tibet, they inscribe the Manifesto into an ancient monastery, then fly on to Mecca in the vast deserts of Saudi Arabia, the birthplace of Islam. Speeding across Egypt and Israel they continue to pull hidden treasures out of the earth. Maya has to force herself to stay focused on her task, but she can still see her grandmother's smiling face as she was pulled into the abyss. Maya almost feels as if she is performing functions that have been programed into her and she is just going through the motions.

Shocked out of her lethargy over Syria, Maya experiences a different form of energy. This is the darkest, vilest, and most evil energy that she has ever encountered, and it hovers over Syria, land of the most recent atrocities and catastrophic devastation. But in spite of this evil and the horrors that have been visited on this blood-soaked land, the people are able to feel the positive energy that surrounds Maya and the group, and they are filled with hope.

The blood has soaked deep into the land for

generations. The drifting sands have hidden much of it and, even though the dragons have cleared the area, there is still plenty of blood for the enemy to replenish its supplies.

And a stronger, more powerful Dark Menace is waiting for them.

Even though they have been flying through many different time zones and climates Maya wasn't prepared for lightning slashing across the sky, and the crashes of thunder that are almost drowned out by the sound of torrential rain, and she thinks of the battle over Ayres Rock. *Is this where it will end?*

Syria has an arid climate, but not today. Wishing that she could enjoy the beauty of the electrical storm dancing around them, Maya has to pull herself back to the present. Maya takes Gustav into a deep dive as the rain streams over her body and Gustav's powerful muscles glow through the torrents. Amul follows on Simone, wanting to restore the archeological treasures to their former beauty.

As the black unicorn prepares to inscribe the Manifesto, Maya and Gustav are hit first by what seems to be a wall of black tar, choking and blinding them; then this is followed by waves of mosquitos. The dragons swoop in breathing fire on the deadly insects and burning up the tar, giving Maya back her vision and allowing her to breathe.

Artemis throws her net, capturing and cremating hundreds of mosquitos, giving Gustav time to inscribe the Manifesto. As hundreds of the insects are incinerated, hundreds more replace them. Olokun and the Spheres swoop in, followed by the fire-breathing dragons. Because of the fresh blood sucked out of the earth by the Dark Menace, the smell of burning blood is even more sickening, and the high-pitched sound of the mosquitos penetrates Maya's eardrums until she thinks that they will burst. The Spheres have found an opening into the core of the enemy and inject the full force of their poison into the Dark Menace. Shrieking, the enemy releases more waves of mosquitos. Maya glances over her shoulder just as Amul is knocked off Simone and, covered with mosquitos, spirals towards the black morass.

Before Maya can react, Artemis takes Pegasus into a dive and catching Amul with one arm, swings him up behind her while simultaneously burning off the biting insects. Simone folds her wings and moves to the side of Pegasus, enabling Amul to leap onto her; but he has deep burns on his face and arms, and his clothing is torn and charred. Relief floods Maya, Amul might be burned, but he is alive.

Olokun sees another vulnerable area of the enemy and guides the Spheres to penetrate the heart of the Dark Menace.

The rage the enemy unleashes knocks the Spheres into one another and, as they bounce, one of them hits Olokun. Realizing that he has struck his mother, the beautiful bumblebee pulls back his poison, but it's too late. The poisonous outer shell of the Sphere has touched her. Because Sirius B is her ancestral home, Olokun has a natural antidote in her blood, but she has been severely wounded and is paralyzed on her left side. Maya has been watching this struggle as if in slow motion.

Suddenly, snapping back into the present, Maya takes Rose's Kali sticks from her belt and, grasping a Sphere with them, one on each side, she holds the Sphere at arm's length, careful not to touch the poison or let it touch Gustav. Trying not to grip the Sphere too tightly, Maya holds it in front of her as she leaps from Gustav and propels herself and the Sphere into the eye of the Dark Menace. As Amul watches in horror, Maya disappears into the void. The enemy collapses, releasing what blood it has left onto the ground, dragging Maya down with it.

After what seems like an eternity, and to Amul's great relief, Maya staggers out of the burning mess, choking, covered in blood and feeling as if her skin is peeling off.

Dropping the Kali sticks she hurls herself towards Gustav, grabbing onto his mane and climbing onto his back. Immediately the dragons attack, incinerating the remaining mosquitos and burning up the blood before it soaks into the ground.

Amul descends rapidly, zooming towards Syria's brutalized treasures, pulling them up from the ground and restoring them to their former glory. The people, confused but awed by the power of the unseen visitors, fall to their knees and touch their foreheads to their sacred ground, their homeland.

Almost overwhelmed, Maya thanks her grandmother. *We have defeated the Dark Menace. We have released millions of people who have been enslaved by the Dark Menace. We are free*, thinks Maya, as she grits her teeth against the pain of her blistering skin.   She is about to take the group to a higher altitude when she hears the Chinese Priestess whispering in her ear.

The Sisterhood has been monitoring areas around the globe where the Dark Menace has had its tightest grip, and the Priestess reports that the blood mist has evaporated and thousands of people are coming out of hiding. They are confused but realize that this monstrous terror has been lifted from them.

Maya slips sideways into the other realm; she wants to see this momentous event for herself.

Darkness has turned to light. People who had previously shuffled as they walked, literally bent over by the crippling weight of fear and oppression, are now standing tall and looking up. Gone is the glassy glazed look of dread; they are seeing with new eyes and greeting neighbors with smiles.

She sees joy on the faces of people in India and watches as Hindus and Muslims embrace each other. She sees North Korean soldiers drop their weapons, strip off their uniforms and race across the border to greet family members.

Maya is able to see a panorama of hope hurtling around the globe. It is racing across her vision at incredible speed; but she is aware of every second of it, and she feels as if her own heavy burden of responsibility has been lifted from her shoulders. She feels free.

Snapping back to the group Maya leads them to a higher altitude so that she can assess the situation.

Artemis gently lifts the Mali Priestess from

Blanca and places her on Pegasus so that she can wrap her arms tightly around her. Artemis strokes her sister's body, filling her with light and healing energy while covering her skin with a soothing ointment projected from her fingertips. Watching Artemis cover Olokun's body with ointment, Amul moves alongside Pegasus and points to Maya. Artemis nods and projects ointment onto Amul's palms. Moving quickly to Maya's side, Amul pushes away her objections as he strokes her face and hands with the ointment. Feeling the ointment cooling her burns, and his caring hands gentle on her skin, Maya feels ashamed that she had even considered that he might have been working against her.

Olokun gives Maya a wan, lopsided smile. Although unable to speak Olokun makes it very clear that she wants to continue the journey with the group, and that she intends to ride Blanca. Moving Gustav alongside Pegasus, Maya calls to Blanca. Together Artemis and Maya lift Olokun onto the white unicorn. After making sure that her sister is seated securely, Maya flicks her wrist and projects golden threads from her fingertips to bind her to Blanca, and then the bumblebees in their Spheres surround their mother.

Maya pulls Artemis aside, telling her that she wants to use her abilities to heal Olokun. Artemis shakes her head, saying that it wasn't Olokun's destiny to be her deputy, and to let the Priestess heal in her own way.

Having seen the joy around the globe, and knowing that the Dark Menace has been defeated, infuses Maya with a rush of adrenalin and, giving

Gustav an almost imperceptible signal, she leads the group unimpeded as they race across the planet inscribing the remainder of the sacred sites.

Chapter 54

Arriving at Stonehenge, Maya tearfully remembers her experience with Vida at this spectacular Druid temple. Maya lingers as the group pulls the sleeping monoliths from the earth, then, unhurriedly guides Gustav to inscribe one of the magnificent stones.

Feeling her grandmother's arms around her waist, Maya knows that Vida is behind her, astride Gustav. She gasps when she hears Vida whispering in her ear, "Come with me to Scotland."

Maya tells the group that they have one more stop. Flying low, wanting to feel the refreshing salt spray in her face, they cross the turbulent waters that separate the Isle of Mull from mainland Scotland, and then they fly across the wind-whipped galloping waves of the Atlantic Ocean. The waves throw plumes of spray into the air as they fling themselves towards the stony beaches of the sacred Isle of Iona. This magical place is the former home of Druids and burial place of Scottish and Scandinavian Kings.

Maya signals for the group to land on this rocky outcropping that is thought to be millions of years older than the surrounding islands or mainland.

Dismounting, Maya can feel her grandmother's hand holding hers as she is guided to a small stone cottage that has moss the color of emeralds covering the shady part of the slate roof. Maya can hear children laughing inside. Their laughter rises and falls, sounding like the bells that are ringing in the nearby Abbey, and almost drowning out the howling wind. This is the cottage where Dinara was born.

Vida guides her granddaughter closer to the cottage, and Maya inhales sharply as a ball of light explodes in front of her. The round white light changes to an egg-shaped bubble of soft blues, pinks, and greens. It pulses back and forth, making Maya feel a little dizzy. Inside the bubble she can see a dark shape. It looks like the stick figure of a man, but it expands and contracts distorting the shape.

Maya looks in wonder as a person steps out of the bubble and she sees a small woman with dark curly hair smiling at her. The woman is surrounded by light, an almost blinding radiant light, and Maya knows that she is looking at her Great, Great, Grandmother Dinara. Desperately wanting to touch her, Maya steps forward and holds out her hand. Instantly the light and energy that surrounds Dinara arcs towards Maya and she feels an electrical charge exploding through her body.

Staggering back from the force of the light and, sensing Amul standing beside her, she leans into his strong body as he puts his arm around her. The power and strength of the island beneath her feet is immense, and Maya understands why she is here; she needed to touch Dinara's spirit and carry the magic of this island with her as she fulfills her destiny to heal the planet.

It is dawn as they near San Francisco and, within moments, they are skimming over the trees of the forest and then land in the garden of Pippin House. Eve and Philip race onto the deck and Frederick dashes ahead of them, almost tripping them on the uneven wooden steps.

Looking at the group, Maya sees that they are all wearing their regular garments but still holding their weapons.

Maya jumps off Gustav and kisses him on the nose as Eve throws her arms around her daughter, sending Horus, minus a few feathers, into flight with a squawk. Then Eve looks wide-eyed at Artemis on Pegasus. Maya looks at her mother with a sad and exhausted expression and nods. As Eve starts to crumble, Philip and Amul catch her before she hits the ground.

The Sisterhood has decided that they will convene a meeting in two weeks and Maya will be joining them as Priestess of the Egyptian Order. There is a lot of planning to do and, once the Manifesto is released, people will need time to comprehend that they now live in a completely different world.

Artemis on Pegasus and Olokun on Blanca will briefly return to their families before the work begins. Before they leave, the unicorns toss their heads and, using their incredible horns, shoot light and sparks of triumph high into the sunrise, surrounding the group with a circle of power.

Amul walks up the porch steps with Maya and, taking her flamethrower and Vida's sword, places them on the wicker bench. Taking her in his arms he sees that she is fighting to hold back tears. Gently kissing her lips he brushes away the tear that is sliding down her cheek, and whispers that he will be back tomorrow.

Picking up Mango, and followed by Frederick, Maya climbs the creaking stairs to her bedroom wishing that her grandmother was with her to place a cool cloth on her burning brow, wishing that she was going to her bedroom for just one more lesson.

Placing Mango on the bed, her eyes move to an object on the dresser, and the pain in her chest is almost unbearable. Seeing Dinara's silver locket confirms what she had already suspected, her grandmother had known that she was going to die. Maya strips off her dirty clothes and drops them on the floor as she steps into the shower. As the hot water streams over her body, Maya starts to sob, then starts to scream and heave with gut-wrenching howls. When she feels that she can cry no more she steps out of the shower and wraps a towel around her exhausted body. Believing that Vida would have wanted Eve to have the locket, she decides to give it to her mother tomorrow.

Just before collapsing onto the bed Maya flicks her hand and releases the Manifesto on this first day of the Summer Solstice.

Chapter 55

Two years after their triumphant ride, there is a new world order. Because the Manifesto was released around the globe simultaneously there is no need for war. Every nation and group was given the same information needed to support a peaceful environment with clean water, disease-resistant crops, and fulfilling jobs. The civilians who fled the terrorists were given shelter, while the rebels who refused to surrender were confined within their borders so that they could fight to the death.

Maya is married to Amul and, whenever she looks at his beautiful face and sees the burns, she feels anger and resolve. She had wanted to heal his scars but he wouldn't let her, choosing to keep his disfigurement. The battle was fought at great cost, but this has strengthened her and she feels empowered knowing that her grandmother and Dinara are guiding her.

Amul and Maya are equal partners and lead a consortium of experts in solar power, crystal energy, and ecology, to regain the balance of nature, ensuring that the people of Earth not only survive but thrive, and that Earth will re-established its rightful place within the Milky Way.

Every person and living thing, animal, fish,

bird, and plant is respected for its place in the chain of life and honored for its contributions. People learn how to control the population so that there is a balance between what they have and what they need, ensuring there are enough resources for everyone. If a group or tribe wants to govern themselves they are free to do so, provided they are able to support their people.

Eve, using her knowledge of plants and herbs, and with Philip at her side, heads the agriculture department, ensuring that the planet has an abundance of food, clean water with reservoirs to hold it, and infrastructure to move it to where it is needed.

Everyone has complete religious freedom and can worship whomever they please, providing it doesn't harm others.

Artemis is in charge of health and education, but Olokum, her second in command, has not regained her full abilities, and so Artemis is training Maya to take her place as High Priestess of The Sisterhood.

Vida and Dinara continue to guide Maya, especially during her training, knowing that one day she will become one of the most knowledgeable, fair, and powerful Priestesses ever to lead The Sisterhood.

Chapter 56

"Magnus, what do you think will happen now?" asks Sagittarius, his voice booming across the Cosmos. "Do you think that Earthlings will be able to change now that the Dark Menace has been defeated?"

Talking over Sagittarius, Draco jumps in, "They'd better change. I'd hate to think that so many of my dragons have sacrificed themselves for nothing."

Everyone appears to want to be part of this conversation.

"I'm sure they will change," says Leo. "Maya, has become a strong leader and she has the help of The Sisterhood."

"Leo, you've always had an exaggerated opinion of Maya's abilities," says Scorpio.

"But," says Leo.

"No he hasn't," Cancer interrupts, turning red from anger. "That's a very unkind thing to say; you're just jealous because you were on the sidelines."

"Well, I didn't see you doing much to help," sneers Scorpio.

"It is a fact that my polar bears are still drowning," says Ursa Major, looking morose.

"I keep telling you all that we have no control over what the Earthlings do, and if they don't change, and change quickly, they are still in a very perilous situation," rumbles Taurus.

"Virgo, you were correct in thinking that the girl, Rose, was working with the enemy," says Aquila. He still thinks she is very beautiful and wants to impress her.

"Yes, what a snake," says Leo.

"What did you say?" hisses Hydra.

"I'm so sorry, Hydra, I didn't mean any disrespect," says Leo, cowering.

"Apology not accepted," says Hydra. "You had better cower in your corner of the Cosmos; remember, I'm so much bigger than you are."

"Enough," shouts Magnus. "I believe that Sagittarius asked me a question."

Everyone falls silent.

"It is true that our universe is still in peril and the children on Earth are continuing to experiment at our expense," says Magnus. "But there has been some improvement. There is less pollution and, because of that, the unicorns on Earth are starting to grow back their horns, and their hooves are healing. If Maya asks us for more help, they may be useful."

"I do empathize, Ursa Major," says Magnus. "But less ice is melting and, although bears are still drowning, the number of deaths is down dramatically. It's also encouraging that the wolves are having cubs again and are starting to resume their place in the food chain."

Lupus, the Wolf Constellation, looks happy at that thought.

"I want you all to work with me," says Magnus.

"It's going to take a long while for Planet Earth to stabilize and we have to carefully monitor their actions. Unfortunately, it seems that some Earthlings always want more than the others."

"But I thought the whole point of the battle was that every Earthling would have the same as everyone else," says Leo, trying to avoid looking at Hydra.

"Yes, those are noble intentions," replies Magnus, "but it seems that a single Earthling, or maybe a group of them, wants to have more power than their neighbors."

"Do you know this for sure, or are you just guessing based on their previous behavior?" asks Sagittarius.

"Let's call it an educated guess," says Magnus.

Everyone looks distressed at the thought.

"Surely we don't have to go through this all over again, do we?" asks Draco.

"Earthlings have fought one another since they crawled out of caves," replies Magnus. "It's part of who they are." He sighs. "How long can it take for a race of people to evolve?"

The Constellations continue to monitor Earth, hoping for a peaceful transition to a self-sustaining planet that is balanced and productive, guaranteeing the stability of the Milky Way. But, like most children, Earthlings are capricious and selfish. Planet Earth is still very fragile, and the smallest thing can tip the balance from rebirth to disaster.

"Magnus," says Leo, "Maya believes that she saved Planet Earth from destruction and therefore saved the Milky Way, and, in her time frame, she has. She was a great warrior and sacrificed much; but, taking the longer view, do you really think that she has won or has she just delayed the inevitable."

"Leo," says Magnus, "you are a lot smarter than some of the other constellations and your empathy and courage have been commendable. I hate to have to say it but it seems that there is evil in some shape or form on Planet Earth; perhaps its people are being tested. Unfortunately for us, this might be a necessary part of their growth process. Peace might not last for much longer and, if there is another battle, Earthlings will have to find a new savior.

Unfortunately, Maya's daughter Ava, although a great administrator, is no warrior. It also appears that Ava is unlikely to have children. If that is the case, Dinara's bloodline will end.

"What will happen to us?" asks Leo, miserably. "There must be something we can do. We can't allow Earth to self-destruct."

"I have an idea," replies Magnus.

Leo perks up, but he is still concerned. *It better be good,* he thinks. *We are running out of time.*

End of Book One

Made in the USA
Las Vegas, NV
15 August 2022